Guard your Heart

About the Author.

Sue Divin is a Derry based writer and peace worker, originally from Armagh in Northern Ireland. With a Masters in Peace and Conflict Studies and a career in Community Relations, her writing often touches on diversity and reconciliation. Her short stories, flash fiction and poetry have been published in literary journals and anthologies including *Her Other Language*, *The Caterpillar*, *The Cormorant*, *The Honest Ulsterman*, *The Bangor Literary Journal*, *Splonk*, *North West Words* and *The Bramley*.

Guard Your Heart is her first novel. In 2019 it was shortlisted for the Caledonia Novel Award and was Joint Winner of the Irish Writers Centre's Novel Fair.

Sue Divin

Guard Your Heart

MACMILLAN

Published 2021 by Macmillan Children's Books
an imprint of Pan Macmillan
The Smithson, 6 Briset Street, London EC1M 5NR
EU representative: Macmillan Publishers Ireland Ltd, 1st Floor,
The Liffey Trust Centre, 117–126 Sheriff Street Upper,
Dublin 1, D01 YC43
Associated companies throughout the world
www.panmacmillan.com

ISBN 978-1-5290-4167-5

5 7 9 8 6

A CIP catalogue record for this book is available from the British Library.

Printed and bound by CPI Group (UK) Ltd, Croydon CR0 4YY

Supported by the National Lottery through the Arts Council of Northern Ireland

For Ethan

Chapter 1. Day.

AIDAN.
Thursday, 16 June 2016.

It was more miraculous than the virgin birth, me finishing sixth form. Not that I believe in holy miracles. Miraculous like the magic millisecond a girl says 'Yes', and you blurt, 'Really?' It was the kind of historic day you only have a handful of in a lifetime. Days that start out all innocent but end up life-changing, for good or bad. Ones that sneak up on you like an unexpected kiss or a kick in the teeth. To be honest, I'd already had my fill of them, mainly the bad kind, but this day was different. My last day of school. Ever.

One last politics exam. Four rows of chairs. Fourteen pupils. Thirteen pages of my black-ink scrawl on lined paper. One varnished assembly-hall floor. Seven years of grammar-school education. Three minutes left. Three minutes till freedom, or something. Mindlessly, I flicked through the exam paper, but my concentration was gone. I chewed my thoughts and my pen lid, gazing round at the wood panelling that gave the room its scent of musty polish. Dust danced in the shafts of sunlight – moving, changing, just out of reach.

Two minutes. Two Nobel Prize winners had escaped from these walls. Mr Seamus Heaney, the famous Irish poet – hope and healing wells and all that – and Mr John Hume, the famous peacemaker politician from that Good Friday in 1998 when the north of Ireland finally brokered a peace deal. The exact day I'd been born. No pressure, like.

Please God I haven't messed up the A levels as badly as the GCSEs in my nuclear meltdown two years previously. Ironic that maybe I'd transformed my own 'Troubles' quicker than the country. Then again, I hadn't had four centuries of being screwed over. Just eighteen years.

'One minute.' The supervisor yawned and shuffled in her chair. It was my last day in the black blazer, white shirt and striped tie. Last day tagged with the dove of Columba and the oakleaf of *Doire*, Derry, my city. *Quaerite Primum Regnum Dei* read the motto – Seek Ye First the Kingdom of God. Yet another thing I'd screwed up with flying colours. 'Guard your heart,' Ma had always said. 'Guard your heart, Aidan.' It had been her favourite Bible verse. I hadn't understood it enough at the time. I twirled her ring in my pocket, smoothing my fingertips over the jet stone set in Santiago silver. My lucky charm, my memory. She would have been there, I know, standing by the red kettle in the kitchen with a pack of chocolate digestives and a coffee to ask me how it went, how I felt. Her youngest, all grown up and finished school. For once, she'd have been proud. Maybe she still was, somewhere. God knows.

'Pens down, gentlemen.'

Conal grinned, handsignalling a drink. I smiled. It took a month of Mondays for the papers to be collected and then, then it was finished. The squeak and scrape of chairs, the thud of the heavy doors on the old hinges and, finally, the sunshine. My luck it would have been lashing, but no, there were blue skies, and the scent of cut grass wafting in the warm air tasted of hope, freedom and endless possibilities.

Like football highlights on a hungover Sunday, most of the post-exam commentary washed over me without sticking.

'That's really it.' Conal slapped my shoulders.

I yanked off my tie, scrunched it up with the exam questions and lobbed it into the nearest bin.

'We getting pissed then?' I grinned.

'Like there's no tomorrow.'

The tidal wave of boys with bags poured out the doors in the race to the buses before the bell even stopped ringing.

'Hennessey!'

I spun towards the unmistakeable voice of my Irish teacher.

'Knew you'd turn out all right in the end!'

'Bye, sir. Thanks.' I waved. End of an era. He'd never lost faith in me; even when I had.

The bus back to Creggan seemed surreal. For the first time amidst the banter and clash of raised voices, I felt out of place, like a Celtic fan in a Rangers stand. Staring blankly through the fingerprint-smeared window, I tuned out from the hum of traffic and the stops and starts of congestion. My shoulders relaxed. The endless studying was over.

I smiled at the loud banging on the windows as a handful of St Mary's girls swanned past in short skirts. My phone bleeped. Conal. An address for the party.

C U there.

Stuff the future and all its *What next?*s. There were no uncertainties or unknowns about tonight – that choice was crystal. We'd be getting hammered.

The daily uphill trek past the Rathmór shops, the cemetery and the chapel to the rows of terrace houses, was a routine trudge; rain, hail or shine. An Creagán, 'the stony place' in its Irish translation, was more of a brick-and-cement place really. Like everything else working class, it still wore its coloured tattoos with pride. Green. White. Gold. Tattered tricolours on lamp posts; misspelled dissident graffiti. I grinned noticing the fresh lick of paint – some wisecrack overnight had changed 'Join the IRA' to 'Join the LIbRAry' on our gable wall. So maybe I couldn't blag like the oul' farts about growing up in the Troubles, but I'd have needed to be tapping a white stick to not see their shadow, especially in a family like mine.

One of the better things about Creggan was the view – like a balcony over the city. From every street corner, I was high above the walls, the cathedrals, the bridges and the River Foyle sweeping out into the Lough and on to the Atlantic. I liked where I was reared; it was home. Doesn't mean I wouldn't kill for a ticket out of the place. It isn't exactly a paradise of prospects.

Seán was out, so the house was empty. Would he ever wash his breakfast dishes before supper? My own room wasn't so chronic. It smelled of sport deodorant and a hint of cheese and onion rather than the stale cigarette smoke of downstairs. I tipped out my blazer pockets onto the bedside table – bus pass, phone, couple of black biros, loose change, house key and Ma's ring. *Worth going for a run?* I toyed with the idea but, remembering the smell of hot dust radiating off the concrete, grabbed my green T-shirt and ripped blue jeans rather than joggers as I stripped off my uniform. I could ditch it now.

Flopping onto the bed, hands behind my head, I stretched and zoned out. Christ, I was wrecked. Three exams in the one week had been draining. I had no idea what was next for me, but right now I didn't care. My phone vibrated.

Hey wee bro. Exam go well? Party time?

My sister Saoirse was somewhere in deepest, or maybe highest, Bolivia. I imagined her in a chilled-out cafe in the Andes drinking coca tea. I was glad for her. When it had all happened, she'd shouldered the responsibility of getting me back on planet earth before heading to explore it herself.

All good. Out later. Skype sometime?

Voices and the barbecue smell drifting from next door's backyard woke me. I'd been out for the count. The phone, still by my hand, showed 18.47, plus missed calls and a message from Shannon.

Take it you're going the night? CU there.

Sitting up too quick, my head went dizzy. I messaged, scooping up keys and money.

There by 7.

Though still early on a Thursday night, many of my mates were already hammered when I arrived at the end-of-term house party. Summer had started; music and atmosphere spilling into the street. My phone buzzed. Conal.

Can't make it. Family stuff. Catch you over weekend.

I had my head down in the hallway texting back, **No worries**, when I felt her arm draping smoothly round my shoulder.

'Hey, Shannon. What's the craic?'

'Missed you.' She smiled, running her fingers down my back. I let her take my phone and slide it into my pocket. She looked stunning. I warmed inside; tiredness flooded by testosterone.

Derry girls are like black magic. They transform at dusk. On Saturday mornings they sneak out to corner shops in onesies and house shoes, but by the time the evening game-shows hit the telly, they're glammed up with fake eyelashes, high heels and skirts the length of belts. You could make a mint here as a hospital frostbite technician, not that I'm complaining – never mind the temperatures, the view sucks my breath away. Shannon smelled of musky perfume and tasted of something unidentifiably sweet and alcoholic as we kissed.

'You're sober.' She pouted.

'Easy fixed.' I smiled, accepting the drink she offered. The unexpected strength of it hit the back of my throat and she laughed as I coughed. 'You trying to lead me astray?'

'Don't see you objecting.' She winked.

People were crammed into the two-bedroom house and the mood, or perhaps more than just the mood, was high. The living room was simultaneously blaring music and Euro football commentary – Northern Ireland versus Ukraine. The banter was edgy. Both Irish teams through to a major tournament. There was a time Ukrainian flags would have clattered Creggan, but things were changing and opinions were split. So what if the north gave a good show? Grand, so long as Ireland did better, or, specifically, that England failed spectacularly – frustrated BBC commentary was a definite highlight of any championship.

The kitchen hosted the biggest crowd. Bottles and cans were jammed everywhere: varying shapes, sizes, colours, empty and full, like the teenagers and ashtrays. We aren't exactly a city known for sobriety. Fluency in the language of drink is part of the dialect. 'I'm not drinking tonight' translates as 'I'm driving' or 'I'm on an antibiotic' or just that I'm not *really* drinking, like only having a couple of pints. Not that a 'couple' of pints or 'a few' necessarily means two or three, either.

Regardless, I was drinking like a drowned fish. I didn't care. It had been my last exam in my last year of school and I was fast approaching the point of being beyond listening to anything rational. Shannon was in my arms. Time, sanity and morality vanished in the fog of sweet smoke, and every movement, every touch, fired me from the inside with the constant beat of dance music.

Her lips smoothed my neck.

'Fancy finding somewhere more private?' she whispered.

I nodded, breathing heavy, trying to read her. We clasped fingertips, weaving upstairs through the jam of people. I clicked the bathroom lock.

My body was hotwired; T-shirt off, skin on skin. An echo stabbed my conscience. Heat. Breath. Hands. I toyed with buttons as the echo persisted. *We're both up for this, right?* Being. Wanting. *Think.* I couldn't even tell which of us was tugging at jeans. *But Christ.* Instead of tiles, the memories of rough fences; bathroom swapped for back alleys; the burned-out shell of me fired up with girls, tabs and recklessness for the smothering of grief . . . *Jesus.* The murder of shame after, the pregnancy risks . . . *Was I still that mental? Shouldn't we talk protection?*

With a sudden jerk of my arms, I shoved Shannon away and, as I tripped backwards from the force of it, I heard her scream, muffled by the loud music. In slow motion I saw every single detail of how she fell backwards, the shower head crashing down from its metal fixture and slamming into her left cheek bone. As I reached to help her, she glared, punching me in the stomach as a trickle of blood flowed from her nose. The scene jarred a childhood memory. My heart raced, blood pulsing through the tangle of limbs, and yet I was on the floor in a cold sweat when I should've felt hot and I couldn't see straight or even feel my way through the blur of emotions. When I tried to speak to her, to see if she was OK, the slurred words wouldn't come out right. It wasn't me, not even a drunk me. My head pounded. I knew what it was. I'd been there before but why was I there now? I couldn't think straight for blackness and light and sound and my heart pummelling my chest. I pulled my T-shirt back over my head as she stepped across me.

'Shannon!' I finally managed to speak, but she'd unlocked the door and was gone in a wave of rage and humiliation. Faces peered round the doorpost. I felt sick, not just from the drink.

Even in the riot of the party I sensed the whispers, the eyes, as she moved through the hall into the late evening air. Stares burned my back as I meandered drunkenly, trying to melt into the faded wallpaper. My heart was in my dry mouth, racing. *What the hell just happened?* There was laughter too and light-hearted punches from some of the lads. I tried to shake it off like there was no issue. The music melted my brain. *Shut up! I need air! I need to think.* Spinning. My mind was spinning. She'd fled the street. I turned every direction to find her, so light-headed I wanted to throw up. The moon, high and bright over the city, caught my focus. Dogs barked. She was gone.

'Shannon?' I shouted half-heartedly, my voice deeper than it should be, and then I shut up and kicked the pavement. As the mess of it all hit me, I shook, like that night in our childhood kitchen when everything changed. *Am I just him? Is this the way I'm going to be too?*

I was at the grave, Ma's grave, not even quite knowing how I'd got there. Sat dry-eyed in shock. *Bloody loser. Spark never falls far from the fire.* My concentration was shot, flitting from one sound to the next as my head throbbed. Had I taken something more than drink? I pulled my knees up to my chin. My soul felt black. Guilt, cold and sharp like the gravel in the grass. Ma would've been ashamed of me. Again.

I dropped my head into my hands. *What the hell is happening to me?* Whatever was in my system overwhelmed my senses. Relentless as conscience. My T-shirt smelled of perfume and I still ached for Shannon.

I heard my voice chattering about nothing as my footsteps drifted down the hill winding through Bogside streets to where moonlight graced the flowing water.

I found myself standing at the Peace Bridge, its white overlapping triangles like a handshake across the river. It was a snake, a ribbon, twisting between the Guildhall and the former Ebrington barracks. My head was killing me. *How bad does pain get before you pass out?* My heartbeat smashed my eardrums like a bass amp about to explode. Past and present blurred as my sweat dripped. Hallucinations. It was a Saturday in June when they opened the bridge – crowds, choirs, symbolic pageantry. I was thirteen. Ma was happy then. The good times in between had been short. Three golden years with Da gone and Ma still here. *What was that mad riddle again? Aye, when I was twelve you were exactly three times my age so what age will I be when you are double mine?* I was back at our old kitchen table as we laughed, struggling with the mental maths; then as suddenly as it came, the picture vanished into the cool breeze like a ghost brushing my cheek. *You never made it, Ma.*

Darkness was closing in. Dizzy, I hit my palm against my head, trying to focus. *Call yourself a man? You hurt Shannon.* I spun around, expecting a troupe of condemning eyes. The deserted bridge mocked me; empty silence except for the sound of water flowing black below my feet. Fate merged nightmare with rose-tinted memories of the day the four of us had jostled in the crowds, walking the bridge together and absorbing the infectious atmosphere of hope in the city. A bridge to help heal the divides of the past; to span the gap between the Protestant Waterside and the Catholic Cityside. Peace in concrete.

My phone buzzed notifications, my head confused, struggling to connect sound to meaning. The bridge was drifting, like when the barges had towed its jigsaw pieces up the river to slot them into place. Everyone had predicted suicides and riots; a bridge from nowhere for no one to cross. A truck banged in a pothole behind me and I jolted, seeing Shannon collapse, over and over. The shock. The crack.

'Away!' I shouted at the mental images fused with haunting childhood memories.

My phone still vibrated and finally my brain clicked, but my co-ordination melted and the mobile dodged my fingers, clattering on the pavement. I fell over my feet to reach it, palms slippery with cold sweat. The Guildhall clock pealed the hour like an alarm buried deep in my skull. Finally I trapped the phone, and the horror of social media slammed me.

Shape of him . . . U C her eye? . . . Heard her scream . . . A shootin's too good . . . All lads . . . She OK? . . . No denying it . . . His da too . . . Toul ye . . . Deserves a hammering . . . Waster . . . Torrents of notifications slayed me – gossip and scandal – lies morphing into accepted truth, trending my crisis and embarrassment publicly. I couldn't breathe. Sweat soaked my T-shirt, hot sweat now, and my heart raced unevenly as I ripped off my jacket and trailed it after me. *I need water.* My eyes wouldn't focus, but they'd read enough. I gripped the cold rail, staring hypnotized by the dark swirls of rushing water below. Lost – mentally, physically and emotionally. Blackness encased me, hemming me into a limbo of hopelessness.

Seconds, minutes, maybe hours – there was no concept of time left, just dizziness, heat and a crazy agitation gnawing my thoughts. Then a shout and the drone of an outboard engine in the current below snapped me back like a starter's gun and I ran in blind panic across the bridge to anonymity amongst trees in St Columb's Park. Running, racing – my energy was back but I couldn't see through the sweat, and I was tripping with the dizziness, tripping over my own shoelaces as the white light of pain blasted my head.

There were voices in the darkness of this park. *Are they real?* They were muffled, distant at first. I was jogging in a furnace: no chill left, just searing heat burning my body from the inside out. *Hennessey. You're dead on your bloody feet. Get help.* I was still legging it, for no real reason, trying to grip my phone enough to find my brother on speed dial. 'Seán. Jesus. Seán. *Cabhair liom.*' My vision was so blurred I couldn't even read the screen and then suddenly I was surrounded by people. Initially I didn't even know if they were real or hallucinations, and then, sweet Jesus, mother of God, for that split-second my world stopped spinning and I realized the danger just before all hell broke loose.

The first blow caught me hard on the chin and I spun off balance, tripping over the empty beer cans as the green, navy and white of the Northern Ireland tops blurred past me. A kick in the groin and a knee in my back followed as swiftly as the abuse.

'Fenian bastard!'

Is 'Catholic' tattooed on my head? How did they know?

Other shouts echoed confusion, uncertainty. In the pause, I found my balance and somehow deflected the uppercut I barely saw coming through the blazing sweat dripping down my face. The next blow to the gut winded me, and though I was wildly swinging my arms to keep them off, there was no real hope. I used to have a good right hook but hit by hit, kick by muddy kick, the pain was mixing with my own blood and sweat, tasting salty and warm in my mouth. Male and female voices, laughing, goading, shouting, but protesting too. Discord on the touchline as my feet were kicked from under me and I fell hard onto my knees on the tarmac path, my hands slamming the ground as the boots to my ribs and limbs flew in. *I don't want to die.* There was a football boot on my head. *Hail Mary, mother of God* . . . A kick in the face jarred my eye socket. I curled in a ball, arms and elbows round my head like a cage, knees pulled tight to my chest. Sustained blows rained from different directions; jeers, taunts, screams, and then a shout.

'Stop it! Now! This is live – I'm filming.'

The voice was a terrified female voice, shaking, trying to hold an air of authority in the madness. A pause. Attention shifted aggressively from me to her and then from nowhere there were lights, new voices, racing steps pounding tarmac in different directions. The pain and the heat were blinding, overwhelming me as I drifted in and out of consciousness on the hard, black path, slippery with sweat, blood and dew from the cooling summer air. People, hands around me, steady voices – and then I was gone. Blackness.

Chapter 2. Night.

AIDAN.
Friday 17 June.

The nurse was kind, answering my questions without judgement in her Filipino accent as I phased back into consciousness. Yes, I was in Altnagelvin Hospital. No, I could not leave; I was still under observation and attached to a drip. No, it wasn't a nightmare, it was real – fragmented memories of the assault; flashes of whitewashed walls and fluorescent lights; tubes stuffed in my nose and throat; stomach pumping; retching; police uniforms. Apparently, I'd been there hours, though at first I remembered only random minutes.

'Know your name?' she asked.

'Aidan. Aidan Hennessey.'

'Grand. Age?'

'Eighteen.' My tongue stuck to the roof of my mouth.

'Good man. What year is it?'

'For real? 2016.' *Please God, I haven't been out for years like in the movies.*

'Day?'

'Thursday? Maybe Friday?'

'Wee hours of Friday morning. You're doing fine. Anyone we could contact for you? Your mum or dad?'

'Seán. My brother.'

'Sure. Know his number?'

I hesitated. 'Mobile's in my jacket pocket. Seán Hennessey.'

'You've no phone. We checked for ID on admission.'

My brain was fuzz. I couldn't get past the 077 . . . 'Please. I think it's the left pocket.'

She gave me that teacher smile, like when you lie about your homework. 'Date of birth? I can check your hospital records for a contact.'

I was slow to react, confused and starting to feel pain through my limbs. The groan was involuntary as I reached my right hand up to touch my eyebrow and realized two of my fingers were taped together in white bandage. 'April '98. 10th April. Where are my clothes?' I felt like a charity case in the cheap cotton trousers they'd on me.

'The police bagged your T-shirt, jeans and shoes. It's standard forensics procedure.'

'Forensics?' My head swam. 'They're investigating me? Did I talk?' My head conjured a blurred image of a young officer, notebook in hand.

She shook her head. 'Relax. You're the victim of an assault. In a day or two you'll want to report it properly. If not, you'll get your property back. You weren't wearing the jacket during the attack,' she added, 'so they left it here.'

'Bloody generous.'

'Calm yourself. I'll be back in a minute.'

I was weak. Everything ached. The ceiling was white and the lights too bright, even for closed eyes, a feat which my right eye was managing all by itself with the swelling. Papery curtains on rails round the beds pretended at privacy but every sound could be heard in the bays around me – whispers, reassurances, shoe squeaks; intense conversations of medical staff, patients and family members. Nothing quiet or relaxing about Accident and Emergency. Everyone was stressed or busy, needing attention or wanting it. Anxiety whirred around me; a repressed panic mixed with the smell of industrial cleaning fluid and human sweat. Like waiting outside the principal's office, isolation and vulnerability hovered around me, as my mind picked through the bits it remembered and pieced them together again.

My bloody fate – screw up, get screwed right back. The cops had even traded my only decent runners for nursery school plimsolls. The metal curtain rings scraped the rail. Same nurse.

'Your brother's listed as your next of kin. We've contacted him. If your temperature remains normal, you can be discharged, providing you answer a few questions. Will you do that?'

Adults thrived on coffee-cream questions, sweet on the outside but impossible to swallow. 'Mm,' I said. *Like I have a choice.*

'If it's too much, tell me. Because you are eighteen and because of the way you arrived here, I need to ask how you are feeling.' She paused for my answer, but my mind hadn't grasped the question. 'Are you feeling OK, Aidan?'

'Yes. No. Are my fingers broke?' I tentatively lifted my hand.

She flicked through medical sheets. 'Remember Dr Mullan talking to you a couple of hours ago?'

I shook my head, wincing.

She read my injuries like a shopping list, 'Right-hand little finger fractured . . . extensive bruising on limbs, left leg, arms . . . right eye gashed, four sutures . . . significant swelling . . . knees, left torso badly grazed . . . rib X-rays clear . . .' A pause. 'Alcohol levels, blood toxins, chemicals . . . Aidan, your temperature was dangerously high. Luckily your organs weren't damaged. Whatever you took was worse than the assault.' Her matron-like tone was mixed with sympathy. 'Anyway,' she continued, 'Foyle Search and Rescue observed you on the bridge and found you in the park. What do you remember?'

'The bridge, the park . . .' It was flooding back, even the bits I would have happily forgotten. *Jesus, Shannon . . .*

'There are support services if you need to talk. Are you feeling suicidal?'

Christ. Was I? I struggled to sit up, staring at the white sheet. I'd been seriously messed up before, low, high – though I was tight on talking about it. 'You're a typical Derry man, Aidan!' Ma had said once in exasperation. 'You bottle it all up. Promise – when I'm gone . . .' The words had caught in her throat as she'd looked at me with her warm brown eyes, mirrors of mine, and touched my hand. 'When I'm gone, promise me you'll let yourself cry, even once, with no one looking. Cry for me, for us, and then remember me with smiles and laughter. Live like the world is your oyster, Aidan, like hope and dreams are possible.'

I crinkled my eyes tight.

'You OK, son?' the nurse said.

'Bloody golden,' I replied. *Shit. Had I been suicidal? Shouldn't watching someone else have to fight for every last minute on the planet hardwire you against that, of all things?* I stared at the floor, like I had at the water. My body tensed as my thoughts skipped back there, then further. *Christ. Shannon's face.* I'd never be able to show mine again in public. Breathing deep, I tried to look the nurse straight in the eye. 'I'm fine, honest.' *Get off my case.*

Her eyebrows raised. 'Just in case . . .' She set leaflets by my jacket. 'I also need to ask about substance abuse, if that's good with you?'

Depends on your definition of 'good'. I was too sore to shrug.

'You had significant levels of alcohol and drugs in your system. From your records, this isn't the first time. Want to talk?'

Like a hole in the head. I blinked. What *was* significant was I couldn't even bloody remember taking drugs. Not this time. That truly was a first. For sure, there was no denying the serious high or the hellish mental anguish before the low, a low I was still battling along with the pain soaking gradually through the medication. Mentally retracing my footsteps, the events of the night before were a clear series of snapshots. Alcohol? Guilty. Illegal highs? Blank. Ripe that drugs could wipe the bits you wanted and frame the memories you'd ditch. Invent tabs that do the opposite and you'd go viral. I sighed. 'I just want to go home. Can I leave?'

'Yes. Once your brother's here and the doctor signs the discharge.' She smiled before drifting beyond the paper curtain.

'You feckin' eejit!' The most comforting words I'd heard in half a century as the curtains parted and Seán appeared, grinning. 'Bloody hell! What'd you do this time? Pick a fight with a lamp post? What's with the prison-issue rig-out? Come on. You're good to go, and I never paid the car park so we're out of here.'

'Since when do you've a car?'

'Since yesterday.'

My brother was twenty-one and held the world record for stringing swear words into single sentences. We'd always been love–hate, but he had my blood and my back and I'd do time for him if it came to it. Despite the banter, he'd paled looking at me. Later we might talk. Right then, though, he knew I needed home and a locked door to shut out the rest of the world.

He parked on the street, opening the passenger door like a butler as I grimaced, hauling myself onto my feet and over the threshold. 'Hungry?' he asked.

'Uh. No. Just wrecked. Still feel sick. I'll try and catch some sleep.'

'*Fadhb ar bith*. No worries. Shout if you need anything.'

Wedging off plimsolls was shit with broken fingers. It ached as I leaned to take my socks off and the muscles in my legs spasmed as I dragged my feet out of the trousers and sat slowly onto the unmade bed. It took three efforts to get my arms out of the jacket. *Feck's sake, Hennessey.* I looked at the blue-black bruising, cuts and swelling. I couldn't face a mirror. Lifting my jacket, I turfed out my pockets. Chewing gum and two coins. Nothing else. I re-checked, trawling the fluff at the seams. It wasn't just the phone gone. The emotional blow hit like a brick, stabbing deep where I didn't think I could feel any more. I froze, palpitations rioting in my ribcage and then, when I knew I hadn't the strength to fight it anymore, I fell face down on the bed and let the hot tears flow silently, soaking the pillow. The ring, her silver and black ring, was gone.

Chapter 3. Dawn.

IONA.
Friday 17 June.

We shouldn't have run. I jolted upright in bed, my brow damp with sweat from the nightmare. Except it wasn't a nightmare – it was real. That animal look of hatred they'd flashed before shouting 'Fenian bastard!'. The crack of the first punch. I flinched. *It'll all be better in the morning* is one of our parents' biggest lies.

Malala, Mandela and Beyoncé glared down at me from the posters on my wall. So much for my own courage under fire. Some people are born epic, others leg it when the opportunity to make a difference is staring them in the face. I pulled the duvet over my head and breathed through the cotton. Was *he* still breathing?

When we'd sneaked home in the wee hours there'd been the initial wave of relief. No hand on the shoulder. No sirens. Nothing. Unfortunately, conscience was a real bummer, mine in particular. I stared at the threads weaving a random pattern over my eyes. If only I were more confident. That, or less honest. It was going to kill me to drop it and say nothing, like Andy wanted. Turning, I wedged my face into the wall, willing the burning in my throat to vanish. Something, anything, had to be better than doing nothing.

We'd learned the word in school – one of a string of isms and phobias straight from citizenship and history textbooks; exactly where it belonged. Sectarianism. No amount of praying was going to make it jump back into the pages. I balled my fists into my stomach as it churned, my mind reliving that split-second choice to run. 'Stand,' my conscience had said, but fear and a tug from Andy had fired my feet. I kicked the duvet into a tangle. There'd been two adults in high-visibility jackets kneeling over him. A third person radioing for help as we'd scarpered in different directions.

About one thing, Andy was right – we couldn't tell our parents. Dad would rage. It'd trigger an off year, never mind an off day, and I couldn't put Mum, or any of us, through that. Dad would insist on reporting it. Grand day out, like, me and Andy in a courtroom dock, with John just joined the police and Dad frowning and shaking his head with former colleagues. Could they jail me for withholding evidence? I groaned at the thought.

'Give me your phone!' Dylan had demanded as we caught our breath in an alley off Bonds Street. 'Call yourselves Protestants? Traitors. Pair of bloody Lundies.' As he'd squared up to me, I'd traded a glance with my brother, only to see him look away, kicking at broken glass. His bravery from the instant had fled. It was something about Dylan's glare at me, pupils dilated, that assumption that he was the big man and I was some wee girl. Behind my back, I pressed my hand flat against the wall to hide my shaking and stared back.

'So you'd hit a girl, like?' I said, stalling, conscience drilling my brain.

'No,' he said, 'but I'd give your brother a kicking for interfering.' Andy looked up, eyes pleading. Reluctantly, I'd handed over my mobile. He'd scoured the photos, hissing slurred questions. 'You lying? Nothing's recorded. It wasn't live, was it?' With deliberate effort, I'd relaxed my shoulders and looked him straight in the eyes.

'I was only kidding.' I'd shrugged and held out my palm for the phone.

'One word of this and you're both dead,' he said, pulling up to his full height. Like bandsmen marching back from the field, there was a definite sway to his step as he strutted off to find Luke. Alone with Andy, I slid down the wall as my knees gave way.

We'd walked in silence through Kilfennan housing estate. Only at our door did I notice my brother's face, whipped whiter than ice cream. 'Say nothing,' he whispered. 'Promise? They'd only dish out the same on me.'

Should I show him the phone? The one with the cracked screen and criminal evidence stashed amongst its photos? The one I'd quickly switched off because of the notifications buzzing? It was his phone, whoever he was. Not mine. Clutching it tightly under my pillow, I drifted back into a restless sleep, just when I'd given up trying.

Mid-morning. The sound of some talk show drifted through the floorboards. My fingers still curled loosely round his mobile. This was not the way the rest of my life was supposed to start. Fourteen years of schooling and I was still clueless about what to do. I flung the back of my hand over my eyes. *God, if you feel like showing up, now would be good timing.* The more my mind and heart raced, the more intently I prayed, letting the words flow out of me in a rambling mess – worth a shot when there was nowhere else to go for answers. Reluctantly, I levered myself off the warm mattress and sat on the pillow, staring at my reflection in the phone. The image would have made the worst selfie ever. Switching it on, I buried it under the covers as a series of missed notifications pinged loudly. It wasn't locked. A smear of dried blood caked the edge of the glass. I grabbed my mouth as the thought of watching the video brought bile into my throat. Not yet. No. *Who was he?*

Scrolling the contact list of Irish names, some of which I couldn't even pronounce, one thing was obvious. Definitely Catholic.

It wasn't that I wanted to think old-school, them and us, it was just there. By nursery I knew my 'good' and 'bad' colours. At primary school, I learned my letters – 'aitch' not 'haitch', my numbers – 'three' not 'tree'. Everyone was tattooed under their skin. 'What school are you at?' people asked. Answer 'Saint' anything and it was dead cert you were Catholic. 'Where are you from?' The killer question. I usually bit my tongue and said, 'The city.' Tourists thought it mad our two communities still couldn't agree on the name after eighteen years of peace. Derry and Londonderry. Same place. Different worlds. Catholic and Protestant. Irish and British. Nationalist and Unionist. Even if we didn't care about it anymore, somehow we still needed to know. Especially in my family.

I flicked into his photos. Group selfies. Lads in a school uniform – St Columb's College across the river. Was he the one grinning at the front, dark hair and brown eyes? A head-and-shoulder shot in a suit with a girl in a red dress. Definitely him. Mischievous, wavy hair on top, short at the sides. He was well fit – tie loosened; top button open. She was blonde, her hair styled in loosely held curls falling beautifully round her face, framing her made-up eyes and bright lipstick. School formal, I guessed, sighing. The cleavage in my own formal dress had been two inches higher, the stilettos two inches lower, yet still I'd felt exposed and wobbly. My night with Kyle had probably finished a lot earlier with fewer smiles. Did this lad have a one-track mind too? I cringed at my own thought process. Maybe his brain was too pulped to think now. Maybe his girlfriend was crying through boxes of tissues. My gut heaved.

Switching back to the home screen, I paused. Facebook. The

app fired up a stream of posts, but I clicked to his profile. *Aidan Hennessey.* Bingo. *Lives: Derry, Ireland. St Columb's College. Birthday: 10th April 1998.* I nearly choked. We were the same age. To the day. I'd never met anyone else born on exactly the same day – the Good Friday they signed the Peace Agreement. If it hadn't felt like trespassing, I'd have delved in-depth through his profile. How could I contact him if I had his phone? With that question, I realized I'd already made my decision. Contact him. Return the phone. Assure myself he wasn't laid out like a sleeping vampire.

Chat show over, Andy's footsteps were shuffling below. Before he would have a chance to change my mind, my fingers tapped the Facebook search into my own phone:

A-I-D-A-N H-E-N-N-E-S-S-E-Y.

There – seventh down, same profile pic.

Hi. Hope you're OK? I have your phone. Message me. I was there. Sorry. A second's hesitation. Send.

'Why does everyone in our stupid family want to play detective?'

When I told him about the phone and the video, Andy was less than impressed. Way less. When I told him about the message, he freaked.

'You what?' he asked for the third time, looking grim. 'For real? Can you delete it?'

'It's my call! Anyway no, I don't think you can.'

'Has he seen it?'

'No. Think that means anything?'

'Like what?' He paced the living-room carpet.

'Is he hurt really bad? Dead?' The thought had festered since the instant I'd hit send. For ten minutes I'd been a statue, praying for an immediate reply. Neither God nor the phone responded.

'Wouldn't it be all over social media if he was dead? Like

dissident punishment attacks and stuff?' asked Andy. 'Could've looked worse than it was . . .'

Though he'd already grown taller than me, somehow he looked small. 'Sorry. I didn't see it coming,' he whispered. 'I don't often hang out with Dylan and Luke since they left the band.' He slumped back onto the sofa, arms folded, fists balled into his armpits.

'No one's blaming you,' I said, sitting beside him. 'You did what you could.'

'Really?' He raised his eyebrows. 'I think you're the only one with a clean conscience.'

'I ran too.'

'For God's sake, Iona – cut yourself some slack! If we'd stayed, we'd be held in Her Majesty's custody. Dad would've gone ballistic. It'd be us would need post-trauma counselling shite. Bloody pulp if we'd reported it, too. We'd be sunk quicker than the *Titanic*.'

The TV blethered. Some granny had found an antique worth billions in her attic. She was off to the Maldives.

'I've to get to work,' I said.

Andy stood, shoulders squared more defiantly. 'Swear,' he said. 'If he replies, do nothing until we talk. Right? Not a word.'

'Fine,' I replied. He wasn't going to get the last say, though. 'Never drink with them again,' I said. 'Better still, wise up and cut your links. Those guys are cavemen. We're supposed to be done with hate. My school's mixed and I've Catholic friends. What if it'd been one of them? We wouldn't even be having this conversation. Fact. Just because we didn't know him . . .'

He eyeballed me, then stared out the window. 'So what are you going to do if he does answer?'

It dawned on me then. I hadn't a clue.

Chapter 4. Aftermath.

AIDAN.
Saturday 18 June.

I'd become a temporary recluse. Yesterday I'd hardly left my room, which wasn't that difficult since I'd slept until tea-time anyway, when the painkillers wore off. Pain jabbed in places I hadn't known could be painful – behind my eye socket, under fingernails – never mind my ribs, head and legs. Pain that makes you moan out loud even when there's no one listening. Seán had been scarily attentive. The moment he'd heard the creak of the bed and the thud of my feet on the floor, he'd bolted up the stairs and tapped on the door.

'You look like shit!' he said reassuringly.

When I didn't reply, he hunkered down in front of me, big-brother–little-brother style, like when I was five and he was eight and the age difference had seemed an era of maturity.

'You OK? Can I get you anything?'

I was slow to speak. The pain was distracting.

'Have we any painkillers?'

'I'll get them. Hospital gave you some. You're overdue a dose but I didn't want to wake you.'

'Wait!' Embarrassed, I realized I was struggling to stand. 'G'on, help me,' I whispered.

'Jesus. You took a right kicking.'

He asked no questions, just hoisted me up, hooking my arm round his shoulders and resting one under my armpit to support me across the landing to the bathroom.

'I'm grand now. Away and get those tablets.' I stared at the scuffed vinyl floor, avoiding eye contact. He closed the door and I stood alone, gripping the sink and staring at the plughole. My fingers messed with water droplets in the basin, then toyed with the tap as I killed time, not wanting to look into the mirror I was leaning my head on. I pulled a thread from the bandage binding my fingers. When I did look, it was with a morbid fascination. I remembered the nurse mentioning stitches above my right eye somewhere under the gauze, but I hadn't anticipated being bruised like a car-crashed panda. The swelling had my eye half-closed. Dried blood caked my nose and teeth. I'd have given Frankenstein's monster a run for his money with the cuts around my hairline, and my ear looked like it had lost a run-in with a cheese grater.

'You decent?' Seán nudged the bathroom door.

'Mm. Am I ever? Not sure if that's a good description right now.' The attempt at humour dropped quicker than a fart in the school corridor.

'Your tabs, sir,' he said, meeting my eyes in the cabinet mirror as he handed me a pint glass of water and two large white painkillers.

'You were right.' Even my voice was hoarse.

'About what?'

'I look like shit.'

'I wouldn't disagree.' He grinned, and just like that it became one of those moments where you have to laugh, because if you don't, you'll cry. Laughing hurt my ribs, which made Seán crack up even more, despite his efforts to be sympathetic. The air was blue with my swearing in laughter and pain, but I didn't care: if anything, it helped.

After, he sat by my bed like Ma did when I was wee and feeling under the weather, chatting about nothing; taking my mind off it until the painkillers kicked in.

'You should eat something,' he said, then disappeared downstairs. He rattled round the kitchen, returning minutes later with toast, the melted butter soaking into it. 'Meds are crap on an empty stomach. How come you're not starving? You normally eat like a horse!' I nibbled the crust till he stopped watching. When you puke there's always carrot; when you're ill, there's always toast.

'So, what's the story?' he asked.

'They jumped me on the Waterside.'

'Who? Why?'

'They called me "Fenian". How'd they bloody know?'

'Did you catch names?' He leaned forward.

'Just let me sleep, would you?'

Saturday morning and my stomach's realization that I was ravenous dawned simultaneously. I tested my body as I lay there, twitching each limb in turn and deducing that although I still felt like I'd been run over by a tank, it wasn't quite as bad as twenty-four hours ago. Mentally I was clearer too, though part of me wished I wasn't. *Shannon.* I'd no phone to know if she'd tried to get in touch. It would take ages to save for a decent mobile again. I hoped my brother had kept his gob shut about what had happened, I couldn't face company. Even with my stomach growling, it took forty minutes to find the motivation to angle myself onto a pillow propped against the wall; longer still to read the dosage on the painkillers to suss it was safe to swallow another couple. My head throbbed. The patter of summer rain on the window was already draining the colour out of the day as I recycled my thoughts around everything that might've happened differently. Snores through the wall. I'd been left to my own defences – Seán was dead to the world.

When we were younger, Da hammered us if we cried. 'It'll toughen ye!' he'd yell, ignoring Ma's protests. With Saoirse, he was different, but with us boys, tears meant he'd grab our chin, forcing us to meet his eyes and man up. His message hit as hard as the slaps – no whinging, no grassing. Take a punch? Throw one! In the end he did shape us, despite Ma's efforts to nurture it out. As I grappled with the dark cloud of emotion hanging over me, it was difficult to judge if he'd done me a favour. I can deal with shit, I just can't talk about it.

Eventually a busting bladder and hunger won. I edged out of bed, testing my feet on the carpet. It was a long and not unpainful process, in slow, single sideways steps, to get downstairs to the kitchen, never mind the struggle to carry toast and coffee and manoeuvre myself stiffly onto the living-room sofa – so much so that I hadn't moved off it two hours later when Seán emerged, yawning.

'How's the head?'

'Pounding.' I didn't want to talk, and he had exhausted most of his limited reserves of supportive brotherliness the day before. The fresh coffee he offered was welcome, though, as we both vegetated in front of Irish TV's Euros highlights and match analysis. Ireland were to play Belgium next. A win was as essential as it was unlikely. We'd need a miracle against Italy later in the week and the Vatican was sure to be biased – but it was in the blood, we rose to a challenge. Any mention of the Northern Ireland soccer team still triggered a stampede of blurred images, sounds and panic. I curled onto a cushion.

'Check your phone,' Seán said as a throwaway thought during

an ad break. 'Conal messaged. Give him a shout – he couldn't get you. Call Aunt Teresa too, but be prepared!'

'For what?'

'I think she saw the stuff on social media. Check that out too when you feel up to it. Bit of a wild night on Thursday?'

'Lost my phone,' I replied.

'Facebook reckons you lost more than that!'

When I didn't take him on, he swore. 'Look, you wanna fill me in? I felt like an eejit not knowing what to say to Teresa. Didn't want to land you in it. What's the story?'

'Am I like Da?' I asked after a moment.

'What in the hell has that to do with anything?'

'Just answer it.'

'You're his double, except for the eyes – everyone says that. You know it anyway.'

'But am I *like* him, you know, how he went on, how he acted when he was drinking?'

'No. You're like Ma. You look like him, but you think, you act, like her – more philosophical, bloody deep. Opposite of me. What's your point?'

'Just – did you read Facebook?' I shuddered as I remembered seeing it in a blur at the bridge on Thursday night. He gave me that all-knowing big-brother look, which implied he had gone through it with a fine-tooth comb and was half relishing my anguish and half sympathizing. Rolling his eyes, he scrolled on his phone and handed it to me.

There are things I love about my city: the wit, the dry humour, the way your friends slag you to your face to show that you're in. But I hate how quick people scorn you when you screw up. Folk are light on forgiveness and heavy on negativity. The comment strings were long and, by my recollection of it, wrong. Ten minutes of silent reading and I set the phone down, swore through my teeth and developed an acute interest in a coffee stain on the carpet. Seán, to give him some credit, let on to be engrossed in the TV. He only glanced over when he thought I didn't see. My head was fried. I'd peeled myself off the sofa and was halfway through the door when he spoke.

'G'on, just talk, man.'

Turning, I looked him in the eye and leaned on the doorframe, my ribs and legs aching just holding me there. 'I didn't do what they're saying, Seán. I didn't . . .' My voice wavered. 'I didn't beat Shannon up. It's lies. Not even remotely near the truth. I wouldn't, I just wouldn't . . . she's my girlfriend . . . was, anyway.'

He waited for me to get myself together to speak again.

'We were just . . . I mean we didn't even . . . Jesus, Seán, I don't want to talk about this. I was hammered, all right?'

'Just hammered? Look, if it's any consolation, maybe you didn't read where Shannon told everyone to stop crucifying you. She as much as said you didn't . . . OK?'

I hadn't seen it. It was like a light flicked on in a dark underpass when he read aloud her comment. 'Quit stirring. It was an accident. OK? Cut him a break.'

I still spent most of the afternoon cocooned in my room. Occasionally Seán's phone rang, presumably Aunt Teresa from the way he was talking, but he didn't venture upstairs until much later to see if I wanted some chips or to watch the match. On any normal day it would have depressed me that we lost 3–0 to Belgium but, ironically, I was beginning to come round. Maybe it was that the pain, like Ireland in the second half, was fading. My head was clearing, too, from whatever my poison of choice had been. It bugged me that I still couldn't remember taking anything, yet there was no denying it. Regardless, ninety minutes of distraction and a bellyful of carbohydrates laced with salt and vinegar picked me up.

'I told Teresa you got attacked on the Waterside,' Seán confessed at half-time. 'It shut her up about the other stuff at least.'

'What'd she say?'

'She wasn't really listening to how bad you got hurt, to be honest. Wanted to know why you were there so late. You should call her. Best wait till after she's back from ten o'clock mass or she'll drag you into confession yet. What in hell were you doing over there anyway?' His question hung in silence while I hesitated. We didn't do this stuff well. Miracle was we'd managed even this much of a serious conversation.

I took an interest in the cracked paintwork over the fireplace before answering him. 'I pushed Shannon away from me. I pushed her, maybe too hard . . . definitely too hard . . . She fell and the shower head fell down and hit her in the face. That's it. End of.'

'Keep talking.'

'You sound like Saoirse.'

'Keep talking.'

It had been Saoirse's mantra with us both, really, after Ma died. There had been no expensive counselling, no fancy therapy, just our sister's wisdom and intuition inherited from my mother. She saved us both, me especially. Seán couldn't fill her shoes. I knew he didn't believe that I hadn't taken drugs. I didn't blame him, I wasn't sure I believed myself after hearing the hospital report. He struggled to avoid ribbing me with innuendo around all the detail I wasn't saying, but at least he was trying.

'That why you asked about Da?' he asked after a few minutes of me stumbling through a heavily censored account.

'I hurt her, Seán. I didn't mean it. Honest. It hit her face . . .

31

Reminded me of that night, you know?'

We never talked about those times, but we both knew the night. We'd been much younger and it was the start of the end. When he'd hit her, his ring had left a red gash in her right cheek. He'd roared at us to scarper upstairs, but we'd sat rigid at the kitchen table. At my mother's silent signal, Saoirse had gripped our hands and led us upstairs where we'd huddled on the bedroom floor, listening to the shouting, crashes of chairs, blows, until the back door slammed after him.

That night when I'd pushed Shannon off me to get space to think, she'd fallen over backwards and held her hand up to her cheek, eyes wide. Just like Ma. I hadn't realized how hard I'd shoved her. I'd been drunk, high and humiliated weaving out of that house, trying to find her, scared of my own hands. But it was the flashback to Ma slumped on the floor, angled against a kitchen cupboard by the sink, that had haunted my mind, led me to her grave and drawn me to the bridge.

'You're not the same as him,' Seán said. 'Don't ever think that.'

Words have a strange power. At that moment, those were precious.

Chapter 5. Waiting.

IONA.
Monday 20 June.

Two days and nothing. On Friday I'd checked my phone so often the battery had run down while I was still serving steaming lattes, cappuccinos and overpriced oatmeal biscuits. I'd smashed a cup by accident, like Dad on a down day. My focus was blurred to the point that I'd had to force myself to stop thinking and immersed myself in the routine of coffee grounds and frothed milk, clearing tables and chatting absent-mindedly to customers. They were always right. Yes, the weather was glorious. Sure, it would break soon. No, I didn't trust the bigwigs blagging about Europe neither. The fact Europe was hanging on a knife edge didn't stave off my boredom with the political posters clattering lamp posts. The vote wasn't until Thursday. *Would he have bothered to reply by then?*

I'd met friends on Saturday, window-gazing round town after the disjointed weeks of A-level exams. Everyone was in limbo, wondering how we'd face two months waiting for results, yet savouring our new freedom and sense of adulthood. Rachel bought new trainers, light green with a flower pattern. 'You gotta get new shoes for a new life in September,' she'd declared.

I was adamant I was sticking to my purple DMs. My stilettos were still stuffed in the corner of my wardrobe.

As we sipped Coke in a cafe, I flicked at my phone and frowned. Typical bloke. Non-communication was almost rude at this point.

'What's up with you?' asked Rachel.

'Nothing. Just fed up.'

She pulled a mad face. I laughed and stopped chasing the ice cubes round my glass. I couldn't tell her – Andy was still freaked. Why hadn't Aidan checked in? I had his phone; maybe he couldn't. Maybe he was plugged into a life-support machine with his family and a priest around him, saying the last rites or whatever they called it. Andy asked me once or twice if I'd heard anything, then, like his friends, turned into an ostrich, as if ignoring it meant it never really happened. Dylan and Luke had dropped off the planet.

'Hey.' Rachel clicked her fingers in front of my nose. 'You're in a different universe! Are you finally over Kyle? If you didn't look so serious, I'd swear you were in love again.'

'No such luck. Sorry. Let's try that wee shop up Shipquay Street.'

Yesterday was Father's Day. A whole family occasion after church. Guaranteed Aidan's family weren't laughing and pushing pavlova round a posh plate. I'd struggled to contribute to familiar family conversations as my mind whirred with doomsday scenarios. John was full of the joys of policing. His training seemed to have missed the mantra of *Don't talk shop when you're a cop*. Dad certainly never talked about picking body parts out of bomb rubble. He had a therapist for that.

'Got my first case!' John had grinned. 'Once the victim files the complaint, I can go at it full tilt. I already interviewed three witnesses yesterday from Foyle Search and Rescue.' I'd glanced at Andy as my dinner lurched in my mouth. The swallow was as distressing as the information. 'It's a real chance to impress and—'

'I've signed up for a course,' said Andy, kicking me under the table.

'Eh . . . what course?' I asked.

'SIA training. Security Industry Authority. They're short marshals for the parades.'

Dad nodded. John looked peeved.

'Where's the course?' asked Mum.

Andy hesitated. 'Creggan . . .'

'No!' Dad and John piped in unison.

'But it's free. Costs 750 quid in Coleraine.' Andy shoved his napkin onto the table.

'No. End of. It's not safe,' Dad scowled.

'There's peace!' Andy glared but his shoulders dropped.

'There's dissidents!' Dad had retaliated. 'The New IRA. Bandit country – they'd shoot each other, never mind us.'

'So you'll pay the fee for Coleraine? You'll be paying Iona's university fees. This is about a real job, not just books.'

My turn to glower at Andy.

'Marshalling won't put a roof over your head like the army would,' Dad said.

I'd been surprised the pavlova hadn't started to freeze over. Andy's head went down.

Mum did her mediator thing. 'Didn't Reverend McHugh speak well this morning?'

'Yes . . . wonderful,' we'd all chimed.

With my constant checking for a response from Aidan, the battery on my phone died every day by evening. I hoped it wasn't symbolic. As I knelt to plug the charger in for the third day in a row, I sighed and prayed. Perhaps I'd been naive to imagine he would message back, but I just needed to know he was OK. Was that too much to ask?

Chapter 6. Aftershock.

AIDAN.
Tuesday 21 June.

As the swelling waned, the cabin fever surged. By Tuesday the walls were choking me, an invisible screw locking the front door and turning my refuge into a prison. Three days of stale sweat and I smelled worse than the school locker room. Showering and shaving were a handling around bandages and bruises, but apart from my eye still shining black at me in the mirror, I was beginning to get back to myself. As if being beat up wasn't enough punishment, I'd finally faced the lecture from Aunt Teresa, from which it was crystal clear that any faith she had regained in me over the last two years was wiped. I was under no illusions that I could ever live up to her butter-wouldn't-melt teenage daughters even if I joined the priesthood. The phone call had been effort enough at communication with the outside world for one day, but I knew I would need to find the nerve soon to contact Shannon. I owed her a serious apology, that is if she would even speak to me again. You can't polish shite, but sometimes you have to try. That was one thing Da never did – apologize.

Seán was still asleep, but his phone was abandoned on the sofa. *Bite the bullet, Hennessey.* I'd bungeed from the mountain top to the gutter in freefall. Would Shannon diss me or take me back? Bloody years vying for her attention, only for it to end up in pure mortification. My pulse raced at the thought of having to speak directly with her. I couldn't risk a text – God knows the ribbing

I'd get if Seán saw her reply. If I used his 4G, though, I could go online into my own Facebook messenger, contact her, then log out. I clicked into my account on the web. One minute I was in a head-spin about Shannon, the next I was juggling my mug and Seán's phone over the sofa. Both chinked, coffee splashing as my head processed the message.

Hi. Hope you're OK? I have your phone. Message me. I was there. Sorry

Iona Scott. I forgot to breathe, staring like my brain was in a glitch, buffering, reading her name and her words over and over. Questions. Fears. Penitence, or a sick joke and a hidden agenda? Unable to suss it, I shelved it. Hard enough finding words for the girl I did know. I tapped the message with my good hand.

Hey Shannon. Sorry. Not sure what to say. You really mad? Wanna talk? I've no phone BTW.

Not the most fluent of apologies, but a start. I could pull that damned-if-I-care swagger as good as the next bloke, but sometimes Shannon pure disintegrated me. Sure, I could talk to a girl, but if I was mad for her it wiped me to show it.

Floorboards creaked upstairs. Hastily I messaged Conal explaining I'd lost my phone but would link up soon. My brother's footsteps on the stairs. I chanced a final flick at the message from Iona Scott, with its arty profile pic of a girl about my age, holidaying in a straw sun hat. Her public profile was limited. I logged out, threw the mobile back onto the sofa and joined Seán in the kitchen.

'You feeling better?' he mumbled through a mouthful of cereal.

'Need to get out for a bit. You got any plans?'

He had runs to do in the car. How he'd got it was one of those Irish sagas, from your-man's-cousin's-uncle-up-the-road's-niece's dog's-friend . . . the long and the short of which was he was on the insurance temporarily, provided he ran some messages when needed. It was a disability car and the owner's usual driver was away all summer.

'You're covered on it, too.' He nodded towards the front door as if the car was parked in the hall. 'I said you wouldn't mind driving a bit if they need stuff, so they put you down as a named driver. Kind of my present to you for finishing school – oh, and I got you a scratch card as well.' He fired it to me from his back pocket. 'Happy graduation or whatever you call it. You going on the dole now or what's the plan?'

'No idea.' I shrugged. I didn't think I was long enough out of school to sign on yet, but my educational maintenance allowance would end soon. I'd have to come up with something. Wasn't my style to go begging off the state. 'Am I seriously insured?'

He nodded, mirroring my sheepish grin.

'Mental!' The last time I'd driven a car was the day I passed my test – I hadn't a hope of affording wheels and insurance for years yet. 'I'm heading out to air my head,' I said, rinsing my mug, 'Catch you later.'

I hadn't meant to walk straight to Ma's grave. There'd been no particular plan as I'd yanked the front door shut, except to try stretching the stiffness out of my legs and see whether I was anywhere near normal yet. Up the street, I chanced a few seconds jogging, but stopped when my ribs throbbed. The cops still had my good runners. I walked on like a pensioner. When Ma died, I'd avoided the cemetery for months, but later it became like time out, a chance to mull over things that bothered me and offload into the nothingness with the thought that maybe she was watching over me somewhere. Other times it was as close as I got to confession, without paying any particular penance. I picked a wee bunch of daisies, buttercups and clover from the grass and laid them at the foot of the headstone.

My fingers played with threads in my empty pockets, then clenched. *I lost your ring, Ma*, I confessed silently into the air. *Sorry. I know it was important.* I scuffed my shoe and sighed. I was never the type to learn things the easy way. 'Rough diamonds,' Ma bemoaned us to the neighbours, 'loveable rogues.'

These days Saoirse was the diamond. Us boys were the rough edges. If Ma hadn't got sick, maybe she'd have smoothed us like she did our school shirts every Sunday. We were always rascals, always in bother, but with no real badness. Maybe our circumstances changed us, maybe not. Ma's disappointment always hurt deeper than Da's punches, yet her hugs healed. But for six feet of soil, she might've tamed my wildness, but then again, she was impulsive too. She'd never have ended up with Da otherwise.

It was on a bench by her grave that I decided it was worth the risk to get my phone back. Now I was coming back to myself, it was like having my right arm cut off to be so disconnected. If she was for real, if we met in public, on the Cityside, then it should be fine. It would have to be our side of the river though, no way was I going to the Waterside right now. As far as I could remember, there'd only been one or two girls that night over in St Columb's Park. I couldn't picture them, but I remembered a voice. It had been lads who had thrown the punches. If Iona came on her own, then it could work.

Internet access was free in the Creggan library. I picked a computer in the far corner, away from everyone else.

Can I get my phone? That what you're offering? Guildhall Square? Just you – OK?

She'd checked her messages recently. So had Shannon, but she hadn't replied. Crap. Conal had written an essay, taking five years to get to the point that he'd been talking to Seán and was worried about me. He'd swing round for the Germany–Northern Ireland match or a jam on the guitars later, if I was up for it?

Maybe, I thought. Only one hour out and I could sleep for Ireland. Call you later.

Her face appeared in a circle by my message. She'd read it. Then her reply landed.

Hi Aidan. Thank God you're OK. 11am tomorrow. Swear you'll be on your own too?

Jesus. She was really real. I winced as I shook my head. Was I walking into another ambush? Was she half wise trusting me? Either she was brave or pretty bloody stupid. Could I charm names out of her with a smile or a poker-faced sympathy card? Should I tell Seán? He knew people who knew people, but that'd be me living up to a reputation black as my eye. Her people had hammered me. The demons and angels spewed in alternate ears.

11am is good. I'll be alone. Just want my phone.

Sweet. CU then.

She was just a girl with my phone. Vengeance or conscience?

Chapter 7. Unscripted.

IONA.
Wednesday 22 June.

All that sixth-sense stuff was pure crap. I couldn't tell if I was being watched. As far as I was aware, only the row of cannons overlooked me from their slots in the dark grey walls backing Guildhall Square. I twirled my necklace, waiting. It was cloudy; the breeze played football with a crisp bag as black clouds threatened rain. At least we'd had a week of Costa del Londonderry. The grey-bearded homeless man wandered by with his battery radio, rollator and shopping bag stuffed with possessions. Watching people fascinated me. I bit a rag nail.

Pigeons circled in front of the Guildhall's burnt-orange brickwork and stained-glass windows, scattering from its gothic turrets as the clock-tower chimed. In winter, storm-battered seagulls roamed in gangs here, colouring the hair white on the sculpted heads of Neptune and Venus carved on the bank. Waiting for exam results was easier than this. As I sat on a stone cube at the edge of the square, I rubbed a scuff mark off my DMs and tightened the rainbow shoelaces. They were the ones Kyle said looked 'gay'. He'd been lucky to avoid a close encounter with one around his neck. Giggling toddlers splashing in the fountains put a smile back on my face. Then I saw him. He was walking from Waterloo Place – slow but purposeful; an athletic six foot tall, in ripped skinny jeans, a grey T-shirt and the same black zipped jacket from that night. My heart beat in my mouth as my eyes scouted the square. He did seem to be alone.

'Iona?' He hesitated a few feet from me, meeting my gaze through dark sunglasses. As I stood, he stepped back, and we both glanced around.

'Hi,' was all I managed, as my words and mouth dried up, making a mockery of the many different introductions I'd rehearsed fluently in my head for the last hour.

'What's the craic?' he mumbled.

'Not much. What's the craic with you?' I cringed as we stumbled on autopilot through the meaningless Derry mantra.

'Been better.' The smudge of sarcasm brought a wary trace of a grin, the kind of smile I couldn't not respond to. My shoulders sagged. He shifted his weight onto the other leg and swallowed. 'It's fine, you know. I am on my own. Just me . . . and half of Creggan waiting behind Magazine Gate for the signal.'

I glanced to the walls before it dawned that he was joking. Despite the veneer of confidence, he was messing with his trainer on the stone slabs, as much on unsure territory as myself.

'Bit mad this,' he said.

'Aye.' I nodded.

The fountains splished.

'I recognize your voice,' he said eventually, cutting the awkward silence and meeting my eyes again. 'You OK?'

Weird he asked the question I'd been desperate to ask him. From nowhere, my tears burst, and I turned, brushing them away angrily.

'Sorry,' he said, stuffing his hands into his pockets and studying the clouds.

'This conversation is all the wrong way round!' I said, recovering my voice after minutes that seemed like an eternity.

'Guess I forgot to read the script.'

'I'm supposed to be asking if you're OK and apologizing to you! You're stealing my lines.'

'Fancy improvising?' He half smiled. 'Your mascara's messed. Swap a tissue for a phone?'

He held out a tissue like a white flag of truce. I fished his mobile from the bottom of my brown leather bag that I'd haggled for in Tenerife. Setting the phone into his hand, I flinched, noticing his bandaged fingers.

'You play acoustic guitar,' he commented, grinning at the confusion in my eyes. His own eyes were still hidden behind the dark tint of his sunglasses. All I could see was my own reflection.

'Yes. You?' I smiled back.

'No. I play bass. Badly. Well, I can mess on a guitar.'

'With broken fingers?'

'Mm . . .' His smile faded as he studied his right hand like it was the first time he'd noticed. 'I'll probably sound no worse than usual! It's just the wee one. I haven't tried since . . . Your nail art rocks, but the blistered bits on your left fingers are a dead giveaway that you play guitar. Hazard of the trade,' he added like an afterthought.

I folded my arms, wishing I'd bothered to lift a hoodie, as the wind blew cooler. Now or never. 'Can we talk about your phone?' I asked, sitting back down on the stone cube. In the script in my head he would say 'Sure', and sit opposite to listen, but he was staring at the dark clouds as he ran his fingers across the side of his hair, like he was scouring for some lost thought.

'I can't pay you for it at the minute,' he said a few seconds later, as the first drops of rain specked the rectangle slabs.

'What?'

'You fixed the screen. I'm broke just now.'

'My friend works at the phone shop. Owed me a favour – but

that's not the point.' My voice lifted. 'I was there when you got beat up. Mind? They were kicking your head in and you dropped your phone and it smashed. I just . . . like I just wanted to show I'm sorry . . . I'm no bigot. Just because I'm Protestant doesn't mean I hate Catholics. I thought you were dead.' I offered no apologies this time for the fresh tears running down my cheeks, and he met my eyes fully for the first time without his sunglasses. His gaze was deep and direct, trying to fathom what to do or say next. Oblivious to the heavy drops of rain, I couldn't help but study the purple-yellow bruising round his right eye, the four stitches clear above it.

'It's going to piss down,' he said. 'You drink coffee? Tea?'

I was quiet until the thunder rumbled like the aftershock of an explosion. As I nodded, the heavens opened and we dove under Magazine Gate archway, sheltering under the city walls where the spiral staircase and twisted rail climb to the Grand Parade. 'Cafe Nervosa?' he asked, 'Just up the street. My shout.'

'Let me pay!' I argued, shivering as the wind blew the rain under the arch.

'Hell no.' He leaned in, raising his voice to be heard over the downpour pelting the cobbles. 'I cracked that screen months ago on the kitchen floor. Hadn't the dough to fix it. I can't run at the minute. Know the cafe? Bright yellow – on the left. Want to run ahead and I'll catch you up?'

'No.' I smiled. 'But I have an umbrella.'

Chapter 8. Nerve.

AIDAN.
Wednesday 22 June.

If I did have a plan, it was banjaxed. I watched her hug the steaming red mug of tea across the table as my hair dripped into my coffee with a splosh, casting a circle of ripples. The intention – mine anyway – had been to get the phone, say a polite thanks and beat a hasty retreat. So maybe I'd thought about digging for names. Maybe I still was thinking. But not this. We were sat in the tiny retro cafe, with its red walls plastered with posters of old films. *Hotel Rwanda* was the faded poster behind her. The African man, the white guy with the TV camera, a peacekeeper with a gun and a family stuck in the middle. I hadn't seen the flick.

'How come you drink your coffee black?' She broke my daydream.

I shrugged. 'We're forever running out of milk at home. Makes it easier.' It was true. Since Saoirse left, Seán and I were hopeless at organizing the messages. It was more like a student flat than a normal family home.

'Looks like summer's ended,' she said. 'Thought you were for being a weatherman the way you were studying them clouds back there.'

Everyone talks about the weather to make conversation, but she was studying me, thinking. I liked her eyes. Hazel. Alive and bright like they were taking in the world and processing it for meaning. Sitting with her was surreal.

'I never talked much to a Protestant before.' It was out of me before my brain censored it. She raised her eyebrows and clanked down her mug.

'Shit. Sorry . . . I didn't mean to say that out loud.'

'Really?'

'Yes really, it makes me sound like a dinosaur. I didn't mean it like that. Sorry.'

'No, I mean, have you really never talked to a Protestant before?' She questioned me like I was some kind of curiosity, a sectarian virgin. I hesitated, but she didn't look riled, just intrigued.

'Honestly?' I asked.

She nodded and cupped her chin in her hands, tilting her head.

'I'm as multicultural as St Patrick wrapped in a tricolour,' I said.

'Crooning "The Fields of Athenry" and downing Guinness?'

Her remark made me grin. 'What about you? Do you know many of us?'

'I go to Foyle College; used to anyway. It's mixed. A couple of my best friends are Catholic. The Waterside is a muddle of everyone, especially where I live.'

'Right.' I flicked a crumb and changed the subject. 'Did you just finish sixth form too, then?'

'Aye. We're exactly the same age.'

'What do you mean?' Her comment was unnerving for someone who didn't know me.

'You were born on Good Friday 1998. So was I. You're the only person I've ever met so far with the same birthday. Our mums were probably in Altnagelvin maternity ward together. You were born here, right?'

I sat back, swinging my seat onto two legs. How'd she know?

Of course. Online. 'You read my Facebook profile?' My heart sank. I'd only recently deleted the crap off it and reset the securities. God knows what she'd read, yet here she was, sipping her milky tea and smiling like this wasn't weird.

'Sorry,' she said. 'Had to suss you out before contacting you.'

My face must have reacted. She blinked.

'What, you think I came up the Foyle in a bubble? Like, I just read the profile and flicked through a few of your photos and contacts.'

'Just?' I dropped the front legs of the metal chair back to the wooden floor with a small thud that rocked the mugs on the table and made us both sit up straighter.

'You and your girlfriend look like a cute couple,' she carried on with a smile that I couldn't read. *Jesus, was every girl in the city slating me?*

'Why did you want to talk about my phone?' I interrupted, praying she couldn't mind-read. The joy drained from her like the rainwater flooding down the street into the storm grates. Again her eyes studied me, lost in thought, edgy.

'You remembered my voice from last Thursday?' She turned a spoon on the table over and over. 'Do you remember what I said? Mind anything else?'

I pulled the phone from my pocket and toyed with it. 'Three lads, about our age?' I watched my foot kick off the wrought-iron table leg as I spoke low. 'I was well oiled, to be honest. Northern Ireland football tops on the guys . . . Can I ask a question?'

'I guess.' She looked resolute now, no tears like before; like we were back on script. This was the conversation she'd expected, and there was a silent strength to her that I hadn't noticed before, as she smoothed her long brown hair back behind her ears where the cute turquoise earrings hung.

'How'd they know I was Catholic?' It had been bugging the life out of me. 'I wasn't wearing anything specific – no crucifix, no Celtic top, no *fáinne* ... Do I just look Catholic or something?'

'Seán. You were trying to get through to a Seán on your mobile.' She sighed. 'And you spoke Irish.'

'Oh.' It came back to me then, the half-lucid SOS call. 'He's my brother. Wrong place, wrong time.' Now it was my turn to study her. Could we really have this conversation? Was I for the naughty or nice list? Swings or roundabouts. Her eyes were steady, if wistful, as she held my gaze. 'How'd you know them? They your friends?'

'Not really. My brother knows two of them from the band.'

'Your brother? Was he one of the guys?'

She hesitated, moving the salt and pepper like chess pieces. 'No. He wasn't one of the two that went for you.' Her eyes flitted and she raised her chin. 'But he knows the score. I told him.'

'What band? Like one of those kick-the-Pope Orange bands?'

'It's just a flute band. Pride of the Kilfennan.'

'Same difference.' There was a distance now in the silence between us, rather than just awkwardness.

'Does your brother know you're here?' I asked, drumming my fingers on the table.

'No.' She looked past me to the rain outside. 'But he knows I'd your mobile and that I messaged you.'

'Shite.'

'What do you mean?' She sat up rigidly, narrowing her eyes.

My hackles rose. 'I don't know ... Like, thanks for the phone but maybe we should just leave, go back to our own lives and forget it ...' I scraped the chair backwards, my hands gripping the metal seat. 'I mean ... this doesn't feel safe anymore, it's not normal ... Like, major reality check – your brother's friends kicked the feckin' crap out of me. You Prods are all the same, thinking we're still second-class citizens in our own country; parading in your wee bands round the walls imagining you still own the place. Well you don't. Go back to the Waterside. Get it? *Sin é.*' I lifted my coffee to gulp the rest of it and avoided eye contact.

'Shin ay? What's that?'

'It's Irish, all right? *That's it.* That's all it means. Our own language. Get it?' My raised voice turned more than a few heads in the cafe as I sprang to my feet, sending my chair clattering. 'And here's another one for you – *Slán. Au revoir, adiós, sayonara,* bye ... and thanks for the phone,' I added. Catching her eye, I saw fire behind her resolution for the first time. She came across confident, but the way she half bit her lip as she looked up stalled me, sparking a fleeting recollection of my father towering over my mother as she sat mute at the kitchen table, deflecting yet another spew of abuse.

'Quite finished your rant, have you?' she hissed.

I swore loudly in frustration as I pivoted a one-eighty, and the cafe customers flinched before resuming their conversations. My feet were still glued to the floor in defiance, knowing I wasn't for going anywhere yet, waiting for my head to catch up.

'We have to talk about your phone.'

I turned to face her, righted the chair and slumped into it, unable to meet her eyes or spit out the apology I was choking on.

'Honest,' she said. 'No one knows I'm here. You think this isn't hard for me too? Want to tell me if I can trust you?'

I ground my teeth, thinking. In the lack of conversation, the pressure seeped out of me; my fists that I hadn't realized were tight, relaxed. She sipped her tea and I messed with my empty mug, staring vacantly at the posters, at the chocolate brownies on the food counter by the till, at other people's shoes, at the chalked menu on the blackboard – anywhere but her. Feck's sake. She wasn't here for some sectarian gameplay. Her knuckles were white, gripped tight round her mug to hide her hands shaking. She was sweet, but no pushover. She minded me of Saoirse, just for sitting there until I spoke – that female gift of patience that could cloak a dagger or a handshake.

'Sorry,' I muttered. 'You OK?' I raised my head to meet her gaze again for the first time in ten stretched minutes. There was the vaguest hint of strain in the hazel now, and I experienced the unnerving feeling of being subtly unmasked, as if there were just the two of us huddled amongst the coffee aroma and background chatter.

'Been better,' she mouthed to me in a whisper tinted with irony. 'That's the second time you've asked me that today. I was wondering, why'd you ask me the first time? It was my question to ask you. It wasn't just a throwaway line, was it?' That quest for clarity was back in her eyes again. I picked at my thumbnail, unsure if I could trust myself to speak. I was bloody like my da sometimes. She hadn't deserved it. The wall of silence I used for teacher's accusations was crumbling. Somehow, she knew my lock codes but wasn't prepared to hack them unless I gave the nod.

'In the square, you looked happy lost in your thoughts. But when you saw me, something clouded.' My voice cracked as I held my broken finger to my eye. 'Bruises and broken bones aren't the only kind of hurt. They heal. The stuff that messes your head? That's tougher. It can't have been a good thing to watch, not if it looked as brutal as it felt. You videoed it, didn't you? You really took it in. That's what's on the phone, what you wanted to talk about, right?'

I didn't need the nod she gave me. I knew. I remembered seeing the same frightened uncertainty in my own eyes reflected in a police-car window when I was twelve. My heart went out to her. For the first time it became simple – we were just two eighteen-year-olds, no agendas, no masks, just an unspoken understanding that we'd shared something which needed working through together, no matter who we were. She jostled in her bag, produced a tangled set of earphones and slipped them straight into my hand. It was the first time we touched.

Chapter 9. Impact.

IONA.
Wednesday 22 June.

I was at the till, hooking my fingers into the handles of two refilled mugs, when he appeared back at the table. He'd started to watch the video on his phone and then bolted to the disabled toilet. He now scanned the room like a toddler who'd lost a parent. His shoulders sagged, arms limp. The change was scary – same skin, different person. Once he clocked me, he headed back to the table, nudging another one on the way and stumbling into his chair, phone discarded with the mess of earphones strung around it. He didn't even acknowledge the fresh coffee I set beside his hand. 'Aidan?'

No response. Two minutes. I shuffled my chair closer as if I could shield him from the rest of the cafe goers as he slid his head into the crooks of his elbows on the table. Five minutes. He moaned into the fabric of his jacket. 'Aidan?' I whispered by his ear. In the silence I chewed my knuckle, wishing people wouldn't keep glancing over. Eejit. How had I not known someone would want to puke after watching their own head get kicked in? I scratched my wrist and slouched in my chair. He'd been right, I reflected, when he'd said the unseen stuff was the hardest. He clearly wasn't OK, but neither was I. How had he known? Intuition? Life experience?

'Aidan?' I touched his jacket. 'You all right? Can you talk?'
'No.'

He lifted his head a fraction and mouthed inaudibly as relief washed over me that he was communicating again.

'No, I'm not all right.' He admitted the obvious and paused. 'It was fucking brutal – excuse my French – and I watched it twice. I feel sick as a dog. And no, I don't want to talk.' He wasn't crying, but his head went down again onto his arms and the backs of his shoulders shifted heavily every half minute or so. I rubbed my neck.

'Want me to call your mum or someone?'

'Ma's dead,' came the reply, muffled through his jacket sleeves.

'Oh God. Sorry.' My throat went dry. I couldn't speak. It hadn't seemed possible that I could have made it worse. After a moment, without thinking, I just put my hand over his on the table and held it there. It was all I could do. He didn't move for ages and I didn't care what anyone else thought. It didn't matter anymore. Outside it had stopped raining and the street was glossed black, steam rising as the sun broke through. When I looked back, his head was lifted and I knew he was back in the room, the colour beginning to filter into his cheeks, although his eyes were still distant.

'You couldn't have known about my mum. It was a few years ago,' he said. 'That video? It's like I'm just a worthless piece of meat.'

'You still feel sick? Wanna get some air?'

'I already threw up. I don't want to move until the room stops spinning.' As he edged up straighter, he withdrew his hands from under mine. 'Thanks . . . Thanks for sticking with me. I appreciate it.' Then, with a deep breath and a nod to his phone, he added, 'I haven't the foggiest what to do with that.'

'I nearly deleted it days ago but couldn't,' I confessed.

'What stopped you?'

'Dunno . . .' I balked at telling him the full truth. The clip was pure gold for justice or John's case. Pure hell for me and Andy. 'Not my choice to make, I guess. It's evidence. You should discuss it with your family; take it to the police. They're identifiable.'

Aidan was quiet a moment, rubbing his brow. 'I'm not reporting it.' He looked directly at me now, returning my gaze steadily. 'Look, I never properly thanked you. Seems I probably am a bigot. You and that other guy with his back turned? You two saved my life.'

I bit my tongue. I wasn't mentioning Andy. That my brother had helped save Aidan was good, but the thought of identifying Andy in the evidence was scary complicated. This was already way too messed up. Aidan's hand shook as he lifted the mobile. He looked round as he spoke, chewing over every word. 'Facing an enemy, I'd stand up for what I believe in . . . facing my friends? Different ball game. You'd some bloody presence of mind to film that. Respect. They were off their heads and clearly for flattening mine. That guy shoved them over right before Pancake Tuesday. I didn't know that happened.' He choked, then whispered low, 'Don't tell me his name. Just tell him I said thanks.'

'I will, especially if you put a lock of sugar in your coffee and drink it. You're in shock.' I nudged his mug towards him and ripped open two paper tubes of brown sugar, stirring them in until they dissolved. He obediently sipped, either lost or locked in thought for a while.

'God, I really didn't mean that stuff, Iona,' he sighed. 'Least, not about you.'

'Forget it.'

He swirled the last dregs round the mug. My tea was long gone cold.

'Are you seriously not reporting it?'

'No,' he said, setting the mug down. I could already imagine John's sectarian rant.

'No, you're not reporting it, or no, you're not serious?'

'I'm seriously not reporting it to the police.'

I frowned and went to speak but he continued.

'Look, maybe for you it's different, I don't know, but my family doesn't do police.'

'My family is in the police.' It was out before I completed the thought.

He looked at me like I was from a different planet. 'You winding me up?'

'No.' I bit my lip in realization that I'd said too much. My chest tightened. How could I have forgotten first my dad's and now my older brother's over-rehearsed mantra? Always spell police c-i-v-i-l s-e-r-v-a-n-t in public. Dad had already quit early on the sick, he didn't need further stress from my stupidity. Just because there were Catholics on the police payroll now didn't mean their whole community was singing from the same hymn sheet. The dissidents were few, but still deadly. They even shot ones in their own estates – dealers and that. I shivered. *Where did Aidan stand?*

'Chalk and cheese.' He returned his gaze from the menu and considered our conversation. 'I'm a Republican,' he said. 'Well, my family is. I'm sort of Irish Republican, half-baked socialist and passportless internationalist for what it's worth. I'd only do police if I'd no choice.'

'What do you mean by choice?' I demanded.

He studied me with a guarded intelligence, arms folded.

'I mean I don't choose police interviews, courts and stuff. Not for all of Ireland am I being handcuffed to this city, justifying what I did or didn't do, how much I drank, what I can and can't remember. Feck it. Half the time they lock someone up they come out worse, so why bother? I just want out of here, to where this shit doesn't matter. I mean that kind of choice.'

'Oh. I thought you meant something different.'

He looked at me for a second before answering. 'If you mean what I think you mean, like reporting it somewhere else, then no – they're just as bad. Worse. Just because I'm Republican doesn't mean I'm *that* kind of Republican. I do believe in human rights and justice.'

'Just not rights for parading culture or justice of the policing kind?'

'Touché.'

His wink would have relaxed me but for the drunken laughs of Dylan and Luke echoing in my brain.

'What if those guys attack someone else? Shouldn't they face justice?' I looked away. *Quit blabbering. Stuff John and his precious case. Keep. Andy. Safe.*

'I thought you'd have been sweet with burying this.' He frowned. 'Think we're all more complicated than the stereotypes?'

'I think you're far more complicated than I read you at first.'

'You read me?' he teased, tilting his head in amusement.

'Complicated is way more interesting.'

He smiled and leaned in with his elbows on the table. 'Well, for what it's worth, I still can't read you. But I can't report this. Real truth?' He edged closer. 'I could put all the political spin on it I want, but never mind community and family, the reason I can't report it is me. I'm raging when it floods back, which it does, and that's exactly what I don't need right now. I don't need two years of being stuck here angry, just when I have a chance to start being something different. I just want out. That's all.' His honesty connected with me as he flicked his phone on and brought up the video. Spinning it round he checked to see I was watching as his finger hovered over the bin icon.

'You or me?'

'Your call,' I said.

We both inhaled as he hit delete.

'Think we could talk about something else for ten minutes to take my mind off this?' he asked with a hopeful sigh.

'Could you stretch to forty-five?' I smiled. 'I've just missed my bus. Next one's not for ages.'

Chapter 10. Driver.

AIDAN.
Thursday 23 June.

Pride of Kilfennan. What a band name. Twats. Were they proud of the bigots marching under their banners too? I'd cut the engine, whistling to the radio as I waited outside the polling station for the two voters my brother had asked me to taxi. *Vote early, vote often*. Since Ireland had pulled off the miracle win against Italy in the football last night, half the folk heading in to X their ballots looked worse than the photos on their ID. Agreeing to ferry the pro-Europe vote was a no-brainer. Seán had promised the car keys for a day next week and I wasn't exactly busy. If only it was as obvious what to do about revenge.

I crunched over my encounter with Iona. Seán wouldn't be this indecisive. A clear lead and clear footage, it had dawned on me, still stashed in my cloud's deleted items. If I as much as hinted to Seán that I had it, he'd be after them, fists flying. Would I? You could proxy vote. Maybe proxy fighting was the ticket. *Grow a pair, Hennessey*. She'd know anyway – and I didn't want her hurt. No way. My head ached worse than my ribs. Whatever.

After leaving the cafe, we'd dawdled over the brick-cobbled crest of Butcher's Gate and past the railings fronting First Derry Presbyterian Church. I smirked at a memory – me, ten, sprinting after Seán like a blue-arsed fly down the banking after paint-bombing its Greek columns one July night. God, but Ma had lit into us after dragging out the explanation for the yellow gloss on our runners. Da's cigarette had wobbled as he tried not to laugh. I could see Iona wondering why I was smiling, but I'd kept my thoughts private. For all I knew it could be her church.

The rain had emptied the walls of all but a handful of Yanks with oversized raincoats and bum bags as we had dandered past St Augustine's. It suited me fine not to bump into anyone I knew. God knows what rumours I'd have generated walking up the town with a new sidekick, and a Protestant at that.

During the Troubles the walls hosted a green British Army observation tower like a misplaced Lego-build. I was around six when I remember Da pulling in our old Skoda at Free Derry Corner and dragging my attention off the Nintendo DS up to where they were ripping off the iron cladding. Changing times. Demilitarization. Days when the walls were gated and locked for every Old Firm match and only the maddest entrepreneurs were wittering about tourist dollars. In the seventies, the IRA blew the ninety-foot pillar topped with Governor Walker sky-high. It had towered over the Bogside, imposing its Britishness on the Catholic houses huddled in terrace streets below. Da had revelled in telling glory stories of chunks of its rubble decorating Bogside mantelpieces. Rose-tinted bedtime stories delivered with slurred words and the smell of beer.

Iona and I had walked past the pillar stump and the trees on Grand Parade to the orange brick of the Verbal Arts Centre. 'To Imagine, To Create, To Learn', read the stone plaque over its door. Fine if you're five and playing with plasticine. 'In the good oul' days we played with grey plasticine that smelled of Christmas and went boom,' my da used to brag. Part of me still wished I was five. It was easier to know who you were in them days. I glanced at Iona. Best to keep radio silence on the IRA family heritage.

I couldn't resist clambering on the cannons at the double

bastion overlooking the Bogside murals. Iona had looked up as I grinned like a maniac, delicately balanced with my arms held wide on the barrel of Roaring Meg.

'Have you ever broken a bone?' she'd asked.

'You my guardian now?' I'd laughed back, raising my bandaged fingers.

I'd broken my left arm when I was five, running too fast down Creggan Hill after a football. When I was seven, I badly sprained an ankle playing Superman off a five-foot wall in our playground. At ten I turned my big toe liquorice after busting it with a brick on a building site at dusk. Ma was a season ticket holder at A&E.

'So what are you for, now school's out?' I'd asked Iona as I straddled the barrel, watching her gaze over the ramparts down the grass to Free Derry Corner. Her heart was set on studying English at Queen's University in Belfast. I must've skipped school the day they taught decision-making. My crystal ball was drowned in slurry somewhere. I'd an offer from Queen's too, but I'd fit university like a fart in a wetsuit. Middle-class bollocks. Our clan were smart, like, but no one had mortarboard photos over the fireplace. Saoirse could make anyone do anything. Seán quit school early over his dyslexia, but he could wire everything – cars, radios, your head with bloody community politics . . .

No one really had any expectations of me except myself after a few pints – then I'd be for taking on the world. Aunt Teresa needed prayer when I scraped enough GCSEs to get back into year 13. My teachers needed vodka. Except for a couple who'd taught me further down the school and knew me better. They'd encouraged me back onto my feet after I'd disintegrated. '*Mol an óige agus tiocfaidh sí,*' – praise the youth and they will flourish – my Irish teacher had whispered, laying an essay with my first A grade in a couple of years on my desk. Along with my politics teacher, he'd gradually sneaked a determination back into me, a focus. It was around then I caught myself reading Irish politics into the wee hours one night. The shock realization that I enjoyed using my brain near put me back on the smokes.

'What do you make of the murals then?' Iona had quizzed me.

Down by the blocks of flats, tourists were clicking selfies at the three-storey historical wall paintings. A people's gallery showing Derry's history in the Troubles. Civil rights. Army house raids. Bloody Sunday. The hunger strikes. Real images of our past, or at least my community's take on it, towering over our present. My teeth gritted on impact after jumping from the oak cartwheel with its black ironwork holding the cannon proud. *Those bigots should pay for my pain.*

'Don't notice them that much,' I admitted, crossing to stand beside her at the parapet.

'You blind?' she said. 'They're like two fingers in your face.'

I'd never seen them like that – the murals were just part of the furniture when you'd walked Lecky Road for the hundredth time. Maybe they did only tell our side of the story, but looking at them made me feel proud. My people. Protesting against injustice. Carrying their banners and placards demanding votes, jobs and houses. Equality. They'd suffered for it too. I pointed out Annette McGavigan on the *Death of Innocence* mural. 'She was fourteen. Went out to spot the talent during a riot and collect rubber bullets. Shot dead in her school uniform by the British Army.'

'You think the Bogside Artists meant to paint the three crosses in the mural?' she'd asked. 'Different kind of shout on the death of innocence?'

I'd never noticed them before, but she was right. Three crosses like on Calvary, hidden in angled planks in the background bomb debris of the image. Her question made me wonder if she was religious. I wondered too what she made of the 'End British Internment Now' slogans on the shopfronts. Neither felt like questions I could ask.

'You live up there then?' She'd gestured at the sprawling estate climbing the hillside.

'See the cemetery?' I'd pointed. 'Move right past the red and white of Celtic Park GAA stadium. See St Mary's Chapel? Near there.'

Like half of Creggan on a Sunday, she'd confused the modern brick chapel with the shopping centre.

'I've never been in a Catholic church,' she'd confessed.

That had made me smile. 'Hallelujah! Thought you'd me marked as a caveman since saying I'd never talked to a Prod before!' She'd laughed with me.

'Like you've been in a Protestant church!'

'Have so! Year nine history trip to St Columb's Cathedral – gawping at padlocks and keys from the Siege in 1689 and the hollow cannonball for the terms of surrender. The guide was going on about the yellowed union jacks and secret escape passages under the pulpit. Kevin Finn stole a drawer knob off an ancient desk and got a right bollocking.'

Leaning back in the car seat, I grinned at the memory of talking to Iona as I waited in the primary school lay-by, then sat upright, wondering if it was the memory from year 9 or yesterday that had made me smile. I was still chewing the thought when my phone in the passenger seat buzzed.

In Magaluf. Back next week. You'd better bloody grovel.

Shannon. A warm wave of something primal rippled slowly through my gut as I closed my eyes and let music from the radio wash over me. Someone rapped on the car window, which interrupted my thoughts and made me remember my taxi duties.

On the last run of the day I went in to cast my own vote, novelty and duty combined. Crazy that in my grandparents' generation Catholic blood spilled on our streets for the right to scribble on a ballot paper. Politics was serious then. It was a joke now.

Seán would've made a good politician. Like Da had on a sober day, he had the passion for Ireland, the charisma to articulate half-truths like they were holy gospel and the ability to talk intelligent-sounding shite and change the subject when he didn't know the answer. I still couldn't decide whether to show him the video.

I glanced in the driver's mirror while waiting for the passengers. Now that the practice nurse had removed my stitches, I looked more like a debonair pirate than Frankenstein's monster. Maybe Shannon and I would look like twins awhile if she didn't give me another black eye for good measure. She *had* texted. There *was* hope.

Alone at home, I fired up my amp and messed on my bass guitar, relaxing to the familiar whack and vibration of the strings. Conal was desperate to get our band playing in the Music City busking competition and a broken finger was too lame an excuse for letting my best mate down.

I was still jamming on my bass about ten o'clock when Seán landed back with a few cans and a sofa takeover bid. I accepted a beer but declined a drag of his spliff. It was a ritual – every so often he offered to test if I'd give him the middle finger. I think he preferred me when I was off my head half the time.

'What you practising for?' he asked, with a nod to the guitar and amp.

'Music City busking. Conal's mad for it. Wasn't sure it'd work with the finger all Egyptian, but it's OK.'

The swingometer guy blethered about the statistical possibilities of Brexit on the TV.

'You don't honestly think they'll vote us out of Europe, do you?' I asked.

'Tell you one thing, if the Brits try to bring back the border it'll make a hell of a target.' He glugged his beer.

I couldn't imagine what it'd be like with checkpoints into Donegal. There were no mad military posts anymore. Illicit border hopping with guns or war-rationed butter in baby prams had gone out with CDs. Then again, vinyl was making a comeback. The border was white lines on white pages, marked only by cheap booze or cheap fuel on either side, depending on the sterling–euro exchange rate. Ma had always bought us chocolate and ice cream at the border filling station, swearing blind they tasted better in the Republic.

I got tired of monotonous referendum coverage and inhaling second-hand smoke sometime after midnight and dragged myself upstairs to bed. Only then did I notice Iona's text.

Random, but I'm for visiting Queen's Monday coming. My friend bailed. Want to join me instead?

Chapter 11. Paths.

IONA.
Monday 27 June.

Typical lad. I knew he'd stand me up and leave me travelling alone on the two-hour trip to Belfast. Maybe it didn't matter. Despite being well past the commuter rush hour, there had been a long queue for the Goldline Ulsterbus from Foyle Street. I shifted in the double seat, staring ahead, wondering how long I dared keep my bag hogging the space next to me.

The bus shuddered as the engine started and the last passenger shuffled up the aisle, wedging a sports bag in the overhead. The pistons hissed our imminent departure and I closed my eyes to consider whether it was disappointment, annoyance or something else I was feeling as the bus lurched into reverse. It stopped with a jerk, doors hissing again and the driver engaging in terse conversation. When I opened my eyes, Aidan was there at the far end of the aisle, scanning the passenger faces until he spied me and, turning back to the driver, dug out a note for his fare.

'Hi. This seat taken?' he jested, grinning, waiting for me to move my handbag. No more shades – his eye was healed and the stitches were gone, although his two fingers were still bandaged. As the bus swung out of the depot and onto the dual carriageway, perspiration glinted on his forehead and he was trying to catch his breath. He stripped off his jacket, shoving it in a ball under the seat.

'Sorry.' He rolled his eyes. 'I probably reek. Had to leg it from William Street. My ribs are killing me now. Thought I'd missed the bus.' He ran his fingers through his black hair, closing his eyes and leaning back onto the headrest. It was the first time I'd noticed his tattoo – a knotted Celtic band in tones of dark greens circling his bicep.

'Like it?' He flexed the muscle taut, having caught me looking. 'Eighteenth birthday present from my brother. Had to hide it in school for a couple of months. Class, isn't it?'

'I thought you'd changed your mind about coming.'

'Almost did. I was still sound asleep forty minutes ago. You watch the football?' He had a coy grin.

'The Northern Ireland *and* the Ireland match. Pity they both got knocked out.' The latter wasn't exactly what my brothers had said about Ireland. The bus trundled across the Craigavon Bridge. We chatted to avoid the strangeness of silence, not knowing quite where we stood with each other.

'That Welsh striker was on fire, wasn't he? Least Ireland scored one against France. Reckon the frogs have it in the bag now.'

'England are still in for the home nations.'

'Home nations? Christ. You support England? Stop the bus and let me off at Altnagelvin. We'll never last the day. Half of Creggan are out Tippexing the "r" in their Ireland tops into a "c" for England–Iceland tonight.'

'Seriously?'

'Aye,' he laughed. 'My brother included. He's a tenner on Iceland for the hell of it – long shot, but after the Brexit vote, anything's possible!'

The bus halted at the hospital bus shelter, but he made no attempt to move – for a split-second I worried he'd been serious about leaving at Altnagelvin.

'So what do you make of Brexit? You raging?' I asked.

We navigated the red, white and blue sea of flag-infested lamp posts in Drumahoe. The shock referendum result was the hot topic on everyone's lips, but Aidan was taking in the parked lorry trailer by the road, its anti-Catholic graffiti thinly blanked out with white paint.

'Not mad. I don't get it though. Like, it's either racist or plain stupid. Wrong too – I mean the North voted to stay. What right's England got to drag us out? You gonna join the run for Irish passports?' He smirked.

'Aye, right.' I whacked him.

'Guess I deserved that. Were you for leaving though? Lots of Unionists were, weren't they?' he said.

'I didn't vote. I don't care if people are different – we're all human. I think I'd like it if there were no borders anywhere, just people.'

Our conversation lulled as the bus hummed past fields of newly shorn sheep and ink-splat cows.

'Know what I think?' he reflected after a while. 'I like your idea. Let's stop talking politics, football too.' He twisted in his seat and produced a half-eaten packet of Polo mints. 'I'm guessing you were more organized at breakfast than me?' He grinned, offering a sweet. 'Mind if I listen to music?' He unravelled a tangle of earphones. 'My brain is still under a duvet somewhere and needs to catch up.'

Lads could be so unsociable sometimes. It was nice sitting beside him though, our knees touching occasionally. The road wound through the Sperrin Mountains, purple with heather, then over the Glenshane Pass with sweeping views of Lough Neagh. I imagined the fields as a green chessboard, stacks of drying turf the game pieces. Music and rhythms filtered through his earphones.

Maybe things happened for a reason, I pondered. My heart had sunk when Rachel had bailed on Belfast. For ages we'd planned on

67

seeing the halls; getting the lay of the land before freshers' week – assuming we got the grades. It would've felt like a pity party dandering around solo. Inviting Aidan had been a bit knee-jerk, but we'd been talking about Queen's. He'd replied with a blurry 'maybe' that I might've been meant to read as a polite refusal. Crazy, we hardly knew each other, but the intensity of the encounter stayed superglued to my thoughts for hours after. He fascinated me. Sure, we were different, but we'd kind of clicked. Being totally honest, I liked him. And so what? The Troubles were history. My stomach had fizzed like a Coke float when I'd seen him at the front of the bus. Maybe that was the real reason I'd invited him. He removed the earphones as we joined the motorway.

'Why'd you decide to come in the end?' I asked him, all casual. He sucked his mint before answering.

'Don't know really. Small part of me still toying with university. Seeing it might help me decide. Don't you feel weird having finished school? It's like limbo – no textbook or directions.'

'Not really,' I admitted. 'Made my mind up a year ago doing the university entry forms.' Our bus had reached the Belfast outskirts: Cave Hill to our right, Harland & Wolff shipyard with Samson and Goliath, its huge yellow cranes, to the left.

'What makes you so sure?'

I shrugged. 'Just feels right. What makes you unsure?'

He rubbed his temples. 'Focused so hard on the A levels I never really thought past them. My GCSE exam results were chronic, so it was either get my head down or end up with a life-sentence on the dole. I suppose I only ever thought on what I didn't want to happen rather than what I did.'

'What happened with your GCSEs?'

He scratched his nose, then turned, gazing at the concrete tower blocks set against the blue of Belfast Lough. 'I was pretty distracted that year. Had a lot of growing up to do. Exams just weren't on my radar. I didn't give a shit to be honest – didn't even turn up or do the coursework for the half of them. Hard lesson learned.'

'Two years' work and you didn't show for the exams?' I asked. 'Were you out of your mind?'

He raised his eyebrows and inhaled. 'You're probably closer to the truth than you realize with that!'

'So how'd you get back into year thirteen?'

'Skin of my teeth. I'd an A star from Irish a couple of years earlier and then a rake of C and D grades. It limited my choices, but I was already doing Irish and they let me pick History, English Lit and Politics. That was fine by me, so I went back.'

'You did Irish two years early?'

'Yeah, I went to a *Gaelscoil*.' He explained it when he saw I didn't understand. 'An Irish-language primary school. All your lessons get taught in Irish so you're *líofa*, fluent, by eleven. That's what the *fáinne* means.' He gestured to the gold circle pin in his jacket.

'Sweet. Say something in Irish.'

'*Thar aon ní eile, bíodh faire agat do chroí, óir is ann atá foinsí na beath*,' he replied.

'Sounds so different. I did French. Our school didn't offer Irish. What's it mean?'

'It's a *seanfhocal* – a proverb – from the Bible. One Ma always said – guard your heart for it is the wellspring of life. She asked us to engrave it on her headstone.'

The conversation lulled in respect as we gazed out at Cave Hill towering ruggedly over north Belfast.

'It's beautiful. When did she pass away?' I asked.

He turned to look at me as he responded. 'Year I did my GCSEs.'

Suddenly the whole conversation made more sense. It must have shown on my face. He half smiled.

'You don't need to know what to say. It's fine. Well it's not, but you know what I mean. She got diagnosed with cancer in May and by November she was gone . . .'

His voice caught as he tapered off.

'So, do you live with your dad then?' I asked.

He shook his head and looked out the window.

'Just Seán,' he said eventually.

I messed with my phone, uncertain what to say. Our bus turned off onto the Westlink, inching through the city-centre congestion until we pulled into the Europa bus station by the Opera House. I was still searching for the right words as he grabbed his jacket and left. He was waiting at the bottom of the steps as I thanked the driver.

'Aidan, I'm so sorry—'

'Don't worry,' he interrupted, as if he had had to deal with the ineloquence of sympathy many times before. 'Right now, Ma would be smiling. I'd never have come to Belfast to think properly about Queen's. She'd have given her right arm to see one of us three remotely considering university. She always wished she'd gone herself.'

We spent a chilled-out morning – the kind I imagined students relishing daily. A take-out coffee in a styrofoam cup along with doughnuts, 'gravy rings', Aidan called them, as we sauntered up Great Victoria Street past student bars, clubs and restaurants to south Belfast.

The green open space by Queen's Lanyon Building had a stilled sense of hibernation; the Students' Union across University Road feeling like it was in quiet storage, waiting for the wave of undergraduates to return in September. As we sat on the low brick wall skirting the grass, I reflected that Queen's was kind of like the orange-brick architecture of the Guildhall – just longer and more castle-like with its ramparts. There was something medieval or gothic about it, like you could imagine rows of knights at trestle tables inside, feasting on suckling pig spit-roasted over a blazing fire. It was nippy enough, so we dandered round the black and white entrance hall with its stone statue of Galileo and into the quadrangle with its corridor of archways and stained-glass windows. The very atmosphere oozed academia even without flurries of students.

'What offer have you?' I asked him.

'International Politics and Conflict Studies. Need an A and two Bs. Yours is English, right?'

'Yeah, with Creative Writing. Same grades, actually. Is it the grades you're worried about?'

He was looking at his trainers, kicking at the grass; same as he'd done in Guildhall Square.

'No, the grades should be fine, hopefully. I did study.'

'So what's stopping you? Don't you want to leave Derry?'

His head shot up, eyes sparking with life.

'I'd leave in a flash. I'd love to travel, or even get a half-decent job I could live off. Nothing in Derry except bar work or flipping burgers – even the dole pays more. It'd kill me to sign on. The way my brother and his mates talk about their dole money as "pay day" – it's soul destroying. Sucks the life out of you.'

'So it's job or university then?'

'Or work-as-you-go globe-trotting . . . University fees scare the crap out of me,' he finally admitted. Then it made sense. Thirty grand average student debt. My parents were chipping in, digging deep for the tuition fees. It didn't sound like Aidan's dad was around to help.

'Mind if we go to the bookshop?' I asked as the clouds started to spit. Queen's bookshop was a wee store crammed with shelves from ceiling to floor. I'd been gagging to spend more time in it on our sixth-form visit. I was a bookworm but none of my classmates had given a monkey's. The stands with postcards, pens and merchandise emblazoned with the Queen's University crest were the supposed customer draw by the entrance, but it was the shelves upon shelves of paperbacks that sucked me in. Novels upon novels upon novels. Poetry collections. I ran my fingers along the shelves, dipping from one volume to the next, lost in browsing. One of my favourites caught my eye – Robert Frost's 'The Road Not Taken'. I wondered about the roads we're expected to take and the paths we choose for ourselves.

I breathed in the atmosphere and felt at home, then realized with a start that over thirty minutes had passed and scanned the shop for Aidan. No sign. Assuming he was outside, I swept past the racks of postcards and checked the Student Union steps and university grounds. Nowhere. I sucked my lip. Boys were allergic to shopping. He might've said. The light rain was still swirling, so I took shelter back in the shop to dig my phone out and call him. That's when I saw him – over in the far corner, stood, shoulder leaning against a tall shelf, engrossed in a book.

My heart thumped as I took a mental photograph – from his wavy black hair, short at the sides and longer on top, overhanging the thick set of his dark eyebrows that almost met in the middle, right down to his faded Converse trainers, beside which his jacket lay dumped in a ball at his feet, just like on the bus. His square jawline had the shadow of a beard, and under his maroon V-neck T-shirt his athletic torso made something in me lift. He wore the same dark-blue ripped skinny jeans and, as he stood poised, skim-reading what appeared from the cover to be a hardback on the

Middle East, three things struck me. Firstly, he already looked every bit the undergraduate; secondly, he had me melted; and thirdly, he was way out of my league. Guys like that didn't even cast a second glance at me, no, they went for blondes like your one in his photos and they played the game by completely different rules – because they could. His mother's proverb was more apt than he knew.

He saw me just before his ringtone blared. Hastily shoving the book back, he glanced at the phone, then at me, and exited the shop in a blur. I followed outside to where he was balancing on the edges of a concrete flower container, listening to the caller.

'But I really thought you weren't due back till tomorrow?'

A pause.

'Sorry, I would honestly but I can't, I'm not in Derry at the minute . . .'

His eyebrows were furrowed in concentration.

'Belfast. Until this evening. A few of us were going to watch the match tonight but if you want to come over?' He scrunched his face, listening.

'Look I'm really, really sorry, it would be good to get a chance . . .'

Whoever it was had obviously cut off the flow of his sentence and he jumped off the container and kicked a loose stone. Speaking through his teeth, the lie flowed off his lips.

'No, I'm on my own . . .'

Suddenly conscious of my presence, he mouthed a silent 'sorry' before turning his back. 'The band is practising tomorrow afternoon. What about after, Waterloo Street? I'll buy you a drink and we can talk . . . if you want?'

The response must've been curt but positive.

'Right, see you then.'

He stared at his phone for a minute before turning. 'Sorry, Iona, I just didn't need that to get any more complicated.'

'Your girlfriend?' I asked, already knowing the answer.

'Yeah.' With not so astute powers of observation, he glanced me up and down. 'Look, you're a girl. Hypothetically . . .' He raised his eyebrows. 'If your boyfriend messed up bad and owed you an apology, what would you want? Like chocolates and flowers just seem so yesterday . . .'

'Hypothetically?' I tilted my head.

'Totally,' he said dead pan, then smirked.

'Sincerity? Honesty?' His blatant lie had jarred me, yet it was me he had lied about being with, so part of me had forgiven him instantly.

Rolling his eyes, he said, 'See, that would work for a girl like you but not for Shannon.'

'A girl like me?' I challenged him.

'I didn't mean it like an insult!' He blinked. 'I mean . . . like . . . you're someone with integrity or something and Shannon's all shoes, handbags and make-up and . . . sorry, that wasn't meant to offend you.'

The fact that he meant it didn't stop the sting. Integrity versus drop-dead gorgeous – easy to see which would fly his kite.

We changed the topic and headed to the student accommodation office to get Halls information. Aidan dragged behind, stuck up his own arse, as I checked off the buildings to navigate the campus. The guy behind the desk was helpful, explaining what I wanted to know – bills, Wi-Fi, twinned options, contracts. Although Aidan half listened; he seemed to have mentally checked out.

'Aren't you hungry?' he asked as we stepped outside.

I was now that he mentioned it. Maybe he wasn't under an emotional cloud so much as needing fed.

'Would you do sushi?' I asked.

'Would I do what?' he asked, confused.

I knew there was a Japanese restaurant down Botanic Avenue with its rows of cafes and student bars. When we'd visited Queen's in sixth form, I'd seen the little conveyor belt circulating coloured plates with rolls of sticky rice wrapped in seaweed. I hadn't convinced my friends then to try it. Aidan was sceptical, but with the assurance that the menu had chips and fried rice he was game. After interrogating me over the main courses, he ordered beef udon noodles, then watched me deliberate. Nigiri with sesame seeds and crab were my favourite, that and the rolls with smoked salmon, avocado and orange fish roe. My family were so meat-and-two-veg, this was like Christmas. Aidan laughed, dodging as I tried to coerce him into trying something new. Eventually he succumbed and, after success with a nigiri block, he dipped some sushi in soy sauce and wasabi before I could warn him that the green paste could be pretty fierce. His face flashed shock. Grabbing his Coke, he gave me a 'You could have told me!' look before coughing.

'Jesus! What *is* that stuff?' He grinned, wide-eyed. The underlying tension that had invaded our day had evaporated and the conversation flowed again. We still had a couple of hours to kill.

'What about City Hall?' he suggested. 'I've seen it on the news.'

'It's right in the centre. We could do City Hall and maybe shopping?'

He looked like he'd prefer to eat pencils.

'Why not buy Shannon some make-up?' I said.

He grimaced at my effort at reconciliation, then smiled. 'Might just work. You know, I really didn't mean that as an insult earlier. I know you took it different, but integrity is a good thing – don't knock it.'

Chapter 12. Centenaries.

AIDAN.
Monday 27 June.

Christ, how I hated lose-lose moral decisions. The ones where you're damned if you do and screwed if you don't.

Iona and I had caught a bus back into Belfast City Centre, then split. We'd meet by City Hall at 3 p.m. Somehow I hadn't needed to explain I'd more aptitude even for golf than shopping. She'd told me there was chemist down the street that would do make-up and I needed a token for Shannon so she'd know I really was sorry. Talk about a foreign planet. You could've painted your granny for centuries there was so much mascara and lipstick and nail polish and blusher and pencil stuff and colours and brands. Endless. Eyeshadow – I'd focused to narrow the options. There was a box shimmering like Christmas on steroids; bold as brass like her. Thinking of her triggered another line of thought, too – it was a pharmacy after all.

So. Deep breath. This was a first. Not the whole expedition, just the dress code. I'd never bought these before, but I was no saint. Like I'd 'never' had a girl, like half our politicians had 'never' had guns, but I couldn't risk hitting the target when it came to pregnancy. Not since I'd wised up anyway. Chances of the invite coming my way again from Shannon were slim, but girls were so unpredictable. How was I supposed to know that would've been the night she'd finally offer to go the full distance? We'd hardly seen each other during my exams. I loitered in indecision, palms sweating, in front of the family-planning shelves, with every bloody emotion imaginable and more coursing through me. Typical that whoever did this shop layout put these next to the feminine hygiene section, as if deliberately heightening the fish-out-of-water feeling.

Was it possible to make a moral decision on top of an immoral one? Did anyone really care? I'd always thought it was the girl's responsibility to sort this stuff, but apparently not. That was what they really should have taught us, but not a hope in a Catholic school. So, I sinned if I used these and yet the alternative was to risk getting her pregnant? Surely to God, on the scale of things, if there was a judge up there counting my trespasses, then one was way worse than the other? Either way I was damned. The condemnation drilling my head every time a middle-aged woman passed me in the aisle was nothing to the motivation of not suffering a repeat of the mortification with Shannon at the party. How I'd had the presence of mind to think about protection when I was so hammered remained a mystery but, even with everything that happened after, I didn't regret it. No way was I for sliding back to the killer cocktail of drink, drugs and girls. Once bitten.

Fumbling for coins at the cash desk, with the eyeshadow and the blue box on the counter for the world to see, was only fractionally less embarrassing.

'Want a bag for the condoms, wee son?' asked the cashier, a pregnant woman in her thirties.

Shout it out to the whole bloody shop, why don't you? I shook my head and buried them in my inside jacket pocket, zipping it tight before exiting to the welcome anonymity of the street. Ten minutes. Shopping done.

In Belfast you had to look up to see the sky; people passed like you were invisible. I'd been here only twice; once to the zoo on a primary-school trip and once with my family when Da decided we should visit his old gaff, which had been scrubbed up for tourists. He'd 'lived' a while, two years seven months to be precise, in Her Majesty's custody at the Crum before I was born; before he met Ma. When he was arrested for IRA activity, he hadn't been that much older than me. Chilling thought. I'd have gone mental locked in a cell. Maybe that's why Da drank, that or trying to wash away other memories. My parents met at the Stardust parish dance when she was nineteen and he was twenty-five. 'He swept me off my feet.' I minded her recounting the story when we were wee. He did. Literally. Whether it was his passion, political or otherwise, or her own free-spiritedness, I don't know, but she was pregnant and married in a shotgun wedding before she reached twenty. Her parents, both good Donegal Catholics, hardly spoke to her at first, but when Saoirse arrived as a smiling bundle of baby girl, all had been forgiven. By the time Seán and I graced the planet, Nan had knit a mountain of blue bootees.

As I wove through the flow of pedestrians, I wondered what Iona would've said on the bus if I'd told her about Da. A policing family and a political ex-prisoner family. Fireworks. Still, she seemed sound; at home in her own skin and different to most of the girls I knew. I didn't reckon it was a Catholic–Protestant thing. There was a hint of fire in her, a strength in her eyes and a curiosity to understand. I'd watched her for ten minutes or so from the row of cannons on the grey walls overlooking Guildhall Square before we met properly for the first time. I was alone. Was she? Mind games had me wary. I hadn't been spying, just observing. She'd sat with her knees tucked up to her chin, arms looped around her jeans, relaxed, people watching. Natural and arty, like she could've stayed all day without a worry.

The lawns in front of City Hall would've been a good place to wait for Iona, but it was still mizzling rain and the political history breathing from the building sucked me in through the entrance pillars. The lobby was striking. A tin of nicked paint wouldn't cut it here. Voices carried high into the fancy plasterwork and split into a thousand pieces by daylight dancing through stained glass. I went to bless myself. It was like a cathedral someone stole the religion out of. Instead of holy statues there were frescos, sculptures and windows showing a 3D history textbook of the city. I loved it.

Like an impostor in Buckingham Palace, I followed a guided group along a corridor of red carpet. Their banter sounded like the smattering of Spanish I'd studied but I couldn't catch the words. If they'd offered me space in a suitcase I'd have jumped in regardless. I'd die if I got stuck in Derry. Whatever was in Saoirse about travelling was in my blood too; possibly inherited from Ma. Scán didn't have it the same way; he'd sit happy in the same pub downing pints every Saturday till he was sixty, solving the world's problems over and over with the same lads until last orders. I wanted to make a difference. I'd combust with boredom if it was just talk.

The corridor led to an exhibition. *Reflections on 1916.* To me, 1916 always meant the Easter Rising. Sure, I'd studied the World Wars, I knew the context, but I was reared on Michael Collins, De Valera and the last stand at the General Post Office in Dublin. It was our cowboys and Indians. After the annual Easter commemorations in the Creggan cemetery, we'd play out the executions at Kilmainham Gaol and the battles for Irish independence up the back fields. First thing I ever googled on the internet was a picture of the bullet holes in the Dublin post office pillars. Da always justified the Troubles, ranting about battles that won freedom for part of Ireland but sold out us northern Catholics. This exhibition was different to my father's Sunday-afternoon versions of history, though. It tugged something different in my gut. People, all sides, caught in a landslide of violence a hundred years ago. For the first time I could see the dominoes lined up: the tit for tat, the hollering for civil war, the screaming over dividing our country into north and south. It was ordinary lads like me born Unionist or Nationalist over the flick of a coin; gun-running for 'God and Ulster' or 'God and Ireland' and both equally duped that a one-way ticket to muddy hell in Europe was their salvation. No God anywhere as far as I could see. Easter 1916 lifted my chest and straightened my shoulders but looking in the photographed eyes of the men in the Somme stopped me in my tracks. They were me too; teenagers dying for a life. Compared to them, though, maybe I had a shot.

My phone bleeped – Iona was at the war memorial outside. She joined me browsing. We flicked through World War recruitment propaganda. It put me in mind of the slogans on the Brexit posters, like they thought you'd only half a functioning brain cell. 'Your country needs you!' seemed to be enough for you to sell your soul back then. Scary thought was, in parts of Derry, I knew it was still enough. 'Now is the time,' stated Erin, symbolizing Ireland as she strummed her harp. It wasn't a long shot off *'Tiocfaidh ár lá'*, 'Our Day Will Come', still scrawled on street corners. In 1916, whether British or Irish, it was plain as spuds that if you didn't fight, you weren't a man.

'So, if you'd lived a century ago, would you have enlisted?' Iona asked.

'Aye.' I tipped an imaginary cap. 'Maybe not how you mean it though. I rather fear, Ma'am, I'd have been buying stamps in Dublin.'

'Glad we don't live a hundred years ago then.' She smiled, understanding I meant the Republican Easter Rising.

'Me too. I don't fancy giving up my life for anyone – especially when it's just starting.' It was cool she didn't care about my politics. She flicked her hair. 'My middle name is James, after James Connolly,' I said. 'Worse, my brother's middle name is Pearse, after Padraig Pearse . . .'

'Both leaders in the Rising, weren't they?' she asked.

'Yes. And executed by the Brits for it. Don't say I didn't warn you I've Republican roots!'

'You've a sister too, right? What's her middle name?'

I laughed. 'Saoirse Erin Hennessey. My parents were pretty intent on blasting our heritage in neon. To be honest, I got away the lightest.'

'What's *Saoirse*?'

'Freedom, in Irish.' I grinned and rolled my eyes. 'Don't suppose half your family is Billy after William of Orange?'

'I've an Uncle Billy.' She laughed. 'My parents went for apostles more than politics – my brothers are John and Andy.'

We stood opposite prints of the Republican Easter Rising text and the 1912 Ulster Covenant some Loyalists signed in blood – warring sides, mine and hers, mixing God and guns from generations past.

'Here's devotion for you – a mate of Seán's has the whole Easter Proclamation tattooed on his back.'

'Do you really believe it?' she asked. 'Like is it what drives you?'

I looked in her eyes. She was asking for real.

'Not really. You ever read it?'

She shook her head.

'Bits of it are mad – linking God with violence and politics –

like Syria or Israel and Palestine. There's good stuff in it too, about valuing all people equally. That's still sound. You realize we're way off not talking religion and politics?'

She shrugged. 'It's fascinating seeing how you think. Most of my friends reckon politics is a waste of space.'

'Most of mine reckon that about religion.'

We drifted to a glass exhibition case full of museum tack – handwritten letters, black-and-white photographs, medals and military cloth badges. It was only when we glanced closer it caught us. They belonged to one family, two individuals from back then. He was a Prod who'd done the signing in blood thing and joined the Ulster Volunteer Force. She was Catholic and had been in *Cumann na mBan*, kind of the women's bit of the IRA. She'd helped the Rising; he'd survived the Somme and Messines. A match made in hell, yet after Ireland tore itself apart, they met in Belfast and got hitched. There was a faded family photo with three kids.

'That's mental.' I studied the three kids in the image.

Iona was hunkered down reading love letters scrawled on yellowed paper.

'Imagine their conversations over breakfast,' I said. 'It's like people like us getting together during the Troubles. Miraculous. Their families would've been killing each other. Can you imagine trying to make that work?'

I glanced at Iona, then gulped, realizing what I'd said. It was the first time I'd seen her blush, the rose colour spreading across her cheekbones beautifully. For a split-second our eyes connected before she looked away and moved to a different part of the exhibition. Something changed. My feet were stuck, but my gaze followed her. From the far side of the room she stole another glance at me, and our eyes connected with a brief intensity I hadn't felt before. This time it was my turn to look away, confused by the unexpected wave of warmth rising as I missed a breath. It caught me unaware.

Staring at my reflection in the cabinet, I wondered if I'd misread her. Was it possible to misread my own reaction? I glanced over again trying to make sense of it. She had her back to me now, the creamy skin of her neck brushed by her long brown hair. From the little I knew of her, being dolled up to the nines wasn't her style, but the bottle-green cotton jumper naturally hugged her frame, and she could have been a dancer in the slim black leggings. I smiled, clocking her sweet DMs and rainbow shoelaces again, like her kick-ass statement to the world. Another wave of emotion powered through me as I observed her with fresh eyes before turning.

Jesus, Hennessey. Two hours ago, I'd been engrossed in thinking about Shannon as we'd trekked to the accommodation office. An hour ago, I'd been in teenage heaven-hell fathoming ribbed, sensitive or safe. There was nothing safe about this. My hand tapped my chest pocket as my mind tried to refocus on what was real – that I was meeting Shannon tomorrow night; that I had been rehearsing an attempted apology for days; that thinking of her even now still fired my bloodstream.

I sensed Iona back at my side and worked to blank my chaos before turning. She smiled, all calm, like it was only me on the rollercoaster.

'Our bus will be heading soon,' she said, her voice steady.

Two stained-glass windows caught our attention in the corridor as we left City Hall. The first was an old factory scene in shades of blue, backed with rainbow shards:

'Not as Catholics or Protestants, not as Nationalists or Unionists, but as Belfast workers standing together.'

The second was for the International Brigades in the Spanish Civil war; the Catholics and Protestants who'd crossed the Pyrenees to volunteer in the fight against Franco. We'd done it in history class. *No pasarán.* I muttered the words from a song about it as I reflected.

She looked at me seeking explanation.

'It's a Christy Moore song.' I sang the lyrics low, about remembering the volunteers who'd died fighting the dictator.

Her expression didn't change.

'In the name of God, haven't you heard of Christy Moore? Seriously? He's only one of the best-known singer-songwriters in Ireland.' *God. We really were worlds apart.*

'You sing nice,' she said.

Lost in our own thoughts, we wove our way on the grey pavements past the mandolins, whistles and guitars of Matchett's Music shop to the Europa bus station. Between those last two stained-glass windows in City Hall had hung a Celtic watercolour of five portraits, its message decreed bilingually in orange lettering:

'*Ar scáth a chéile a mhaireas na daoine.*'

It is in the shelter of each other that people live.

Chapter 13. Reflections.

IONA.
Monday 27 June.

Times I hated liking boys. They thought we were complicated? Didn't they have mirrors? Without even knowing it, in five minutes they could mess you up so many ways it wasn't fair. Apart from a mother and her toddler twins excited by the view at the front window, the top deck was empty. Aidan commandeered the back seat and jammed in his earphones, leaving me chewing my nail polish. It was the same way he'd been after the nagging from his girlfriend – too self-absorbed to be bothered with me. I stared at our reflection in the bus window as I fixed a hairclip and sighed, then studied the traffic.

On one level, I should've seen it coming. Only an airhead could dream it would work to spend a day with their . . . 'nemesis' came to mind, but it wasn't quite the word. 'Opposite' maybe? In fairness, the day hadn't been a complete write-off, it had been fun except for that one moment. I knew my cheeks had gone lipstick red when he'd described being in a relationship with me, even a made-up one a century ago. When our eyes had reconnected, he'd looked weird, then turned away. What odds if I couldn't tell whether it was a 'Don't you know how hot my girlfriend is?' death stare or a 'What planet are you on?' put-down?

That first day in Cafe Nervosa his emotion had been raw. I'd thought I could read him; like he wore his heart on his sleeve. Today he'd had more mood swings than the weather. Was it even worth trying to understand someone I might never see again? I could've been orange as King Billy with fake-tan trauma and he wouldn't have noticed me on the double-decker bus for the first half of the journey home.

'Listening to Christy Moore then?' I jibed, bored senseless on the motorway. He tapped the music off and swung his feet round to face me.

'Sorry.' He wound up the earphones, looking at me for the first time in twenty minutes. 'I was listening to a set list Conal wants us to play soon at a busking event. I thought focusing on the bass tracks might clear my head.'

I wondered what he was trying to clear his head *of*. He looked beyond my shoulder as the bus started the slow climb over the Glenshane Pass. He had the kind of personality that, when he switched it on, lit the room. One smile and he had the forgiveness dragged out of me. It was disarming, but since the exhibition earlier my guard was superglued in place. I was never for being ridiculed by a boy again.

'What do you want to talk about?' he asked.

My brain went to sludge. *Anything*. I scavenged for something to say. 'We played this game once, Soul Search, on a sleepover. It's way random. You take turns – pick a topic, or a question, and then talk on it for five minutes solid. No lies, no avoidance, no hesitation, no straying off the subject.'

'So girly! Must've been an all-female sleepover?' He raised an eyebrow.

'But it's good! It's harder than you think!'

'All right. Shoot. We've a long journey to kill,' he said.

I went first. 'What do you want to be when you grow up?'

Something skipped inside me when he laughed and started to spiel on – open, real. He straightened an imaginary tie and introduced himself as the BBC's Middle East correspondent. He was for going to foreign places for the news, strutting in a flak jacket and writing the headlines. His face shone. It was a cool idea; suited him too, with him being all political, plus, I thought, he had the looks and charisma for TV. Alternatively, he was also for saving the world somewhere a chunk at a time: building wells, volunteering in refugee camps, pulling people out of earthquake rubble. 'More than likely though,' he finished, as his mobile's stopwatch beeped the end of the five minutes, 'I'll just be a bouncer in Waterloo Street. What about you?'

'Don't laugh . . .' I said.

He didn't. He sat back and looked at me intently with his dark eyes.

'I want to write kids' books and do all the drawings, too.'

'That's beast,' he said. 'I could see you doing that.'

'Really?'

He nodded and gestured for me to keep going. Anyone else I'd ever mentioned it to just went, 'That's nice,' and changed the subject. I nattered on about seeing a documentary about refugee kids being helped through picture books and how I'd scoured the children's section in the library and discovered kids' books on parents splitting, goldfish or grannies dying, even kids who were sick. I wanted to write smiles onto little faces. If I couldn't do that, I'd be a primary teacher.

Aidan listened, nodding at times. 'What were your A levels?'

'English, Art, Music, Religion.'

'Sounds like perfection. Makes sense, you doing English and Creative Writing now,' he said.

We smiled.

'So, are you any clearer about university?' I asked.

'Ish. Honestly? I thought today would help me rule it out. I've never really seen myself as the university type. Problem is –' he ran his fingers along the back of the seat – 'I liked it.' He paused, then picked up. 'My turn anyway. Music. If your life had a soundtrack, what would it be and why?'

It was a killer question. Unusual. We chatted way on after the countdown bleeped. It turned out Christy Moore would not be his soundtrack – it was more his parents'. A South African band were his current favourite, rock but with an alternative edge. We talked about my guitar and his bass. He'd got into it at fourteen because his best mate was awesome at lead electric and songwriting. I blethered about singer-songwriters and mentioned that Mum had named me after a Celtic Christian band. That intrigued him.

'It's also a Scottish island. Mum liked the Christian spiritual connection.'

'It's where St Columba went after Derry, right?' Aidan leaned in.

'Yeah. Mum went on a residential there about Celtic Christianity.'

'A retreat? Is she wild religious?'

'Kind of. She's into faith. Most of my family is like that.' I didn't brave saying that I was. He'd probably think I was bananas. Besides, it still felt like a tightrope talking about religion and politics. I breathed deep; my lungs tight as I contemplated the subject change. His eyes fleetingly crossed mine.

'Next topic,' I said. 'Relationships. Ever been in a serious one?'

He groaned theatrically.

'Five minutes. No lies, no avoidance, no hesitation, no straying off the subject!' I reiterated the ground rules like a year head nagging about make-up infringements. 'No hesitation' was on the edge of my lips when he finally took on the topic.

'Mm. Definition of serious?' He blinked and leaned his head back against the window, pulling his leg up towards his chest. 'Like, serious as in length of time, serious as in emotions, serious as in . . . whatever?'

'As in, have you ever been in love?'

It wasn't my imagination, he *did* blush. Revenge was sweet.

He looked at me intensely with a 'You are really stringing me out to dry' kind of a grin, but he was playing.

'This girl up the street. I was thirteen. She'd blonde hair, was class at gymnastics – cartwheels and stuff. She could spin three in a row, all pro. Same primary school till we were eleven. I fancied her for ages – took me a year to bottle the courage to ask her out. I was so scared she'd knock me back. Crazy. Seán teased the life out of me. I was broke to the bone anytime she even walked past.'

'*You* were nervous?'

'Course! You think I'm made of steel? I'd never asked anyone out before. I was just this kid and my voice was breaking; you have no idea!'

It was hard to imagine him shy over a girl turning cartwheels. 'Did she say yes?'

'Yeah.' He grinned. 'First kiss same day. Got to be love. Broke my heart three weeks later and snogged someone else. Your turn – ever been in a serious relationship?'

It struck me what he *hadn't* said. Coy, like. No mention of Shannon the entire conversation. I struggled to fill five minutes without sounding like Cinderella before the slipper. They were always 'the one' until they weren't. School discos, formals – some good, some, well . . . Aidan kept his eyes full on me, getting his own back rightly. Finally, I mentioned Kyle, just not the bit where I'd wanted to whack him with a stiletto. I still regretted the missed opportunity. We'd broken up just before Easter.

'He said I was boring – like, he actually used that word. Am I boring?' I asked Aidan.

'No,' he said straight off, sliding his hands down his jeans. 'I think . . .' He chewed his finger. 'That guy was an eejit. Don't take him on. We're lads – we don't think, we don't expect girls to go over our exact words for weeks in their heads. You're not boring. You're . . .' He rubbed his stubble. 'You're interesting, intelligent, you're really intuitive and genuine . . . and you've got shedloads of integrity.' He winked.

I figured it wasn't chronic that it had sounded more like a dictionary entry than a chat-up line. *Interesting. Intelligent. Intuitive. Genuine.* They were meaningful, but definitely spelled *friend*. Neither of us mentioned anything about meeting up again once the bus pulled back into Derry. He high-fived me a goodbye as I got off at the Waterside. I watched the outline of him through the back-seat window get smaller as the bus trundled off to the Cityside.

Chapter 14. Encouragement.

AIDAN.
Tuesday 28 June.

It had been the best afternoon of the school holidays so far, if I could still call them 'school' holidays. The cops had left my clothes back. I'd scrubbed the blood from my runners but kicked the bag with the T-shirt and jeans under the bed for another day. Like a bashed ornament Nan had attacked with superglue, I was nearly back to myself. Granda, God rest him, used to say Nan could mend anything except her own memory. Apart from my finger, the bruised ribs had caused me the most grief after everything else healed, but I'd managed a short jog across Creggan Heights on only one ibuprofen. I'd tried a few weights in the living room against a backdrop of daytime TV. People were crooning on about sentimental antiques, then sniffing onions and selling their heartaches for holidays in Barbados. Seán was still out for the count, hungover from the joys of the cherished Irish national pastime the previous night – watching England crash out prematurely of yet another football cup. We couldn't have sung louder for a united Ireland. A rake of his friends had piled round for the match. A couple of new faces. Iceland – of all the countries! Half their population was in the stands doing some Viking chant and, after a few beers, half of Creggan was fluent enough in Icelandic to join in. Having failed to find anything in our cupboards more effective than a Pot Noodle to fend off the hangover, it had dawned on me that shopping may not be avoidable much longer.

The fridge at Jess's house that afternoon was the perfect prescription. I'd linked up with my mates and we'd spent hours jamming; prepping for the busking gig and raiding leftover pork adobo and some random Asian peanut snack. Jess's real name was Jésus, but he dropped it within hours of landing in a Derry primary school – the teachers couldn't control the weans smirking over being allowed to swear all day in the classroom.

Conal had a new song and was giving it lilty. It was seriously good, but of course we weren't for telling him that. Instead, he earned a right ribbing. Despite his denials, it was clearly about this girl he'd seen up the town and hadn't had the nerve to chat up. He was a master of bottling teenage angst into lyrics – that or a bloody talented liar. My broken finger, taped like a Siamese twin to the one beside it, throbbed with the thwack of bass strings but survived. We jammed sequences and riffs until Jess's ma came back from her shift, then, evicted for her sanity, we headed up the town.

The Gweedore bar was the third in a string of pubs up Waterloo Street. Tracy's Bar, Peadar O'Donnell's, and then the dark greens and blues of the Gweedore paintwork, with the flags of the four Irish provinces hanging off the second-storey windows above the Guinness sign. None of them were exactly high end, but at the weekends you got a good crowd and great music – trad was more the scene in Peadar's, and live bands of all kinds upstairs in the Gweedore. The red seats and varnished tables were surprisingly full for a Tuesday. I fidgeted, shredding the edges off my beer mat. Shannon was due to join us. Conal watched me glancing to the door every time it swung open and didn't question that I asked for water when we went to the bar.

Her entrance turned more heads than just mine; in a tight blue dress, her blonde hair flowing like an expensive shampoo ad. Wiping the sweat off my palms and fixing my shirt, I went over, pulse racing. She smelled great, coconut and tropical to go with her holiday tan. I breathed easier noting that there was no mark on her cheek and bought her a vodka and Coke. We were talking low, leaning against the bar, close enough to hear each other without being overheard. I was scared to touch her.

'Shannon, I am so, so sorry about the other night.' My voice wavered with having to dredge it up again. 'I never meant it to happen like it did. Are you OK?' I struggled to keep eye contact. 'Are *we* still OK?'

She reached out and toyed with the Celtic cross on the leather cord round my neck, like she knew it was slaying me to have to wait for her answer. 'I'm fine *now*.' She sipped her drink and rolled her eyes. 'You going to make it up to me? Screw up one more time and we're done.'

Her hand cupped her hip and she raised her chin. My heart pounded. Christ but she could play me.

'I swear it won't happen again. I drank too much. I was way out of line. Look, it's really not in my character to . . .' I searched for the right word; *domestic violence* was not something I wanted to be labelled with, having witnessed enough of it for one lifetime. 'I was off my head,' I admitted. 'I'd no clue how hard I shoved you away until it was too late and . . . were you hurt bad?'

I reached out and ran my thumb across the soft skin of her cheekbone. She didn't flinch, just looked at the floor and then back at me gently, moving closer. I could feel the warmth of her body stirring mine. Remembering the make-up, I produced the small case of eyeshadow and put it into her palm, folding her fingers round it. 'It's just a token. I didn't know how to handle this. I felt so bad after . . . and I looked for you but I couldn't find you anywhere . . .'

'You're really sweet sometimes. It's fine. I'm fine . . . Why wouldn't you . . . Why didn't you want to . . . ? You were like a priest during your exams. I thought you were for dumping me. I needed to know you were still mine.' The hurt glistened in her eyes.

'I was just cramming. I didn't want to mess up. The results are my ticket out of here.'

'And when were you planning on telling me you were leaving?'

'Look, I don't know what I'm doing next. I haven't thought it through yet.'

'But you were at Queen's the other day, checking out being some bright spark, thinking you're better than everyone else.'

It was simpler to divert off the topic; I knew she was a homebird and I was aching to stretch my wings.

'About that other stuff . . .' I began, fluent as a monk on honeymoon. 'It wasn't that I didn't want to . . .' I leaned in closer and spoke low.

She had a coy look back on her face, like she knew fine rightly she could outplay me on this without a second thought. 'I've a confession,' she said, touching her finger to my lips as I went on fire inside. 'It was partly my fault what happened.'

'No. It was all on me. You didn't deserve what happened.' I smoothed her shoulders and then it came back to me, what I'd wanted to ask. 'Look, did I . . . take something at the party? The hospital said they were hard pressed to find blood in my veins amongst the chemicals. I was out of my mind, not just drunk, and I don't remember taking anything.'

'Well, you've nailed my confession now.' She smiled and kissed me lightly on the lips, pulling me close.

'What do you mean?'

'I might have put a little . . . "encouragement" in your drink,' she said.

My mind was filtering the information in slow motion as she laughed.

'Encouragement?' I questioned.

Her breath was warm on my neck.

'Look it was just a tablet. It was supposed to relax you, get you in the mood . . . It was a present for finishing the exams.'

'You thought I needed encouragement?' I stepped back. 'Do you know how amazing you look? You honestly thought I'd say no?'

'You did say no!' She flicked her hair, pouting.

'Not that way!' The heat flushed my cheeks as I floundered, out of my depth in the conversation. 'I just didn't want to get you pregnant, OK? That's all!' My voice was barely a whisper as I glanced around.

'Trust me, I have that covered.' Her confidence was sassy and attractive, but something in me had caught up with what she'd said.

'Can we wind this back a minute?' I stood straighter and looked into her teasing eyes. 'Did you just admit you *drugged* me?'

'Like you're really going to shoot me down for wanting to give you a good time? Wise up, I know you do drugs . . .'

'*Did* drugs, Shannon. I'm clean ages now,' I interrupted, temper rising.

'. . . and I heard,' she continued with a smirk on her face, 'it wouldn't have been your first time anyway. You think girls don't talk?'

As she paused for dramatic effect, the blood was draining from my face.

'So what's the story? Once bitten?' She studied my silence. 'I was doing you a favour. Get real. I'd you down as interesting, but these last few months you switched off. You're *boring*. You think I'm going to hang around as your girlfriend on the off-chance that you'll put your stupid books away and get back to the races?'

Her hand slid across my jeans. Suddenly her proximity to me made me sick to the core.

'We're done!' My voice broke as I stumbled backwards, shaking.

'You think *you're* dumping *me*? After making me hide my face for half my holiday with the bruising?' With one swift movement that I didn't see coming, her vodka and Coke was round my face, dripping onto my favourite black shirt; for the second time in a fortnight I wished the ground would swallow me up as I lifted my jacket off the bar stool and stormed out of the pub without a backwards look.

It was still bright outside. Embarrassment and rage were flaring through me in equal measure as I paced head down, hair still dripping, past the row of black taxis queued in William Street. I was angry, hating myself as well as her. Mad that, despite feeling violated, half of me still wanted her, specifically the lower half. I'd save the fare and burn off some of the frustration if I hiked the hill home. I was well past the kebab shops and Pilot's Row Community Centre along Lecky Road before I heard the shout from behind.

'Hey! Aidan!'

It was Conal. I strode on, ignoring him. 'For the love of Christ, wait up!' He was running now and spun me round by the shoulder as he caught me, stooping to catch his breath at the railings of the Bloody Sunday Monument.

'What's wrong?' he panted, straightening up.

'Isn't it bloody obvious? Girls are shite!' I shouted at him, pacing the pavement, kicking my foot hard off the kerb.

'Singular, plural or generic?' His humour failed to hit the mark.

'All of the above!' I ranted. 'Leave me alone, Conal. Go back to the pub and chatting up that girl at the next table.'

'Hell no!' He squared up, eyes narrowed. We'd never fought in seven years. 'Calm down, Aidan. And stop marching like a maniac for feck's sake, you're making me dizzy. Talk!'

'I don't want to calm down. I don't want to talk. I've just had a drink thrown in my face by my girlfriend, my *ex*-girlfriend. I want to be on my own, so feck off and leave me alone.' I strode off again.

He hesitated before following and catching me outside the black frontage of the Bog Inn on the corner of Westland Street. 'Aidan!' He grabbed my shoulder with a jolt until I faced him again. 'Shut up and listen. I've known you since you were eleven. I've stuck with you through gold and shite. I've watched you deal with your da; bury your ma; put yourself through hell and come back from it. I don't know everything that went down a fortnight ago with you and Shannon, but I know you went to the bridge. Then you got a serious kicking. You were in hospital, for Christ's sake. Your brother said it was real bad. All that and you hardly break breath to me about it.' He looked at me and swallowed. 'You're my best mate, Aidan. Did I read that wrong or did you nearly jump, then almost die anyway? Enough bullshit. Talk!'

Neither of us were sure what to say when he finished.

'I just want to help you,' he murmured apologetically as I stood there, empty. 'Is that so wrong? I know you'd do it for me.'

I hung my head. 'I was wired that night. The bridge . . .' I hesitated. 'Believe me. None of it was intentional.'

It was his turn to look blank.

'I've been beating myself up for days thinking it must be genetic, like something toxic in my blood that was turning me into Da: drinking and treating women like crap. I couldn't face myself if that was me.' I sighed. 'Turns out it wasn't – she put something in my drink. I think I went mental with whatever she doped me with. Like imagine *I* drugged *her* – I'd be in court over date rape and taking out insurance on my kneecaps. The hospital had to battle to get my temperature under control. If it hadn't come down after they pumped my stomach, I could've died. I knew everyone would assume it was my fault; that I was back on drugs. I'm not. I swear. On top of that, I was hoping to get back with her tonight. Now I'm single for the summer.'

'Join the club,' he said.

'I'm a mess, Conal. She said I was boring. Surely to God there's a scale between boring and psycho with a death wish? All I want to do is not be at either end of the scale.'

He didn't respond for a moment, then said two words. 'Curry chip.' I looked at him with the question. 'Yip,' he continued, 'if in doubt, male and eighteen, buy a curry chip, sit on a wall and meditate. Eventually it solves all the world's problems.'

'Deep wisdom indeed. How many years up a mountain in Tibet did it take you to come up with that one?'

He grinned at my sarcasm, knowing it was progress.

'Make light of it now, mucker, but in the future people will pay me for this therapy.' He smirked. 'Never forget I'm four and a half months older. I *know* stuff.'

So that's what we did. Ten minutes later we were sitting in a kind of agreed silence on the window ledge outside the Celtic chippy on Stanley's Walk with a plastic fork and tinfoil tub each of chips glooped in curry sauce.

'So,' he said, when the sounds of the plastic prongs were scraping the last chips round the bottom of the tinfoil to mop up the last drop of curry. 'I've just one question.'

'What?' I mumbled through my last mouthful, much calmer.

'When I asked singular, plural or generic, you said, "All of the above." Generic I get. Girls are girls. They're as frustrating as they are essential, even when you're born lucky like you. Singular I get. Shannon and all that. Plural? Am I missing something here?'

Chapter 15. Colour.

IONA.
Wednesday 6 July.

Rachel wanted to make it up to me for bailing on the Belfast trip. The novelty of no school had worn thin; the routine of work and lounging around making my life drier than a mouthful of porridge oats. I couldn't even find the concentration to read. What kind of eighteen-year-old is slouched in pyjamas at 9 p.m.? Even I couldn't kid myself anymore that beauty sleep was a positive option. Anything to alleviate the monotony was welcome.

This specific anything was sitting like a marinated hedgehog in a black swingy chair, tinfoil and hair dye pasted all over my head. Rachel had devised the whole menu – hair dresser's for appetizers; main course, men's Wimbledon quarter-final (complete with tight white shorts, sweaty T-shirts and new balls commentary); dessert, a popcorn overload and bubble gum for the eyes at the cinema. The most complicated question of the day should have been 'Blonde highlights or copper lowlights?'. Not so.

'You'll feel like summer,' Rachel argued. 'New season, new style.'

I stuck my tongue out at her. She was always threatening to pierce it like hers. It felt like summer already anyway, with the gaggle of markets setting up along the Quay for the Maritime Festival and Clipper yachts.

'Wanna reschedule Belfast?' She pulled a sad face in the mirror, apologizing again for the fact that her cousin's unexpected visit had botched our plans.

'Actually, I went anyway.' I flicked nonchalantly through glossy celebrity gossip in an out-of-date magazine. 'How were your relatives?'

'Pains. Wished I was in Belfast. You'd have had far more fun with company.'

I swallowed. As my brain ticked, she seemed to catch my thought process in the mirror.

'Unless . . .' Her head tilted, eyes narrowing as I chewed a fingernail.

Cornered. There was no wriggling out of it, so, instead, I chose my words carefully. 'I went with another friend. You wouldn't know them, though. Did you go bowling in the end?'

Rachel was studying me intently now from under her own wig of tinfoil. 'Iona Scott –' she patted a hairbrush into her palm – 'you're changing the subject! Who'd you go with?' She snatched the magazine from my hands and eyeballed me, her sixth sense already picking up on gossip.

'It's a long story . . .'

'Sure, haven't you a captive audience here for at least the next hour?' She raised her eyebrows and spun her chair on its casters, making the tinfoil flutter ridiculously.

Caught. I leaned back, slowly twirling my chair. 'His name is Aidan and before you ask, no, because he already has a girlfriend.'

Rachel should have applied to study forensics. Not inclined to explain the whole St Columb's Park incident, I said it was a chance encounter in Guildhall Square. Near enough the truth, except that Rachel was the relationship inquisition.

'Iona!' she burst out. 'You spent the whole day with a guy and you didn't tell me?'

'It's no big deal. He's thinking of going to Queen's. It made sense to ask him,' I protested.

'Everything! Now! Is he smart? Fit? Where's he from? Spill the beans!'

'You're missing the point,' I reiterated. 'He has a girlfriend and he's not interested!'

'No, girl!' She wagged her finger. 'You're missing the point – two points, in fact. Number one, you avoided telling your best friend that you spent the day with Mr Mystery Man and your protests and blushes clearly mean you like him. Number two, no guy spends the whole day on his own with a girl if he's not interested, girlfriend or no girlfriend. Like, maybe he's not showing you he's interested, but he's not *not* interested either.'

I liked her logic, but that was different to believing it.

'Photo evidence? Any selfies?' She clicked her fingers in my face. I shook my head. 'Facebook then!'

'He hasn't friended me on Facebook.' I bit my lip. 'But I can find his profile pic – it's one with his girlfriend so you can see it really is pointless . . .' I hesitated when I found the image. He had changed it. A streetscape torso shot with damp hair and a black shirt unbuttoned at the front. God, but he was gorgeous. Distracted by the heat low in my belly, Rachel grabbed my phone before I could blink.

'O-M-G,' she spelled slowly, looking from the screen to me and back again with each letter. 'He's an absolute babe! About time you hit the jackpot.' She flicked the screen a couple of times. 'Don't say I never do you any favours.' She winked and giggled. 'What d'ya know?' she said. 'You've just sent him a friend request. Fiver says he accepts it!'

Chapter 16. Our Father.

AIDAN.
Wednesday 6 July.

Christ, but this was surreal beyond bloody belief. I was sitting in a mass, a funeral mass, in the backwater of Strabane town and I didn't even know the corpse in the coffin. Ash Wednesday had been the last time I'd endured the holy mantras and that was only because they'd caught us mitching in the locker rooms. The benches in this chapel were polished wood but smelled of incense, not BO. I sidled into the back corner. My brother was near the front, sitting saint-like with his new friends. They'd become like blood brothers since the elections in June and Seán was walking the taller for it.

'Rise and bloody shine! I need a favour!' He'd burst into my room less than politely not long after eight this morning when I was still in bed, wrapped up like a fish supper. They'd to go to this funeral of some guy and they'd want a pint afterwards and would I drive? On the promise of having free car use for a day, I had donned black from head to toe; mourner in chief. Since splitting with Shannon a week ago, I felt dour anyway. I'd done little more exciting than phone for pizza and venture to the supermarket to restock our cupboards, but only when the toilet paper ran out, making it a non-optional activity.

In my pocket, my fingers fidgeted with the Celtic cross from my necklace. I'd lent its black leather thong to Seán's mate – an emergency replacement for a broken shoelace on the way up in the car. Gerry had been like a diva till he sorted it. He'd killed the buzz in the car and scowled when I turned the radio up. As if anyone would notice his bloody shoe. Stuck in the standing ups, sitting downs and mumblings of a mass, phone switched off in respectful silence, I was reflecting. The curry chip – the conversation rather than the carbs – was repeating on me. My feelings were clear as midnight muck in a pigsty. *Singular, plural, generic*. Apart from that moment in the exhibition at Belfast City Hall, I hadn't much thought of Iona. Who was I kidding? I *had* thought of her – after a couple of days' self-therapy being pissed off with girls in general and Shannon in particular. She'd come to mind, frequently, but like the Virgin Mary at Christmas. *How could this be?* The cultural barriers were higher than Croagh Patrick. *Opposites attract*, my hormones jibed. She was different, too, not like other girls I'd taken a liking to – floaty yet grounded, brunette, not blonde. Mainly it was her character, an honesty and a quiet kick-ass edge to her, that appealed. What freaked me wasn't what she thought of Mary, the chapel or church stuff; she had family in the police. That fazed me.

'You sly dog, there is someone else, isn't there?' Conal had pressed in the banter after the chips, as we'd steadily ascended the steep hill to Creggan.

'Maybe . . . yes . . . no.' I was all over the place in the immediacy of the row with Shannon.

'Do I know her? You weren't two-timing, were you?'

'No and no. Look, it's nothing. Nothing that's going anywhere anyway. Give me a break. I just split with Shannon. What about you? That girl at the other table?'

'Never mind me. Who is she? Seize the day and all that.'

'You don't know her. She's from the Waterside.' We slowed with the exertion of the climb up Eastway.

'Sure I'm from the Waterside. What's her name? Try me, I might know her. What school does she go to? St Cecilia's? Thornhill?'

Conal had made the automatic assumption I'd known he would – that she was Catholic. As I looked round the backs of the heads in the mass and considered my circumstances, nothing Conal had said about being my own man made much difference, it was still impossible.

'She went to Foyle. Look, you won't know her. She's called Iona.' We paused to gulp cool night air.

'So, what's the big deal? *Maybe, yes, no, won't go anywhere . . .*'

I smirked as he'd mimicked me annoyingly accurately.

'She's Protestant.' Finally I'd come out with it to shut him up. Conal rubbed the back of his neck and eyed me to check I was telling the truth.

'So what?' he said eventually. 'Since when were you a sectarian bigot?'

'Since I was born. Look, it's different for you – maybe for most people these days – but take a juke at my family history. Get real! "So, what does your father do then, Aidan?" "Well, Mr Scott. Glad you asked, *go raibh maith agat* – thanks. I'm from Creggan, me da ain't around but he's an unemployed IRA political ex-prisoner." Aye. Taxi for Hennessey!'

'Hands off my daughter, you Republican deviant!' Conal grabbed my shirt collar, role-playing Iona's da. It felt bloody good to laugh. Conal had spun round and snapped a photo – me caught unawares, smiling skewed, my hair still a mess from the vodka and Coke. 'Right, Hennessey, at least do me the honour – that's your new Facebook profile. If you've really broken up with Shannon, get your image changed and get back on the pull.'

The mass was only half done. I yawned, counting the ceiling rafters.

'Our Father . . .' began the priest, and there was that low stammer of a delay while the congregation joined in the prayers by rote.

'. . . who art in heaven, hallowed be thy name.'

Our father. My da, now there was a story. Nothing hallowed or heavenly about it either. I wondered if he was still in Liverpool, or if I gave a shit anyway. The invisible man since that night when I was twelve and he finally pushed it too far. The miracle was it hadn't happened sooner; that residue of community respect for former volunteers meant Ma had endured it longer than she should have. If I was brutally honest, I didn't mind that Da had been in the IRA. The Troubles were different times. Mad with injustice. Only after peaceful civil-rights protesters faced guns did many men like Da lift guns to fight back. My superheroes growing up had been the protesters, the fighters and the hunger-strikers I'd heard about. Real men. Spider-Man was just make-believe.

Sometimes it was hard to see fiction from fact, though, in the yarns of other wasters living on faded dreams and rose-tinted memories. That was the real rub. The Troubles were bollocks. They screwed everyone over – especially my da. He drank increasingly through my childhood. I remember him egging me on to take my first sip out of his can at ten; me curious whether it would make me a demon or a god. He wasn't all bad all the time. I'd some good memories of him hiking me around on his shoulders, spinning tales. He was the life and soul of the party on a good day, the death of it other times; days I balked at even offering him a wine gum. There had been too many school nights with Irish music blaring in the kitchen till past 4 a.m., when he'd finally fallen asleep in an armchair with the whiskey bottle empty on the carpet by his feet; too many days at a school desk where the learning had been a fuzz of tiredness and worry I couldn't fathom, despite Ma's hugs at the breakfast table. Too many family occasions, first communions, confirmations, birthdays that ended in embarrassing displays of drunken revelry to the point that we were scared to look forward to anything, even Christmas. Especially Christmas.

The congregation roused to give the sign of peace, the handshake with those around us.

There hadn't been much peace in our house until he left, or rather, had been finally taken away in handcuffs. The one time in our lives we – Saoirse, actually – called the police. The one time we'd been glad to see them. When we were younger, times when it got really bad, Ma used to just routinely pack a plastic bag of our underwear and toothbrushes and escort us out the door to Aunt Teresa's spare room for a night or two until he had drunk it out of his system. He was a binge drinker; in and out of cycles of depression and nightmares you could hear through walls. He could go two months being virtually normal, sucking Polos and nipping to the yard when we didn't need coal, handling the crushing boredom of life on the dole and the haunting from his past. Then suddenly he'd crack. We'd come home from school to find he'd cleaned the house from top to bottom for the justification of sitting slouched at the kitchen table with the beer cans crushed around him, the ashtray overflowing, and my mother tense as a bent school ruler right before it snaps, letting on all was grand. I was too young then to wonder how she coped. Budget beans on toast for a week was just code for, 'Your da gambled his benefits again.'

As Seán and I grew older, so did Ma's fear that one day we'd sense our manhood enough to take him on for her sake. Instead of us leaving, she'd throw him out to drink elsewhere, but he would return; she'd ban drink but he would hide it; he would make honest-to-God promises, only to break them weeks later and with it Ma's heart all over again. We'd hear her sobbing. He would swear in the morning that it was the last time he'd hit her, but we saw through her make-up. Our hugs couldn't heal everything. It murdered me to watch her get ground to dust. Only in the months after he left, when she slowly recovered her lightness, did we realize he wasn't the only ex-prisoner.

The final explosion had come when Seán was fifteen, Saoirse sixteen. Da had picked his moment more carefully, as he always did by then; calculated the day that Saoirse and Seán, who was now as tall as him, were away from the morning, so that he could drink all day uninhibited. He hadn't counted on me being furious and desperate enough at twelve years old to take him on in a battle I could only lose.

The kitchen was a war zone when my siblings turned the key in the front door at dusk. Glass everywhere, my screaming, his goading, a riot of testosterone and anger with a backdrop of rebel songs at full volume on a CD player as I pitched myself at him again and again, taking the blows, dodging the knife he held. My sweat, Ma's blood, my yells, her silence and his demonic laughter. It was an enraged combat I was sustaining on adrenalin alone. Ma was unconscious, in a crumpled pile on the floor against a cupboard, bleeding.

In the hellish stretched minutes it took for the ambulance and police to arrive, Seán had torn into him like a man possessed. The neighbours had gathered as the fight had spilled into the street, and for once no one had jeered or attacked the police car as the officers dragged my brother and father apart, restraining them and then forcibly removing Da from the scene. She didn't press charges. He never came back.

The funeral mass continued for the young man, a thirty-one-year-old shot dead in some drugs thing in Dublin. Relatives in black passed tissues to each other and struggled to hold back tears. You couldn't help but be moved by the silent weeping of his mother in the front row during Prayers of the Faithful. I wasn't that faith-filled anymore. Ma was the praying one in our house right to the end. My final loss of faith, my last dance with religion, was when she was dying. I prayed then. It made no difference.

The bell rang out for the Eucharistic Prayer and again as the priest at the white altar raised the wafer and chalice for the Body and Blood of Our Lord. Himself, carved beautifully onto his smoothed wooden crucifix at the side of the chapel, glared down at me. Rather than joining the silent waves of those queuing for Communion, I stayed on my bench, stuck in the condemnation I felt every time I had to endure mass. The 'Thanks be to God' after the priest announced the end were always the most meaningful words I uttered. The congregation filtered out after the coffin to the chapel grounds.

In the swell of the crowds I could see Seán and one of his three friends across the car park. That's when it happened. The colour party. Six men in khaki-green army jackets, black gloves, black berets and black glasses appeared from round the side of the chapel and, passing through the crowd like Moses parting the Red Sea, unfolded an Irish tricolour, the green, white and orange, onto the coffin with military precision. Hoisting it onto their shoulders, they carried the weight of the pine coffin step by co-ordinated step behind the hearse with the grieving in their wake. It was the first time I'd ever witnessed this. In the past, before my generation, it was more common to see IRA funerals with flags on coffins, but we were supposed to have peace now. This wasn't even the funeral of a veteran Republican of the Troubles. Suddenly

I was flooded with doubts; angry, uncertain questions I wasn't sure I wanted to know the answers to, questions I needed to direct at my brother, especially after I clocked the familiar makeshift shoelace of one of the Republican volunteers in the colour party.

As we squished round a table in the pub after the burial, my silent glares at Seán tried to communicate a mixed sense of betrayal, disbelief and concern, but he wasn't taking me on. Had we not learned anything from our da? Perhaps we both had, except in totally different ways. Seán avoided eye contact, busy downing pints as they all were. After two packs of salted peanuts and an ocean of Diet Coke, I was fit to be tied, gagging to get Seán on his own. It didn't add up, my brother in all this, unless there was a whole other level we weren't talking on. Even then I didn't know if I could ask, or if he could answer. Didn't he see this shit had a cost? It wrecked the people who carried guns, as well as the lives they targeted. Couldn't he see the north of Ireland was different now? My brain buffered, circling and circling, as the others soaked in alcohol. Seán was propping the bar up like the latest lotto winner and two others were outside for a smoke when Gerry, shoelace Gerry, piped up. Was I as into politics as my brother? Innocent enough question, yet it felt every bit like a warped priest asking an altar boy if he'd a girlfriend yet. Maybe it was the difference in sobriety by that stage, maybe personality, but it wasn't a conversation I cared to be in.

'No, I don't give a shit about it,' I lied. 'I'm leaving Derry anyway.' I shifted round the table and went as if to help Seán carry back another round. He fired a venomous look when I issued my ultimatum – outside in half an hour or they could hike home.

I was stone-cold sober, thank Christ given the 'coincidental' breathalyser test I'd later get pulled in for at the roadside going home – two firsts for me in one day I could've done without. As I ticked over the car engine and listened to the radio, waiting for them to finish their pints, I fumed. If, *if* it wasn't just my imagination, *if* they had been trying to groom me, recruit me, into dissident Republicanism with or without Seán's knowledge, it had backfired with spectacular brilliance. The timing of my reflections during the mass: Da and all that he'd done to us; my thinking about Iona despite the barriers; what Conal had said about cutting my own path; all of that, combined with the sinister chat-up line from Gerry, were turning me in a very different direction. I found myself in an imaginary conversation with Ma. Her three-word answer was predictable. *Guard your heart.*

My phone, which had been on silent in the pocket of my black leather jacket, buzzed – Conal, setting up band practice. Only then did I cop the Facebook request from Iona. She'd sent it during mass. It brought a sliver of warmth, hope, into a bleak day. So she'd been thinking of me the same time I'd been thinking of her? I visualized the way our eyes had locked in City Hall. It stirred the same hot wave of emotion now as it had then. So maybe she liked me? Maybe I liked her? Maybe, given the day that was in it and everything else that had gone down since school ended, it was time to go against the grain and prove their assumptions wrong. Maybe there were different routes to being a man these days. I looked across at the pub.

Her ex had devastated her by calling her boring – same jibe Shannon had fired at me. I couldn't remember the exact words I'd reassured Iona with on that bus journey. Even I knew it was out of line to lead a girl on when I was hoping to shag a different one. Plus, she was a Prod. Was it even legit to have her in my sights when our das probably targeted each other in a very different sense? I closed my eyes, offered up a silent prayer to the universe, then typed.

Hey. Your ex, the one that called you boring, was a jerk. So was I. I messed my lines. Should've called you beautiful. Don't shoot me if you don't want to hear that from me, I'm just saying . . .

Chapter 17. Connection.

IONA.
Thursday 7 July.

The bonfire builders were out in force on the Clooney football pitches as I walked our dog, Maddy, in the afternoon sunshine. It was a male Protestant rite of passage, younger teenagers gathering wooden pallets, sofas, tyres – anything you could take a match to and pile in towers high as houses. An older teenager, or some eejit in a balaclava, would assume the honour of igniting it by petrol bomb and the Loyalist crowds would cheer as the cladding of Irish tricolours and Republican election posters went up in smoke on the 11th Night. It was supposed to be a celebration of 1690 – the Protestant King William beating Catholic King James II for the English throne. These days it was pure tribal. The silly season, they nicknamed it, when, for a few weeks, Northern Ireland descended into its two camps again, in flags, flames, parades and protests. The attitudes hadn't changed, just the tools. We fought with culture now, not guns.

I had to admit, though, the Twelfth of July itself had a buzz about it. Crowds, deckchairs and picnic bags lined the streets every year. Even the chip vans, ice-cream trucks and bouncy castles donned the British red, white and blue along with the stalls selling orange regalia and everything King Billy. Since we were eleven, me and Rachel always went talent spotting amongst the bands and banners.

By fourteen, the lads in band uniforms had lost their appeal.

I'd got bored with their prancing like toy soldiers and knew their four tunes backwards. My family weren't in the Apprentice Boys or the Orange Order, but both my brothers were committed wood scavengers, camping out on dumped sofas in makeshift huts guarding bonfires in the build-up to the 11th Night. It drove Mum mad. She hoped it was just a phase, and it kind of was until Andy came in one evening wielding a Bb flute and announced he'd joined a band. My parents' protests fell on deaf ears, the same as you needed to listen to the band. John ultimately opted for a different uniform; the same one my father had recently retired from on the sick.

Maddy barked and set off, racing faster than my head when Aidan's message had landed. She sniffed hedges and christened lamp posts while my brain, or maybe more than just my brain, throbbed. Rachel and I had been watching Wimbledon, having abandoned the thought of the cinema – there was enough male muscle on show between tennis and the Euros. When my mobile had bleeped, my effort at cool disinterest was so see-through she'd swiped my phone quick as an ace down the centre line and waltzed round the room singing 'You're Beautiful'.

'Text him back! Now! What are you gonna say? Oh . . . play it cool! Leave him hanging.'

To my shame, I'd left him hanging overnight and a pretty sleepless night at that. *Was he messing? Might he be serious?* What if I did say yes to a guy from Creggan? I could feel my heart pounding. It had never crossed my mind that he would message, or feel, something like that. Complicated felt like a distant shoreline. One thing liking him in fairy tales; scary when 'we' became possible. No one but Andy knew about the fight in the park weeks ago, and no one but Rachel knew I'd been to Belfast with him. Then there was his politics. I didn't really care, but my dad and brother still had to check under their cars every morning – peace had a price. How would they feel about me cashing in on it? Would everything explode anyway if John turned into Sherlock, investigating the attack? It already felt like I'd drunk fifty Red Bulls. Maybe it was me. Had I the confidence to risk getting hurt again? My faith had a line, and at eighteen, boys demanded to cross it. Chances were, Aidan would be no different.

'Iona!' Rachel had pestered me on the phone this morning. 'You're eighteen going on eighty! Stop over-analysing. I never meant leave him hanging that long. He's saying he's into you. It's not a proposal. What've you got to lose? He's gorgeous! You like him. Give him a chance!'

As I padded the pavements with Maddy, I reached the obvious conclusion – the only way to find out if it would work was to give him a shot. Terrifying and awesome, like the stirrings of rebellion. Sitting on a low wall round Kilfennan Country Park, I watched white butterflies flutter past and finally summoned the nerve to phone him.

'Hey, Iona!' he answered, after about eight rings.

The audio backdrop was a loud mix of drums and electric guitar. I jammed the phone to my ear in case I missed what he said.

'Hang on!' he shouted over a din now laced with wolf-whistles and slagging from male voices. There was a muffled retort from him as door hinges squeaked and footsteps sounded on a path. 'Hey,' he said again. 'How's things?'

'You busy?' My breathing was erratic.

'With a few mates. You? Get my message?'

'Yeah. Thanks. Sure you were sober when you sent it?' I screwed my eyes tight, focusing everything on listening for hints of half-truths.

'Come on! It was early afternoon. So . . .' He coughed, hesitating.

'What about Shannon?' I said.

'We split. About ten days ago . . . I just wondered . . .'

I could hear him shuffling. I'd thought he would be mad confident, but he kept taking sharp intakes of breath and clearing his throat.

'Am I just a rebound, Aidan?'

A pause at his end of the airwaves.

'No.' His voice was steady again. 'You're not a "just" anything. It was a compliment – and I meant it. Look, maybe I read you wrong . . . I thought . . . You know I enjoyed hanging with you in Belfast . . . but if . . .' He faltered to a stop and inhaled.

'You read me right,' I whispered.

'Yeah?' The hope strengthened in his voice. 'Em . . . fancy linking up again sometime? I could try to get the car and we could go up the coast or just get a coffee . . . whatever?'

'Sounds great.' I hugged myself. 'I'm working tomorrow. Maybe Saturday?'

'Saturday is sweet.' He laughed nervously. 'You know, I really thought you'd shot me down when I didn't hear from you. So good you called.'

'Even with your mates slagging you?'

'Hell yes! And they'll wind me mental when they hear you said yes.' His words raced. 'I'll check out the car and message you later, all right?'

'Perfect.'

'Beautiful!'

I sat on the brick wall, all sugary in the moment with the

mobile glued to my hand, until Maddy bounded back across the park, tongue out, panting. I stroked her glossy coat, whispering, 'I've a date! With Aidan. Our secret.'

She barked and ran. Suddenly the butterflies weren't just in the park. They flooded warmly across my stomach. Maybe I'd tell Rachel, but no one else; not yet.

Chapter 18. Siblings.

AIDAN.
Saturday 9 July.

It took a few moments for the sleep-fuzz in my brain to clear. Worming my arms from under the duvet, I fumbled around the bedside table in the dark to locate my buzzing phone. A half-yawned hazy 'Yeah?' was all the coherence I could muster.

'Ha! Shape of you! Bed-head!' my sister taunted. Only then did I realize it was a video call.

'Christ's sake, Saoirse. What time is it?' I sat upright in bed and leaned back, rubbing the sleep from my eyes and holding the phone out to focus.

'Two a.m. with you. Weren't you still awake? It's Friday!' Technically it was Saturday morning, but I wasn't awake enough to argue.

'Give me a second . . .' The wall was cold on my bare back. I stretched for my leather jacket.

'You look like a male stripper now,' she teased. 'Bare chest and black leather. Could be a positive career plan . . . I see you're feeling lucky?'

'What?' I missed her drift.

'Table behind you . . .'

She laughed at my groan from across the other side of the world, where she was sitting in some cafe-bar place, the lottery ticket Seán had given me and the unopened Extra Safe box from the Belfast chemist visible in her screen. I swore as my cheeks reddened.

'I was out sound. Give me a break!' I grinned sheepishly.

'You are on your own, I take it?' She raised her eyebrows.

I turned the phone three-sixty degrees around my bedroom. 'Pure as the driven snow, your wee brother! Angelic as always, like yourself.' I laughed.

'Ha! No need to lie to me. Refocus your screen. I'm not Aunt Teresa!'

It was so good to hear from her, even if I had been out for the count. Between Bolivian Wi-Fi and my 4G limit, we hadn't FaceTimed in weeks. It sounded magic – volunteering with street kids in La Paz, kayaking in the Andes, trekking desert dust in the Altiplano. The people smiled straight at me in her photos – wrinkled, dark-skinned people in bowler hats and bright woven blankets; street vendors with rainbows of fruit on dusty mats; kids leading llamas through mountains. This time, though, she hammered me with questions about the attack; my Facebook; the incident with Shannon. I was itching to talk about Seán. Was he a dissident? Sworn into the New IRA? It was frying my head. We'd been ships passing in the night for two days. When our paths had crossed, he blanked me, tense as if he were about to turn green and rip his shirt. It had made me clam up anytime I'd tried to talk.

'I'm sure it's nothing. Maybe he's dealing with something.' Saoirse shifted in her seat.

'Like what?' I said.

'Dunno.' She hesitated. 'Like, you know, after Ma died. You exploded. Scary to watch, but in the end, you grew up and faced it. You're the stronger for it. Seán's still stuck. Give him space. Maybe he needs a girl, maybe he's pissed off on the dole. I'll call him, all right? Promise. Don't get involved.' She looked away. 'Trust me.'

My shoulders relaxed, sagging back into the pillow. She made it seem easy – like there was no big issue. I sighed, looking beyond the screen to the damp in the wallpaper. I could've used the escapism of talking about travelling but she kept turning the conversation back to home. When I mentioned about losing Ma's ring from Santiago, she went quiet.

'Did you look for it?'

I'd scoured the house on the off-chance that it hadn't been in my pocket that night. No luck. Searching further was pointless – a needle in a city-sized haystack. For the first time since packing her rucksack many moons ago, my sister seemed homesick.

She sang a line from an old Bobby Sands song my parents used to sing, wishing she were back home in Derry. We reminisced about the better memories. 'Any other bars? Tell me good stuff!'

I told her about the Clipper yachts, the markets up the quays. I hadn't been to them yet; I was pretty broke. We were going to busk though, me, Conal and Jess. It would be a laugh and might net us enough for a few pints.

'So are you a millionaire with your lottery ticket?' she asked.

'I never scratched it yet! Right. Beaming live from halfway across the world, this is the moment we win the airfares to emigrate to New Zealand . . .'

'Tickets for Broadway?' she jested.

'A Harley-Davidson?' I held the ten-pence coin poised to scratch.

'University fees to get my wee brother a break?' she added.

I scratched the card and she shouted for my attention as the grin spread across my face.

'God's honest truth . . . I actually just won fifty pounds! Yes, lads!'

'Hey, big spender . . .' she sang.

'Don't laugh. This is my salvation for tomorrow. Exhibit A . . .'
I turned the phone camera towards my freshly ironed shirt,
pristine on a hanger in front of my wardrobe.

'Aidan Hennessey!' she exclaimed 'You've a date and you didn't
tell me till now? Please God you're not back with Shannon, are
you?'

I told her about Iona and our day in Belfast. I hadn't told Seán,
it might have wired him to blow.

'You're so cute when you fall for someone!' Only my sister
could get away with saying that without comeback. I blushed
again, then confessed what was still worrying me, especially
since the funeral at Strabane. *Would my own family be OK with
me seeing Iona?* Saoirse seemed fine about it, the Protestant bit,
the police bit. Later she harped back on it though, in the
middle of talking about something else. 'Tread carefully,' she
cautioned.

'What, you don't think I should see her?' I frowned. 'Isn't that
what peace is supposed to be about – life beyond labels? We like
each other – what's so wrong with that?'

'Nothing. Nothing at all, Aidan. It's just . . . perceptions. People
might see it different, no matter what the truth.' She looked
down, then back at the camera. 'Ignore me!' She smiled. 'If you
like her, go for it! She's a lucky lady. You're a gem, even if you are
my brother, even if you don't see it yourself . . . but *faire agat do
chroí*, and I'm not just talking about your love life, all right? And
go down to Dove House and get benefits advice. You must be
entitled to something to live off.'

We'd barely hung up when the banging downstairs began.
Seán was obviously too drunk to get his key in the door. Again. I
dragged myself half naked out of bed and turned the latch.

'Jesus! Shannon?'

'I need a gun. They only gave me two weeks. You've gotta get me a bloody gun.'

She'd burst into our hall, tripping on her hysterics, hitting me, hugging me, snot and tears streaming. 'They threatened me. They'd hurley sticks and balaclavas. I need you. Bastard. You owe me.'

'What?' I asked.

'Gonna make me stand in your hall?' She shoved past to the living room.

'They threatened me. Over drugging you,' she said, cowering by our mantelpiece. 'Said it was anti-community behaviour. That I've to take the blame for you getting beat up.

'Who's they?'

'Are you asleep? The dissidents!' She was shaking. 'They were all screaming about defending Creggan against anti-community behaviour. Said it was about justice. Equality. They had it from a source. Said if I was a lad drugging girls, there'd be no negotiating – I'd already be bleeding in a back lane.'

'Bloody self-appointed vigilantes! They're not threatening that in my name. Honest.'

'They said it was as bad as dealing. That they're protecting people. Can't you see I'm scared? I'm shot in the knees in two weeks unless I can get them a gun.'

'For real?' I tugged my leather jacket tighter, self-conscious in bare feet and boxers. 'Seems extreme. Even for them.'

'Not like you couldn't already name the lads they shot by the shops so far this year . . . Look, it's either a shedload of cash or a gun. You've brains. Help me. Please. I've to get them a gun or I'm shot by appointment. Didn't your da have a gun?'

'I'm not my da.'

'He must've kept it somewhere . . .'

'Like I'm supposed to know? I wasn't even born. You think guns grow on trees? Can't you get cash?'

'Christ! My whole family's on benefits. Will you help or what? Don't I mean anything to you?' She hesitated, then in the silence, stepped close. Eyes wet. Hands trembling as she touched me.

Fallen out of bed, half dressed and fully mortified, I hardly knew up from down, let alone right from wrong. I hated that she still turned me on. And that she knew it. She slid my hand up her jumper, her bra as present as my moral compass, and parted her lips slightly as I failed to control my roving fingers.

Sensing my weakness, she pulled me tight, hands all over me. 'Sort me out and I'll give you one . . .'

As her lips brushed mine, finally my brain kicked in and I slumped into an armchair. Thinking for a minute, she changed tack as my heart and head raced.

'Heard you've a Proddy bitch now? Yous were seen on the Belfast bus. She's from the Waterside. Does she know about your wild days? Bet she'd love to know about your da and—'

'No way I'm getting you a gun. It's not like you can just walk into a shop.'

She stepped back, hands on hips and studied me. 'You know,' she said, 'it's dead easy to hype stories online. Drink, drugs? With your past, you know it would stick . . . Doubt your new girl will go with you again if she thinks you beat your girlfriends to a pulp.' She did a fake sniff, then buried her face in her hands. 'I should've listened to what everyone was warning . . . He made me swear not to tell you . . . but he's violent. Just like his da.'

'Liar!' I lurched to my feet.

'Pants on fire?' She glanced at me and laughed. 'I don't give a shit. People heard me scream. Saw my eye.'

'You wouldn't!' My hands were fists as our eyes locked.

'Believe me. I'd do anything . . . or everything . . .' she said, stroking my chest, 'to avoid being shot.'

'That's blackmail!' I argued. 'Where'd I get a gun anyway? Two weeks?'

'Think you're so smart now? Use your brain.' She smirked. 'And your family history.'

'Two weeks?' I sighed, wondering where the hell I'd even start tracking down a gun to avoid being slated for life. My head was fried with the onslaught in the middle of the night. 'At least give me a fighting chance!'

'Fair enough. Let's keep this simple – you've a month before you're screwed one way or another. Only choice is heaven or hell.'

Chapter 19. Mussenden.

IONA.
Saturday 9 July.

The view was stunning. I wasn't sure if Aidan was considering it or something else entirely. Candyfloss clouds skated across the blue sky, and in the distance the arcs of a double rainbow connected the peaks of Inishowen. Below us, patchwork fields edged the Foyle to the Atlantic. It made me want to write or sing. Aidan had been quiet at first, but the further we'd travelled from Londonderry the more his shoulders relaxed. The water glinted as the sun played between clouds, hiding, then reappearing with beams of light. I studied him as he took in the black cliffs and rugged grasses of Coleraine Mountain. There was a comfort in being away from people who would recognize us. For some reason, I'd known we had the same type of soul; something in us connecting with being outdoors. We were both still, the silence broken only by the low whistle of the wind whipping around our ears. I tightened my fleece.

The narrow back-road had forced cars to hug the grass verges and dodge ditches, passengers breathing in sharply when they met an oncoming vehicle. I was glad he'd driven; I'd hung out of the car window and relished the scenery as we wound our way to Downhill. We were almost there when we came across the tall statue of Manannán Mac Lir perched on the flat mountain top, imposing his will, arms outstretched over the choppy waters far below.

Aidan was stood in the carved stone boat, beside the bearded Celtic god – a life-size Irish Neptune. The statue was bare-chested, but wore thick Celtic bracelets, a flowing cape, long skirt and a sword sheathed on his hip. Aidan, still lost in the view, was in a dark green shirt, black jeans and Converse trainers; his front foot was balanced on the ship's bow, hands high like a charismatic preacher and jacket whipping behind him in the gusts surging up the cliffs. He beckoned me to his vantage point and I clambered to join him at the prow. Looking at me, he smiled properly for the first time. I glowed. His moodiness had vanished, replaced by a playful free-spiritedness, openly flirting with my emotions. Our silence felt golden, like the Broighter treasure that had lain hidden for centuries in nearby fields, waiting patiently to be discovered: a boat with oars, a bowl, two bracelets and two necklaces, the visitor information panel had indicated. I imagined two lovers on a perilous voyage, sacrificing it to calm this ocean god from the sandbanks beyond Magilligan. Places like this made me feel mystical; faith felt so real here.

'Makes you feel alive, doesn't it?' He turned, moving closer so that I could hear him above the wind.

I nodded, returning his smile. I loved the power of the statue; it stirred my bones.

'Did you grow up with Irish legends too?' He motioned to Manannán Mac Lir. I had. The Hound of Ulster; the Children of Lir; the Land of Eternal Youth, and Finn MacCool, the causeway giant from round the coast.

'I used to dream of the warriors and the gods,' he said.

'Do you believe the legends?' I asked, without thinking beyond it. 'Or what exactly do you believe?'

The spiritual feeling of the hilltop drew the deeper

question from me. His eyes reflected a hint of surprise. Drawing an imaginary halo, he clasped his hands and rhymed off, 'I believe in one God, the Father, the Almighty, Maker of heaven and earth, and of all that is seen and unseen . . . I believe in one Lord, Jesus Christ, the only Son of God, eternally begotten of the Father, God from God, Light from Light . . .'

Part of the mass, he explained. Liturgy sounded weird.

'Should've been an altar boy.' He winked. 'Missed my vocation.'

'Aye, you look wild upset,' I said. 'For real though, what's actually true for you?'

He hesitated. 'I believe in life before death. I believe in justice. Human rights . . .' His eyes sought mine before he continued. '. . . I like big places, wildness that makes me feel small, yet part of something.' Hands clasped behind his head, he lost himself in a train of thought. 'If you push me on it, I guess I believe in God, probably the Christian God, but I don't think he believes in me much anymore . . .' The sentence hung in the air. 'I do believe in heaven. I have to. Ma's there. Hell? Who knows? Maybe I'll be hanging on in purgatory by my fingernails hoping someone will pray for me . . .'

His answer struck me as beautiful in its honesty, but sad too. 'I don't believe in purgatory,' I said.

'Guess I'm fecked then!' He grinned, jumping from Manannán's boat to the packed earth at its base and turned to help me down. His hand was warm.

'There's more religion in the Pope's toenail than me,' he said, as we dandered back to the car. 'Like does all that really matter to you? I don't honestly care if we don't share that stuff.'

'Yes and no.' I wasn't sure how to talk about it with him. I didn't care if he drank holy water or ate rice-paper circles under statues. I did need him to know I wasn't insane, that it was as human to believe as not. I wanted him to understand me.

He looked at me curiously. I liked that he seemed quite spiritual, whether he recognized it or not.

'We'll get there, I think.' He smiled as we approached the car park. 'Try and convert me if you want, but I don't rate your chances.' He winked.

The mountain road drew a steep zigzag to the bay at Downhill. The beach, a finger of beige, darkened to grey-brown. Mops of seaweed decorated the tideline. We walked with the dry sand pulling at our shoes until giving in and going barefoot, socks stuffed into our trainers, trousers rolled up. Aidan carried all four shoes dangling by their laces as we let the waves suck the sand from beneath our toes. The sea was cold, the salt air blasting our senses. We cut a ragged path through the foam of the shallow breakers, shifting back towards the shore if a larger wave pulled at the shingle, toppling the pebbles over in the drift. Neither of us changed course as our shoulders touched, sharing warmth through our jackets.

'What do you write?' he asked, as we sat further down the strand, gazing out to the horizon.

'Stuff.' I shrugged.

'No, seriously. If you're going to do a degree in it, you must write?'

'Short stories. Songs. Poetry.'

'Tell me a poem.'

I never shared my poems. They hid in a greenbacked notebook in my bedroom drawer. No one had ever asked before. I played with the hair hanging in front of my face. Sensing my hesitancy, he leaned his knee against mine. After a few minutes of silence, he cleared his throat.

'Glory be to God for dappled things . . .' he began, looking out to sea.

  'For skies of couple-colour as a brinded cow;
   For rose-moles all in stipple upon trout that swim;
Fresh-firecoal chestnut-falls; finches' wings;
  Landscape plotted and pieced – fold, fallow, and plough;
   And all trades, their gear and tackle and trim.

'All things counter, original, spare, strange;
  Whatever is fickle, freckled (who knows how?)
   With swift, slow; sweet, sour; adazzle, dim;
He fathers-forth whose beauty is past change:
    Praise him.'

His voice had steadied through the poem. It stirred me.

'Course, I'm only after realizing I'm quoting you a Catholic priest.' He tipped his palm off his forehead. 'Hopkins,' he added. 'Just in case you thought I'd gone all virtuoso. We studied it in school. Felt pretty apt for today.'

My mouth was dry. He didn't pressure me to share a poem, yet somehow he'd made being vulnerable feel safe. I studied where the horizon met the green-blue water and breathed.

'Have you ever tapped the half-haze of morning wakening?
Read real dreams before their unmaking
In the light
Of what might
But will probably never?

'At the seams of our dreams,
We are,

129

It seems.
At least I am, and always shall be.
Whether you join me may be psychology,
May be mentality,
May be causality.
It is where I am me.
And keeping the mind-mist makes vision clearer.
At the heart of the centre of self, breathes a hero.

'The trick of life's trade is in transposition,
Imaginings plausible, wonderings feasible.
Constructing the bridge between the dimension.
Being ourselves and living invention.
Blind to the limits.
Doing intention.'

'You wrote that?' he whispered. 'It's beautiful.' His dark eyes looked deep into mine, like in sharing poetry we'd glimpsed each other's souls. He might have kissed me then. I'd have let him. Instead he played with a lock of my hair that the wind had freed to twirl around my face. As he tucked it behind my ear, my doubts about being with him evaporated, blowing over the wild horses topping the waves to that Land of Eternal Youth, or wherever random thoughts roamed.

'You like it?'

'No.' He tilted his head. 'I love it.'

I laughed as without a further word he wiped the caked sand off my feet. It tickled. Rolling down the ends of my linen trousers to meet my ankles, he handed me my shoes with a coy grin.

'Flirt,' I said.

'Don't hear you complaining. I've never been to Mussenden

Temple.' He stood, offering his hand. 'Have you?'

Perched on the edge of the cliff over the beach, the temple was a Mecca for weekend strollers, but the mixed weather meant it wasn't thronged. We wove across the field to its dome. The sign said it was once a bishop's library. That intrigued me. It was necklaced with Latin round the top:

'*Suave, mari magno turbantibus aequora ventis e terra magnum alterius spectare laborem.*'

Aidan googled it.

'*'Tis pleasant, safely to behold from shore the troubled sailor, and hear the tempests roar.* Don't know if I like that,' he mused, as we tried the door to the stone building and found ourselves alone in its damp interior. 'Wouldn't you feel guilty not wanting to rescue the troubled sailor?'

'So what would you engrave round the building?' I asked as we stood side by side, looking beyond the film of sand and salt on the square windowpanes to the sheets of rain beginning to blur the view.

'Life is an ocean and love is a boat.' There was a glint in his eyes as he turned to me again. 'It's sung by this really obscure Irish singer-songwriter guy, Christy Moore, you won't have heard of him—' I punched him gently in the ribs. He groaned, taking a step back from me on the tiled floor.

'Sorry!' I gasped, having forgotten they were still healing. When I touched his shirt, he set his hand over mine. We stood close; his breath warm on my face.

'Ma swore blind a kiss always made it better . . .'

It was like a surge of electricity, the warmth and saltiness of his wet lips on mine as his hand, soft in the small of my back, pulled me close. We didn't stop for ages, lost in the passion of our first kiss, until the door clicked and the moment was interrupted by a tourist couple. Holding my hands, he turned me until we faced the window again. His strong arms wrapped around me from behind; his chin rested on my shoulder.

'I find Christy Moore quite inspiring,' I ventured. 'If he has that kind of effect on you.'

'More than an effect . . .' he whispered into my ear. 'It's a miracle, me and you. I mean, I never really knew a Protestant before you. I'd no idea what I was missing.'

'Suppose I taste different as well?' I raised an eyebrow.

'I'd never have believed it if they'd told me in advance,' he said, deadpan, arms still warm around me. 'Like, I'd have assumed it was some sectarian jibe about the orange centre . . . but it's true, Protestants really do taste of Jaffa Cakes.'

He dodged out of my way with that same smirk, palms upright protecting his ribs. Instead, my mouth found his again, and I didn't care about the other couple at the far rim of the old temple.

Outside, we stood by the damp stone wall, which secured the precipice from visitors. Leaning over it, we sensed a rush of vertigo looking down at the breakers on the beach below, the click-clack and horn of a train carrying up from the rails beneath us, the sound mingling with the roar rising from the turquoise surf. I stooped to search for a four-leaf clover by the path.

'You're religious *and* you believe in luck? Isn't that illegal?' he asked.

'You going to arrest me?'

'Daren't,' he said. 'Family allergy to handcuffs.' He dodged my eyes for a split-second, then interlaced his fingers with mine and led me back across the meadow, the swish of the grass brushing our shoes. We followed a mown track through the carpet of buttercups and daisies, the meadow springy beneath our feet, the wind whispering secrets through the wild grasses. Under the cover of the woods, with the twirls of climbing ivy wound round conker trees, we kissed again. The heady scent of pine mixed with his aftershave making my head light. Already I loved him.

We ate chips on a wall in Castlerock, swinging our feet against the stone. Driving home in the car, the radio belted out summer hits, and more than once I caught his gaze straying off the road onto me. I made eyes at him and stroked his leg until he pulled into a lay-by, choking with laughter.

'I can't concentrate! G'on, please let me get you back in one piece! I really want to see you again!'

Stealing a kiss as he was strapped into the driver's seat, I promised my best behaviour. He rolled his eyes. Was that really what he wanted? As we drove on, we chatted about all sorts of nothing. Food, films, teacher crushes, music, gigs. As I juked in the passenger mirror to tidy my hair, he complimented me on the new 'red bits'. Sweet he'd noticed.

My driveway was empty when he pulled up outside my house. 'You want to come in?'

He was hesitant. 'Is your family going to be like the Inquisition?'

'No one's in.'

'Did you say coffee?' He followed me into my house and nosed about. 'Remind me to renovate my entire house before you set foot in it,' he said ten minutes later, sipping coffee in the living room.

'It can't be that bad!'

'Wanna bet?'

He'd explained that he lived with his brother. The thought crossed my mind that John and Andy couldn't keep a house tidy if their lives depended on it. *Oh God. Our family photos.* I hadn't told Aidan yet that it was Andy who'd intervened in the fight. Would he recognize him? I glanced back at our mantelpiece and angled myself in front of a portrait. It was a different picture that caught his attention – John's police graduation. My older brother was all uniformed up with a gun at his side. I cringed. Was it really only two weeks ago we'd had that conversation in Cafe Nervosa? There was no way Aidan could know John was investigating the attack, was there?

'Your brother?' he asked.

'Yes. John. You OK with it?' I watched his face.

'It's a bit . . . surreal. Fine. I just need to get my head around it . . .' His pupils narrowed. 'Mind if I use your bathroom?' He set down the empty mug as I gestured upstairs, scrambling the moment his back was turned to hide Andy's image in a drawer. I needn't have rushed, his footsteps traipsed around above, lost in transit.

My breathing had calmed by the time he was back in the doorframe.

'This was good today,' he said, fiddling with the back of his shirt. 'What are you up to the next few days?'

'Church on Sunday, working Monday. You angling for an invite to the Twelfth parades?'

'Bollocks,' he said. 'Even miracles have limits. Wednesday? I've to head now. Promised Seán I'd have the car back for three.'

As I nodded, he held his hand out to me and was leaning in for a kiss when we heard the back door. He straightened. 'Who is it?' he mouthed. My stomach turned as I looked over his shoulder. Andy. No doubt he'd seen us.

'My younger brother,' I whispered.

Andy plonked his jacket on the kitchen table and sauntered

into the living room, expecting an introduction. I was tongue-tied, waiting for the moment the penny would drop. Heads or tails. Aidan's eyes flashed my direction before he stepped up, my brother accepting his handshake with a look like he was processing something.

'Hi, I'm Aidan . . . I was just leaving . . . I'll call you later, Iona. Thanks for today.' He swept out, the front door clicking behind him. There was shell shock on my brother's face when I turned back.

'Was that him?' he said.

Chapter 20. Twelfth.

AIDAN.
Tuesday 12 July.

My head was as fried as the halal burgers I was flipping on the oil drum barbecue. I couldn't stay pissed off with Seán for long. When he'd asked if I'd help at a community barbecue welcoming Syrian refugees, I'd shrugged and said, 'Sure.' I needed something to get girls and guns out of my head. Well, one girl and one gun anyway. Iona had a VIP invite to stay front and centre, even if I had near split my skin with the shock of meeting Andy. My brain catapulted almost an hour later, when it finally processed where I'd seen John. The image of bright lights and paper curtains was still blurry. Crazy. I'd met both Iona's brothers before.

The meat fat was dripping, hissing on hot charcoals, infusing my T-shirt and skin with the reek of smoke. *Very attractive*, I thought wryly, happy as a pig in muck. Could you be mad and on a high at the same time? I was. Something manly about cooking on coals was helping me slow the hurricane in my head. I smiled hearing Seán laughing in the crowd. 'Anger is only one letter short of danger,' Ma used to cite, splitting us from a sibling scuffle. I'd remembered her words clearly as I'd hit the permanently delete icon on the phone footage a couple of hours after my date with Iona. I'd bolted when I'd made the initial connection – Andy was the one who'd intervened to save me. A bandsman. A Loyalist. I'd always assumed they saw us as subhuman. Maybe the thinking worked both ways. Iona hadn't exactly lied about her brother, just hidden the truth. I wiped the sweat from my brow, still reaching the same conclusion – I'd have done the same. I kind of was doing the same. It had provoked a serious case of the headstaggers that afternoon. Ultimately, I'd faced a simple choice: kissing or kicking? Revenge may have been sweet. Kissing Iona was magic.

It wasn't like being freaked or angry was new. Processing anger was why I'd taken up running. Saoirse had *made* me. Pounding pavements somehow kicked the pressure into touch. As I'd changed, so did my motivations. It powered me to keep positive, busting my frustrations. Endorphins had become the chemical of first choice in my bloodstream and thankfully I'd never looked back.

When Aunt Teresa threw me out, I'd more than merited her wrath. But for Saoirse's tough love, I still couldn't have babysat a goldfish. 'Go running,' she'd ordered, 'but run to a dealer and you're out on your arse.'

After Ma died, Saoirse and Seán stayed on in our family home, until the rent hiked. Saoirse was nearly twenty and Seán was eighteen, so there was no issue. I'd still been a minor, so my aunt took me in. There hadn't been any other cards on the table, with Nan losing her marbles. They might as well have stood me in a firing range – three months of hell watching Ma deteriorate crowned with being stripped of my home and siblings. With two pre-teen cousins more angelic than Mary Magdalene, I fitted my new family like a penguin in the Sahara. I only had to survive the length of my supposed final year at school but the arrangement collapsed spectacularly one night when, not for the first time, I landed back to their house plastered at some ungodly hour and sprayed the stairs with beer infused vindaloo. Them finding the half-dissolved tabs in the vomit was the last straw. If I was going to wreck my life, it wouldn't be under their roof.

I remembered shivering on the beige carpet, a spare part in their spare room. The message, filtering up through the floor from the raised voices of my aunt and uncle in the sparkling kitchen, was clear. I would be leaving. I didn't matter. Not to them; not to me; not to anyone. There was no place for me in their home anymore. Wound tight into a ball, I'd chewed my fist, overhearing the logistics of my eviction. Two days after my sixteenth birthday: my wake-up or die moment. I still couldn't put words to how blown apart I felt without Ma and didn't dare confess how screwed I'd become. They'd hate me like Da. I was becoming his double in more than looks. I'd tugged at my hair, firing the dark strands at my feet. *White-trash Hennessey. Unwanted. No tears.* I'd forgotten how to cry. *Man up.* I'd packed my own bag and slid out the front door, leaving my key in the latch.

At the barbecue my eyes were watering from the smoke drifting in swirls over the burgers. I stepped back to watch the gathering families – local and Syrian. The hijab rig-outs were new to me. A few wore black top to toe, others had coloured silks around their faces, long dresses and leggings. They were smiling at our Derry families – middle-aged men in cringe-worthy khaki shorts, white sports socks and milk-bottle legs; women enjoying 'the bars', the gossip, over plastic cups of Coke; kids kicking footballs, blowing bubbles and leaping like mad bucks on sugar-highs round the bouncy castle.

The sun was shining. It always did for the Orangemen parading on the Twelfth; not that they'd be parading in this neck of the woods. The barbecue was to keep young hoods away from protesting. Would Iona be watching her brother strutting his stuff with the Pride of Kilfennan or taking in the rays in a bikini in her back garden? My heart beat faster with the mental image.

To say I hadn't stopped thinking about her was understatement. It'd have been a blast if it weren't for Shannon's ultimatum the night before. It had been a mind-blowing day. I'd snogged a Prod. And. I. Bloody. Loved. It. Physically, I was healing rightly, and emotionally, well, I was turned on just thinking about her, never mind the memory of kissing her, like velvet in my mouth.

Seán approached me with a large plastic tub of sausages to see if the burgers could shift over. It caused a near riot of Arabic hand gestures and words until we twigged that mixing pork sausages with halal burgers was out. Multicultural education in a Catholic school had been as expansive as a whale swimming in a teacup. As we dished out burgers in baps with ketchup and onions, I was picking up the lingo. '*Marhaba*', 'Hello'; '*Wahid? Athnan?*', accompanied by a finger pointing at one or two burgers. '*Sukhran*', 'Thank you'. It didn't need many words. Kindness was language enough.

I liked watching how people connected. It made my feet itch to travel. Like, what was it other than a twist of fate which left us born who and when we were? I could've been Syrian – the coffin ships sailing from Derry's quays in the Famine weren't much different to the swarms of dinghies spewing across the Mediterranean. I could've landed in last-century London with 'No blacks, no Irish, no dogs' glaring at me from windows. Fate could've even had me born bowler-hatted, parading down streets I wasn't wanted in the name of 'God and Ulster'. Scary thought.

'Mind when Ma used to take us on a hike up the back fields on the Twelfth to get away from Da drinking?' I elbowed my brother with the memory.

'Aye.'

Seán went quiet, stirring onions on the tinfoil. He cricked his neck, then looked at me. 'Mind Da taking you on a walk up them fields one time too?'

'No. It was always Ma.'

'Not on the Twelfth. He took you one time. With Saoirse. You were about seven?'

I thought hard. 'There was one time. Was he drunk? It was supposed to be a picnic, but he took the wrong tin. We trekked our feet off, then sure it was just a broken water pistol in it. No crisps or Coke. Were you there?'

'No.' He shrugged, looking away. 'Just you and Saoirse.'

'Why'd you ask then?'

'No reason. Looks like it's more than the barbecue drawing their attention over here.' He nudged me, glancing in the direction of some Derry girls our age, definite eye-candy, leaning on the wall near the queue for the kiddies' face painter.

'All yours.' I grinned.

'What's with you? Still wrecked over Shannon?'

'No.'

'Come to think of it, you've been quite the smiler this last couple of days. I thought you were pissed off about me dragging you to that craic in Strabane.'

'I was. It's OK now.'

'Dog! Did you pair up with someone new already?'

My cheeks touted me. I told him about Iona but left the details scant. When he asked what school she went to, I said she worked in a coffee shop. Like Iona with her brother, it wasn't a lie, just avoidance of some truths I didn't want to share yet. We'd only just got together, the complicated stuff could wait. That was the exact moment she texted. I near choked trying to swallow my laugh. Passing Seán the barbecue tongs, I sauntered away to the quiet of the community centre, smiling. In her snapshot she was posing in a deckchair, sporting a British flag plastic bowler hat with a 'Made in China' sticker. I stared between her and Andy, saluting in red and gold military-style uniform in the background with a Pride of Kilfennan Lambeg drum.

Happy Twelfth, read her message. You mad at me or am I forgiven?

Sexy hat, I retaliated. Mad about you, not at you.

Wish you were here?

Anywhere with you ☺ . . . unfortunately busy washing my hair all day x

The Lambeg was a beer belly of a drum. Colossal. We could hear them banging even across the river. It was impressive. I thought about Andy, proud in his uniform, as I loitered inside the community centre, waiting for Iona to jibe back.

The noticeboards were cluttered with community posters: computer classes, parent and toddler stuff, and some history project. Faded snaps were spidered with scribbled comments, names, memories. My eyes flicked from images to ink scrawls roadblocks in the Bog with ranks of skinny youths in balaclavas and flares; women and kids jammed in pick-ups with chairs and suitcases; army with guns on street corners. The seventies. *Guns were easy got in them days*, I thought grimly, reminded of Shannon's deadline. Da would've been too fresh out of nappies to be holding one at that stage; stones maybe.

My best wee mate, Alan: an inked arrow pointed to a photo of a boy gripping a teddy in a street emptying itself of residents. *One of 14,000 Protestants who fled to the Waterside in the Exodus – never saw him again.*

Shit. Did we do this? I'd studied history, but I didn't know about this stuff. Was that why we'd Protestant churches on our side of the city turned into music venues and offices? If I hadn't heard *their* history, had they heard *ours*? I knew they called Da a terrorist. He wasn't. He fought for freedom, but maybe they didn't get that. Would Iona? Were we building peace only knowing half the war story? In our charity-shop jigsaws as kids, there'd always been pieces missing, we never got the whole picture. Key bits were brushed under someone else's carpet. I remembered wincing at Ma putting antiseptic on my grazed knees – 'If you don't clean a wound it won't heal.'

My phone buzzed in my hand.

Glad you like the hat. Bought it especially for you. Wear it and I won't care if your hair is washed or not . . .

I liked her style.

Back outside the crowd was swelling. Sunshine brought everyone out, from the blue-bag brigade in Brooke Park to the grannies with woollen skirts and walking sticks. It made me smile to see the families bonding over ice creams. Made me think I was overdue a visit to my own nan in Letterkenny over the border. Long overdue. I hadn't seen her since Easter and now that I could loan the car off Seán, it would be far easier than getting the bus into Donegal. Before catching up with Seán, I pinged Iona a reply.

I'll eat my hat if you ever get it onto my head . . . call you tomorrow x

And then it dawned on me. It was never a water pistol in that tin.

Chapter 21. Fireworks.

IONA.
Saturday 16 July.

Chips. Coffee. We'd hung out a bit since the Twelfth. Cafes felt much less 'them' and 'us' places than pubs. For once I wished I wasn't getting so many hours covering holiday leave for other staff. On the plus, I was loving the flow of banter and one-liners texted at random moments from Aidan. He had brains to burn and his wordplay, laced with innuendo, made my heart skip.

Thankfully he seemed to have forgiven me over Andy. His curiosity had become like a quick-fire school test. *How had Andy reacted? Was he mad? Why had he stopped the fight?* I was wobbling on a tightrope between two universes – Andy equally pestering me about Aidan. They were culturally opposite sides of the same KitKat. After another peppering of questions, I'd finally shut Aidan up by inferring that he must fancy my brother more than me. He'd looked at me wide-eyed as if I'd slated his very manhood, then leaned in across the cafe table, his mouth and nose moving close around my face but not quite touching, his now familiar aftershave wafting around me. Under the table his legs slowly, deliberately, tangled with mine and his hand brushed my thigh, generating fire through my nervous system.

'Are you inferring I'm *gay?*' He teased. 'I'm all for equality but I'm more than happy to prove I'm as straight as a ruler if you need any kind of convincing. Please feel *exceptionally* free to ask.' He had winked.

Tonight, though, it wasn't just us. I sucked my necklace as Rachel and I scanned round Ebrington Square. Conal and Aidan were messing around, typical lads, when I'd spotted them by the live stage.

'It's such a waste,' Rachel whispered through her teeth, all ventriloquist, when I pointed him out. 'Why do all the drop-dead gorgeous ones have to be Catholic?'

She laughed when I elbowed her. Aidan's T-shirt rode high, showing off his muscles as he twisted around fake punches from his mate and held a Sprite can in the air, just beyond Conal's reach. As I called, his attention shifted and his friend lunged to recover the drink.

Aidan played the perfect host, introducing his friends and high-fiving Rachel before mouthing a quiet 'You look great' to me. Did he mean it? I felt like a brown paper bag compared to Tala, Jess's girlfriend, who was Filipina too, with beautiful long dark hair and chestnut eyes. They'd been together, like, forever, and though they both spoke in Derry accents, they'd share quick comments in Tagalog like a lover's secret language. I ached to get Aidan on his own, yet found myself smiling at how he interacted with his friends. He played to the audience, but threw regular glances my direction.

'Quit acting the maggot!' Conal slagged him, still equally as engaged in the rivalry half an hour later.

It was like a circus of gothic-gypsy performers had spilled across town. As we crossed from Ebrington over the Peace Bridge, we passed acrobats twirling under glowing hot-air balloons. Everyone chatted, but even in the positive carnival vibe it felt stilted. Rachel was quieter than usual, messaging on her phone as she walked.

'Mind if I slip away?' She nudged me. 'Kinda feeling three's a crowd.'

'But there's six of us,' I said.

'Don't you guys want some time on your own?'

'Sure.' I shrugged and watched her head off.

The crowds were flocking in the dusk for the last night of the Clipper festival, browsing dreamcatchers and carved wood statues in the continental market, waiting for sunset and the fireworks. Conal, Jess and Tala loitered with us a while longer but split the moment they bumped into other friends. Aidan squeezed my hand. Speakers strung along lamp posts blared African rhythms and pan pipes into the aroma of street food from around the globe.

'No wasabi anywhere . . .' Aidan faked his disappointment. I smiled. We wove through the crowds and bought fizzy cola bottles, flumps and other kiddies' sweets from the pick 'n' mix beside an incense stall further on down the riverside.

'My game this time,' he said, stopping in front of a plant stall and rooting in the sweet bag for a strawberry lace. His finger tapped my lower lip and I let him place one end of the lace between my teeth. Putting the other end into his own mouth, he then tried to explain through his teeth that it was a race to the middle – no hands allowed. There wasn't an iota of self-consciousness in him as we sucked and chewed to the inevitable kiss somewhere near the middle.

He was startled by a tap on his shoulder from a middle-aged bearded man speaking to him in a different language. Aidan reddened when he turned but spoke back relaxed, in a stream of what I assumed must be Irish. He didn't grow horns or sound political like Dad said. Poetic more like. Cool. The language flowed out of him with a lilt and collection of different sounds mixed with occasional English words. The gentleman nodded to acknowledge me and Aidan switched back to English.

'Iona, this is my Irish teacher, Mr Ó Súilleabháin. We were just saying how class the Clipper festival is.'

'He was recommending the pick 'n' mix,' his teacher said tongue in cheek before bidding us 'Slán' and waving goodbye.

'Absolutely not embarrassing at all. Not remotely,' Aidan commented low as we passed a toy stall. 'Hands where I can see 'em, lady!' He'd grabbed a cowboy hat and gun, targeting me with a playful wink, then, as if they'd burned his fingers, dropped both toys back into the bargain bucket. He stared at them, then grabbed my hand and pulled me onwards.

At the pontoon there was a flotilla of smaller boats: orange kayaks and yellow canoes; bored dads and enthusiastic kids splashing around on the river. The floodlights from the quay lit the Clipper yachts in their racing glory, their rigging clad with colours and shapes of sea flags I couldn't decode. Typical our boat had the longest name, *Derry~Londonderry~Doire*, and choreographed colours to make sure she didn't resemble any national flag. She took pride of place with her purple, pink, yellow and red branding and an open invite to venture across her gangplank.

Inside the yacht was ultra-compact – the shining galley, stacked coils of ropes, high-tech navigation equipment and tightly strung hammocks. Aidan glanced round before launching himself into one and pulling me in beside him. He snapped our first selfie and we simultaneously posted it as our profile pics before being reprimanded and ushered on round the ship.

'You're bad.' I laughed.

'But that's good, right? . . . So,' he ventured, 'a hypothetical mysterious windswept dark and handsome traveller buys you a plane ticket to journey with him anywhere in the world – where'd you choose?'

'He's a very generous stranger . . .'

'Yeah but he's dead handsome . . .'

'South Africa. For the people. For a safari. Robben Island would be crazy. I read Nelson Mandela's book.'

That spiked his interest. 'You know he was a political prisoner?' he asked.

'Sure. He was fighting apartheid. It was pure racist.'

'Kind of mad, jails becoming tourist attractions.' He bit his lip. 'Ever visited Crumlin Road Gaol?'

'No. Why?'

'Just wondered,' he said.

'So where would the handsome stranger want to wander in the world?'

'The Camino de Santiago,' he said instantly.

'What's the Camino de Santiago? Why'd you want to go there?'

'Who says I'm the handsome windswept stranger?'

'Call it a hunch.'

'Already blew my fortune, I'm afraid. Penniless. The Camino is a pilgrimage. Santiago, some saint, James, I think. His relics are in the cathedral in Santiago and people walk for weeks to think about life and stuff. In the mass at the end there's this huge incense burner that they swing on a rope right over the pilgrims.'

'I thought you weren't religious?'

'I'm not.'

'So why the Camino de whatever?'

'Because of Ma. You don't have to be holy. You can walk for penance, as a tourist, to find yourself . . . Whatever. When Ma got her diagnosis, before she got really sick, she joined a parish group hiking the Camino for a week. It gave her strength. Helped her face the crap. I'd like to walk it in her memory. To be honest, I'd walk any road out of Derry at the minute.'

His eyes were bright, deep. He wasn't just a head-the-ball from Creggan; my first instincts had been right – there was more to him, and I was still only scratching the surface of understanding who he really was. Fair enough. There was a lot I still wanted him to understand about me too, I just wasn't sure how he'd take it.

A single rocket boomed upwards from the barge anchored in the middle of the Foyle, signalling the imminent fireworks. Dad would be in the house, windows tightly closed for fear of the noise triggering Troubles' memories. Definitely not the night to announce I was seeing a Catholic. Explosions of colour, red, yellow, green, blue, flowered outwards high over the city. Yellow lanterns and blobs of purple fire floated mysteriously in the tidal flow of the Foyle. The night air was cooler now, and as we walked back down the quay towards the Peace Bridge, Aidan pulled my back close into his body, wrapping me in his warmth as we craned our necks skywards. I loved the strength of him wound around me even more than the showers of rainbow fire decorating the heavens. Secretly, I thanked the chill for the excuse it gave to generate a different kind of glow.

After the finale, we began crossing the bridge. As we made our way over, I spotted my brother sitting with a group of friends on the ramparts around the former military base. Andy returned my wave, catching Aidan's attention.

'Come meet my brother properly,' I suggested, embracing the evening's positivity.

Aidan tensed, dropping my hand. Too much too soon. It was barely a month since he'd been beaten up, not more than a stone's throw away. He went silent, studying the line-up of my brother's friends, all of whom were now staring in our direction.

'It's fine. It's not the same ones,' I whispered.

His eyes narrowed, the muscles in his arm stiffening as I touched his shoulder. 'I've got to make tracks. Can you head home from here?'

Words might have been his strong point, but it was clear he was doing the maths and didn't like the odds. Six versus one. Not an acceptable calculated risk. These were different friends; they were sound – not the louts who had pulverized him. By the second, though, Aidan was morphing back to the bloke I'd shared coffee with at the cafe that first day. That angry and broken version of him was light years from the Aidan I'd spent the last few hours with. My shoulders sagged, heart aching as he walked away. If he couldn't cope with Andy, would he ever handle meeting John or Dad? The Foyle Search and Rescue boat skimmed under the bridge. How much had their volunteers witnessed when they'd rescued Aidan from the attack? How long had I before John started piecing the evidence together anyway?

Sorry to abandon you tonight, Aidan messaged later. Promise I will meet your brother sometime if you still want me to. Just not tonight and not there. x

There is something intangible about how we heal, just as there is something intangible about how we fall in love.

Chapter 22. Digging.

AIDAN.
Thursday 28 July.

Pistols at dawn were no craic. Not when you couldn't bloody find them. And what if I did find it? Leaning back on the gate, I threw the stone after the trowel, sighing. *Clink*. It hit with accuracy and ricocheted towards the hedge, where small twigs marked my digging like a geography project. This was my third trek up the back roads. I wasn't sure if I'd crossed the border, but two things *were* certain – it was the right field and the clock was ticking.

Iona was all I wanted to think about, yet she'd be out of my life if she knew the half of it – never mind what Shannon could spin to make it worse. Chatting about Mandela had been the perfect chance to tell Iona about Da, but I'd chickened out. Right now, guns were too touchy a subject. I needed Shannon like a hole in the head, but I didn't want her to end up with holes blown through her knees or any other kind of punishment. Thank God I'd argued back. I had a month. No solace now, with nearly three weeks gone.

I'd not slept a wink the night Shannon had come over. Instead I'd surfed the net, becoming a self-educated expert on how you couldn't buy a gun; not if you're eighteen, broke and stuck in bloody Northern Ireland anyway. Thanks to the Troubles you couldn't even buy fireworks here without a licence. Shannon's ultimatum was as sick as she was; the only way Iona was hearing about my past, or my da, was from me. That, I had to control. My way. My timing. The truth was bad enough without added lies.

I had to find this gun or Shannon would trash what little was left of my reputation, and being with Iona would dive from complex to done. I sighed. The whole thing was twisted. Would the dissidents really shoot a girl? Beat her up? Even for the New IRA, it seemed severe. Not a question Shannon or I could gamble on – question their version of justice and you risked facing it.

I swore as the next stone missed the target and I traipsed after it to grab my trowel, orienting myself again by my blurry childhood memories. The gate where I'd sulked; the ditch Saoirse had jumped. Somewhere, just there, Da had dug. Maybe the hedge had grown broader. Maybe me being taller skewed my sense of distance. Maybe it was gone: dug up and decommissioned properly.

At least digging felt honest. I'd been many things, but never a thief: except for occasional chocolate bars or my uncle's cigarettes. Sneaking around upstairs in Iona's had felt so wrong. Especially after a morning that had felt so, so right. Her parents' room had been clinically neat. I couldn't have farted without disrupting its military precision. Opening the drawer of the bedside table had only revealed neatly folded men's reading glasses and a black bible. Load the guilt like. What had I expected? A revolver and two pristine silver bullets like the movies? I hadn't expected three strips of tabs. Pain, depression and relaxants. Worth a bob too – swallowed like smarties you'd be high as a kite for three hours, but wouldn't get it up for three days. The crap I carried in my head. Give me a bloody degree in that.

No. It was find this gun or face a loaded one. As I set again to digging, the sun was rising. So were my doubts. I was shite at maths, but something didn't add up. She'd definitely been scared, that was real, but if Shannon was the victim, how could she renegotiate the deadline?

Chapter 23. Jolt.

IONA
Friday 29 July.

Stretching both arms, I reached for the edge of the pool with my fingertips, letting the bubbles fizz from my nostrils as I finished my final length. Forty. Forty was a kilometre. Enough to clear my head and bleach the vanilla-coffee scent from my skin after work. My goggles were fogged, my breathing still heavy with the exertion as I hauled myself up the metal steps. A cloud escaped the steam room as a lady emerged with a shiver. The sign by the open door was trilingual. Cultures side by side. Ulster-Scots. English. Irish. The letters didn't touch. Would it kill to sneak in for ten minutes even without the proper wristband?

Alone in the privacy of the cloud, the warmth of the wet tiles soaked into my thighs as water from my hair rivered with sweat down my back. I relaxed, playing with the bubbles of air trapped between my toes and the sparkly mosaic, the squelch of my hands in the condensation. My nostrils flayed as wet heat hit my lungs and, closing my eyes, I imagined Aidan's fingers interlacing with mine, the touch of his shoulder on my skin. Sometimes he tasted of cinnamon.

A suck of steam left the room as the door opened.

'Traitor all alone?' Dylan's voice iced my blood. First time I'd seen him since the attack.

In two steps he towered over me, fencing me into the corner. I froze. Luke sniggered, silhouette blocking the door.

'Wee birdy tells me you're too rainbow-shoelaced for a shag. Least you were after your school formal anyway.' He licked his tongue along his teeth, staring me up, down and over again in my swimsuit. I tightened my arms and legs into my body.

'Understandable Kyle was cut seeing you plastered over Facebook with a new man. Thing was –' he leaned in – 'when he showed us the photo, Luke here reckoned his boot remembered your man's face.'

I flinched as his fingers slid round my ear and grabbed my chin.

'Laugh was, I defended you. Can't be ugly *and* stupid, says me. So.' His grip tightened. 'Squeal.'

My brain told my mouth to speak, my hands to move, my feet to run. Nothing. Nothing but palpitations, rapid intakes of breath with no exhale, no release. As he slid his hand from my chin, to my neck, to the elastic of my swimsuit, he shoved his knee forward, splaying my legs. I gasped with the jolt of it.

'Frigid is easy fixed,' he whispered. 'Think you're the big girl now?'

My back was glued to hot tiles. As his face pressed against mine, my stomach lurched with the smell of fried fish on his breath. A moan slipped from my throat.

'It's your lucky day,' he said into my ear. 'Big things happen to big girls.'

I winced as he grabbed my wrist. My fingers starfished, rigid in spasm as he shoved my palm against the groin of his swimming trunks. A strangled cough from Luke at the door halted him.

'Fucking forgot,' he said. 'Eejit here likes ye. Not second-hand after a Taig, mind.' As he turned to consult, the door swung. My brain clicked. I jerked my wrist from his vice and dug my nails into his trunks. He hollered. Doubled over. *Run.*

'Jesus. What's the story? You marathon training?' Aidan tried to grab my shoulder as I careered along the side street, swimming bag skimming the pavement behind me. 'Bloody blue-toothed myself here after your phone call and you've hardly spoke.'

I turned. Shoved him in the chest. He reeled. Stepped backwards. Stopped.

'Is it me?' he said. 'My family? Did I do something?'

I met his eyes. He dipped down to my level and saw me blink away tears as I shook my head over and over. My heart drummed my ribcage. He reached to touch my arm, but I flinched. He jerked back.

'Iona? Are you OK?' His voice was low.

I leaned my head against the pebble-dash wall of a terrace house, not caring about the jagged pressure of it on my temple. 'They came for me,' I whispered. 'The two who attacked you. Luke and Dylan. I was in the steam room. They saw our photo on Facebook and . . . and I . . . he . . . I couldn't even scream.' I lunged my arms round Aidan burying my face in his chest. It took a few seconds, then his arms wrapped like a safety blanket around me. No words, just the warmth of him, the deodorant on his T-shirt, the fresh sweat on his skin. He held me steady until the trembling stopped, his lips gently touching my forehead.

'Want me to call your mum?' He paused. 'The cops?'

I lifted my head and studied his worried frown. That the offer was genuine, was powerful. Family. Police. When it mattered, like really mattered, when it was about me, he was offering to cross his own fault lines. Some kids were kicking a football at the far end of the street. The steady thud of it focused me.

'Did they . . . ?' Aidan swallowed. Fingers in fists on his head.

Something in me calmed and I told him. He went quiet.

'I feel . . . degraded. Ugly.'

He locked eyes with me, and gently held my face. 'Never. Never let them in your head. Every morning spit the peppermint, stare in the mirror and tell yourself you got this. You're a walking miracle. You're beautiful.'

His gaze was chocolate. My breathing steadied again. 'Did your ma say that?'

'No. Just me.'

'Does it work?'

'Mostly.' He hesitated, biting his lip. 'Listen, Iona, you and me, it's explosive. I can't keep you safe. I can't risk you getting hurt over me.'

I lifted my chin. 'That's not your job. It's not your call.'

'Doesn't stop me feeling it.'

The tangle of emotions churned in me. 'I'm no doormat. I want to kick them for this! We are not over. They're not winning. Not now.'

Aidan looked to the sky. 'I love your fire.' Touching his thumb to my lower lip he studied me. 'Don't ask me to fight them. Please. Not that I wouldn't . . . It's just, in my shoes, that's a one-way slide. I'd lose even if I won.'

'I don't want your fists.' I lifted his hand, feeling the rough of his knuckles, the smooth of his palms. The urge for him was overwhelming. I tugged his head towards me, locking my lips fully on his. He was startled, then responded.

'But we can't do *nothing*,' I said afterwards. 'What if there's a next time?'

'This is my fault. If I hadn't deleted the evidence, you'd be protected. Bloody ironic me saying it, but you've got to report this.'

'What's the point? It's not like they'd get forensics off a damp swimsuit.'

He stared at me, then his trainers, then back at me. 'Look, it wasn't just Andy I recognized at your house,' he said. 'The photo. Your older brother. John. He was at the hospital that night in uniform. He was given the initial investigation on the attack, wasn't he? Think he'd still take my clothes for forensics? Or bend a few rules if it kept you safe?'

Chapter 24. Breadline.

AIDAN.
Monday 1 August.

I was standing in the Rathmór supermarket debating whether I could afford to buy both deodorant *and* shower gel, and still have enough for a week's budget pasta and sauce, when it had really sunk in how desperately broke I was. I'd £13.23 left to my name and no clue what I'd live off afterwards. I hadn't been joking when I'd told Iona I was penniless, even if I had already ditched the thought of paying to launder my stained jeans. Iona had them now anyway. I'd thought I'd have felt weird handing her the evidence, but it was simple. She mattered. So did finding an income. The busking and the lottery ticket had tided me over taking Iona out for a few cuppas, diesel for the car, a phone top-up and the night at the Clipper festival. All well and good, but our electric meter was nearly out, and the cupboards were empty bar cream crackers and a few tins of beans. Gun or no gun, I still needed to bloody eat.

I hoped to God my brother would produce a few quid for everyday stuff, but I couldn't bank on it. Seán was wired these days, and I was tired walking on eggshells. He was irritable, skulking in at 3 a.m., acknowledging me with an occasional grunt over brunch as he poured whiskey into his coffee. Sometimes he was fine, but increasingly he was drinking, smoking more than just nicotine, or becoming argumentative over nothing. I was tasting my own medicine from a couple of years ago. When I'd asked if Saoirse had been in contact, he'd near bit my head off.

'No! None of your feckin' business who I talk to!' he'd shouted, barging past me and out the door. He didn't come home for two days. My anger was shifting to concern, a growing unease that all was not right with the world. There would be even less right, though, if the cupboards echoed. One thing we shared as brothers – feed us and the world rotated so much better on its axis; left hungry, our world imploded.

I'd taken my sister's advice and called into Dove House armed with my National Insurance number. Sure, I'd be entitled to something eventually. Problem was 'eventually' could mean six weeks, and I'd have disappeared down a grating from eating thin air. Dating Iona would definitely require both shower gel *and* deodorant, and at least a fiver in hand. That she'd risk everything for me was mind-blowing. I needed to treat her amazing. Hunting down a job was fast becoming as critical as hunting down a gun.

I'd never had a proper paid job. Truth was, I'd never thought to try. The only thing higher than the Derry unemployment rate was half the city on a Saturday night but, I reasoned, if Iona could find a part-time job then, surely, I could too. I didn't want her to think I was a complete waster. No matter what my future held, I needed a basic bank balance to get started.

There hadn't been much joy at the job centre. The handful of posts listed experience or qualifications I lacked. I'd filled in a fast-food and a labouring application. Christ, I'd perforate tea bags or empty dog-shit bins if they paid me. Next, I'd taken to padding round Creggan shop by shop, bookies, pubs – anywhere I could think of – and had felt increasingly depressed. My final call before giving up had been an old man's bar, a former haunt of Da's which I never frequented. Not because of its renowned Republicanism, it just wasn't the kind of place my generation hung out in. Still, I'd pull pints and wash glasses anywhere that paid.

'Paddy! Look what the wind just blew in,' the barman had called out in a Belfast twang across the counter to a heavily tattooed middle-aged bloke downing a Guinness in the far corner.

'Well, there's no denying you.' He'd laughed, making his way over. 'You're the absolute spit of your old man.' He slapped my back as if I should know him. 'Liam's youngest, right?'

It was a while since anyone had publicly related me to my father. We tended not to reference him anymore. I nodded. The barman intervened, 'Kid's looking for work. We've nothing here but I thought you might be interested.'

Paddy looked me over. 'Can you paint?'

'I'm a fast learner.' I'd shrugged. 'Give me a shot. If I'm useless, don't pay me.'

'I hear you and your brother are wild ones, like your da. Can you turn up sober, on time and do a hard day's graft?'

'Absolutely.'

'Right then. I'll try you. Cash in hand. Eight pound an hour. No tax. Zero hours paperless contract – I'll call you as and when. I've a fair bit of work going now, though, so I can use you if you're up for it?'

We'd shaken hands on it and I gave him my number before leaving the pub with a spring in my step and blowing my last three quid on a large bag of chips to celebrate. I'd still been licking the salt and vinegar off my fingers when he'd called with an address to turn up for work the next morning.

A day or two in, I was getting the hang of it rightly. My jeans and T-shirt bore all the tell-tale trademarks of a painter – splashes and hand-wiped white paint down the front like a rite of passage into the working class. The bathroom at home bore a new smell of white spirits and my muscles ached contentedly after the sweat of each day's hard work washed off under a hot shower. A shower with, I might add, decent shower gel, shaving foam, deodorant *and* aftershave. Aftershave I knew Iona liked because she'd said so.

It was the start of my third day on the job. This morning felt like the first Monday since school I'd any real purpose to throwing off the duvet.

'So how exactly did you know my da?' I asked Paddy as I straightened up from glossing some skirting boards in a hallway. Turned out he'd known him a lifetime. Best mates the whole way through primary school – same class, same playground antics, same misadventures – and then on to St Joseph's at eleven together. Paddy reminisced like my nan as he rollered the ceiling in the kitchen, Radio Foyle on in the background.

'He was the class clown in primary school.' He chuckled at some unspoken memory. 'But smart too. I remember him acting the maggot one time at school swimming lessons down at the City Baths. Came out of the changing rooms with his boxers over his trousers letting on to be a superhero. Earned him a caning but that was par for the course in them days. He hated secondary school though. Loathed exams. Never did well despite his brain.' I thought of Seán and his dyslexia. Maybe Da was dyslexic but never knew it? I'd never seen him read books, come to think of it – it had always been Ma who did the Roald Dahl voice-overs that had the three of us in fits at bedtime.

'He dropped out early, didn't he?' I encouraged Paddy to continue. It was rare to hear anything about Da other than his drinking and his politics.

'He did, kiddo.' Paddy sighed. He always called me kiddo. Apparently, he had known our whole family when I was a toddler and the term of affection seemed to have stuck. 'Mind, it was different times then. We fed off anger and adrenalin – Brits, bombs and H-blocks. In them days, the Saturday matinee wasn't the pictures, it was the weekend riot. Crazy times.'

I paused to think. 'That why he joined up?' I chanced.

'That's why we joined up together, kiddo.' I heard him step off the ladder and set his roller down in the tray before he appeared in the kitchen doorframe. 'Didn't know that, did ye?'

I shook my head, but wasn't surprised either. It was par for the course in Da's generation and Paddy's tattoos told a familiar story. I was still having no luck hunting up the back fields. Maybe Paddy could get me a connection to a gun.

'Strangely, my luck was that I got caught earlier,' Paddy continued. 'Sweet sixteen. Served two months before they let me out for good behaviour. Still had a record though. Makes getting insurance, work or visas a handling. My mother beat the living daylights out of me before shipping me to the back end of Connemara. Your da, on the other hand, didn't get caught until he was twenty-one. The Brits gave him hell. It changed him.'

I painted on, dipping the brush in the white gloss and smoothing it onto the wood; digesting what Paddy was saying. Da's nightmares had freaked us worse than horror movies. He'd wake up shouting and screaming in the next room. We would hear Ma whispering, soothing him, thinking we couldn't hear through the plasterboard. Paddy's eyes were on me, watching for a reaction. What he said next got my attention. 'I hear you and your brother play your cards close to your chest. That you've both had your moments over the last few years, too. Especially you.' His comment hung as I stood to stretch, thinking. I was uncertain how to take his words.

'What are you saying?' I looked him straight in the eye.

'Nothing in particular, kiddo. Just what I hear. Like father, like son. You'd a couple of pretty reckless years. Now you seem . . . focused, into politics, community. People you hang with. Taxiing to polling stations. Makes me wonder.' Paddy retreated back into the kitchen and lifted his roller again. 'You were at that funeral in Strabane, too.' His thick Derry accent carried to me in the hall. 'And your borrowed wheels have connections . . . Time I spent inside was for being a driver. Nothing more, nothing less. You've been stopped a couple of times driving that car, haven't you?'

I strode into the kitchen, oblivious to the gloss dropping off my brush onto the sheets covering the tiled floor. Paddy carried on working.

'What exactly are you saying?' I challenged him.

'You didn't come up the Foyle in a bubble, lad. Neither did I. You don't need me to say it.'

I hesitated. My brush dripped paint on my shoe. Paddy said nothing, just returned my look. Heart in mouth, I risked the question. 'Paddy, are you still involved? Like, do you still have a gun?'

'No, kiddo.' He lowered the roller, staring. 'That ship sailed long ago. No call for guns when the Brits have gone. Mark my words, that Brexit lark is like the winning lotto numbers for a United Ireland. Politics will carry it over the line. Get out of it. Leave well alone.'

'Jesus, Paddy. I'm not involved!'

He looked at me cynically. 'Sure, lad. Get back to work. I believe you.'

I painted in concentrated silence for two hours until tea break. I desperately needed a gun and it was crystal he thought I already had one. It made me think. Deep. Scary thing was, it confirmed something I already knew, just not about me.

'Paddy?' I ventured one last question over a mug of black coffee. 'You said you went to Connemara?'

'Aye, kiddo.'

'How'd that work? I mean, I thought if you were involved with the Ra you couldn't just walk away?'

'Are we talking then or now?' He furrowed his heavy eyebrows and scrutinized me.

'Back then.'

'It was complicated. Depended how much you knew. My mother's credit-union book came in handy. These days I don't know though. Like I said, I'm not involved. Though maybe you already knew that.'

Chapter 25. Labels.

IONA.
Thursday 4 August.

'I've been meaning to ask,' Mum said as she drove us back from Limavady, 'is anything up with Andy? Girl trouble or something he wouldn't talk to me or your dad about? He seems ... restless.'

I coughed. Her question had caught me on the hop. At least she hadn't noticed my own sanity was in the blender. 'Don't think so,' I said, chewing my lip. 'Don't you worry more about our John joining the police?'

Mum looked at me. 'How so?'

'Like, with Dad's post-trauma stuff or the dissident threat, the new IRA.'

'Why the sudden interest? Dad's fine, John's fine, even if he's miffed his first case went cold.' She smiled reassuringly.

The conversation hung for a moment. Maybe they were OK, but Andy wasn't, especially since I'd told him about the pool. There was an increasing nagging in my gut telling me he wouldn't be fine unless he talked, and, maybe, that talk needed to be with Aidan.

'How did Dad get over all that ... stuff? What he saw in the Troubles.'

Her foot touched the brake as she looked over. I'd never had this type of conversation with her. She smoothed her hand over the steering wheel.

'Sure you want to talk about this?'

I nodded.

'Trauma's a funny thing. Well, not funny, but it impacts people differently – drink, depression, stress. Takes its toll; years of wondering at breakfast if you'll see supper.'

I looked away, relating more than I could show.

'Hard for a strong man to admit he's struggling, but your dad is so much better now. He'd say it himself, the counselling, him so sceptical about it at the start. Talking through it was key.' She paused and looked at me, wiggling her eyebrows. 'And on the topic of men and talking, how come you're so quiet about this new boy?'

Dylan and Luke hadn't been the only ones to spot my Facebook profile picture, the selfie from the Clipper yacht. The defiance in me had refused to change it, even with a crick in my neck looking over my shoulder every time I stepped out. John had remarked on it, and Mum had picked up on me swiftly switching the conversation topic. I hadn't wanted a barrage of awkward questions. Sucking my nail, I glanced at her sideways. Mum was great. I loved her to bits, and she hadn't had one of *those* types of parenting conversations with me since I was fifteen, but then, who was I kidding? *Those* conversations hadn't exactly covered the topic of me dating a self-proclaimed Republican from Creggan.

When we were alone together, Aidan and I laughed about our labels – would she? Would Dad? I'd tried to convince myself they'd be fine. It was normal enough these days. I'd even prepped a religious defence – our faith taught us God didn't judge from the outside. Although, the fact I'd prepped the argument said it all.

Mum's fixed smile indicated I wouldn't be getting away with changing the conversation a second time. It wasn't like I hadn't realized the excuses were wearing thin. She knew, fine rightly, it wasn't always Rachel I was chatting with on the phone. Her suspicions were well founded that it wasn't Rachel I'd met at the cinema either.

'Sure, we can talk about him,' I answered. 'But he's kind of shy about the whole meet-the-parents thing.'

That bit at least was true, although 'shy' wasn't exactly in Aidan's dictionary about anything else except family. Mine and his. He was frustratingly vague about them. Was it the whole Protestant–Catholic thing? Did he tell them about me? What did he think I couldn't handle? Or what couldn't he handle me knowing? I remembered his jibe about handcuffs. Last time we'd met, he'd handed me a forensics bag still stuffed with his bloodied clothes from June but had still balked at talking to John. Or Andy. Then again, even I hadn't found the guts yet to raise the topic with John.

I loved Aidan's blend of fierce independence, playfulness and vulnerability. It was cute, though he'd have killed me for saying that. It connected with something deep in me. I was proud being with him. Sometimes he'd an edginess, though, especially since the pool. When he couldn't sit still or seemed lost in thought, I glimpsed an uncertainty, hurt, behind his eyes. Bits of his life, his dad and brother in particular, were like a closed book on a top shelf. He was fine with me knowing it was there, so long as it stayed dusty and unread. Saoirse was different – he'd smile and chat of her global adventures, hands gesticulating wildly.

'Where did you meet him?' Mum interrupted my thoughts.

'Guildhall Square.' My standard half-truth. Her eyebrows raised as she drove. She'd expected school or faith circles to be the connection. Maybe telling Mum would be practice for telling John. I still hadn't handed him the evidence.

'Do you remember any other mothers from Altnagelvin the day I was born?'

'Not especially. I was rather preoccupied with having you. Why?'

'Aidan was born the same day.'

Her intake of breath was barely audible. It was the first time I'd mentioned his name, and her mind was doing Northern Irish arithmetic. The name Aidan definitely added up to being Irish, and in her book that equalled Catholic. Her hesitation was momentary. 'I see. Where's he from?' Code for, *Is he definitely Catholic?*

'Creggan.' *Yes, Catholic for certain.*

'Oh.' *Your father won't like this.* 'Are his parents working?' she said. *Is he from a decent family?*

'His mother passed away. He doesn't talk much about his dad.' *So, no. Not in Dad's eyes anyway.*

Several miles of hedges passed as I slouched in the seat, waiting.

'I see.' *Houston, we have a problem.*

She hummed as she thought. Maybe Aidan was lucky to be so independent. No, that was unfair, I didn't envy his shoes. Ironic. He'd already bleached them. Only his blood-stained T-shirt and jeans were bagged at the back of my wardrobe waiting for me to find the courage.

'Pet, you know we trust your choices, but have a think, will you? Maybe it's not wise getting in a relationship when you're about to head off to university.' *Iona, cowboys are good, Indians are bad. Stick with the cowboys.*

'Mm.' *Robin Hood used a bow and arrow too. He was awesome.*

The road sign for 'Londonderry' whizzed past. The 'London' bit was never spray-painted out on this side of the city.

So much for hoping they'd see the Aidan who I could chat with for hours snugged in cafes. His mad enthusiasm for global stuff, big issues, politics. Sure, it was like blood from a stone getting him to open up about his family or his past, but so what? Given that half the guys I knew struggled to string a meaningful sentence together, he was virtually Shakespeare. Plus, he snogged amazing. Compared to other lads, he at least acted interested – cupping his chin, listening like I mattered, eyes furrowed in concentration. It was a far cry from Kyle, all hands and no brains in a cinema seat – though come to think of it, I couldn't actually remember the ending of the last film I watched with Aidan. I crossed my legs and blushed. Things Dad would never know. 'You're nuts for him,' Rachel had slagged me. Too right. If I could get away with it, I'd spend every waking minute with him. If I wasn't a Christian, probably every sleeping minute with him, too. Now there was a conversation bound to be harder than this one, especially with the mixed messages my hormones sent him. I'd need to swallow a bible to hold out at this rate.

Aidan was clueless to how he melted me; those flashes where he dropped his guard, dark eyes seeking reassurance. He'd look right at me, telling me a million stories with no words in his lost-boy look. From the brief gulp and the flicker of his eyes, there was more than a couple of times he'd had something on the tip of his tongue to say but stalled. Me too. Though there were places we couldn't go just yet, intuitively, beautifully, we still connected.

'That him?' Mum asked as my mobile chimed. It was. Maybe I would meet his family after all.

Visiting my nan in Letterkenny 2moro. Fancy coming ;-)? Might be like watching paint dry but I'd shout you lunch after?

Chapter 26. Memories.

AIDAN.
Friday 5 August.

It was one of those crisp summer mornings in Creggan. The ones where the whole city below was still blanketed under mist; only the cathedral and church spires sticking out the top. When the sun burned through, it was going to be a scorcher. No way was I letting Shannon's pestering over a gun screw this day up. She could stuff her bloody deadline where the sun didn't shine. Years ago, I'd have been off to Brooke Park with cans and a football, but like Ma's old CDs used to sing out, the times were a-changing.

Iona's Alsatian, Maddy, was in the back seat of the car – a bundle of canine muscle and energy bursting to please. Her lolloping tongue made me laugh. I'd half expected her to bare her teeth, like she'd be trained to sniff out the enemy. Instead, she slabbered over me like I was T-bone. After visiting Nan, the plan was a long walk either up by Grianán or down round Inch Island.

'Nan's got mild dementia,' I explained to Iona as we joined the dual carriageway past the Noah's Ark chapel over the border. 'You never quite know how you'll find her on any given day.'

Ma used to say Nan was blessed with a unique superhero power – the ability to forget the last thirty years in three seconds. Times I thought she was jealous. Nan thrived on oul' anecdotes, stories spilling out of her if you caught her in the right frame of mind. Her memory was razor sharp for details from ten, twenty, fifty years ago. I knew Iona wanted to meet my family. God knew what stories Nan would spin, but compared to an absent sister, an aunt who would happily deny my existence, or an increasingly unpredictable brother who'd go ballistic if he knew I was dating a cop's daughter, Nan was by far the safest bet. Plus, she was sweet and somehow still felt I could do no wrong. Far be it from me to disillusion her, much as I was sure Aunt Teresa had tried.

Maddy's whines carried from the half-open car windows as we headed through the heavy swing doors into the musty odour of the nursing home. Something like potpourri or talcum powder mixed with over-cooked cabbage, mashed spuds and a hint of something medical. The four-digit corridor code hadn't changed since my last visit. On a good day my Nan knew the codes through the entire building. On a bad day she couldn't find the way back to her room. I rapped on her open door.

'Aidy!' She returned my grin from her recliner chair, stretching her arms wide for a hug. She was frail, light as fluff as I bent to wrap my arms around her blue cardigan. As she held me tight, I felt a pang of remorse that I'd neglected her since before my exams. She never complained, never made me feel guilty. She reminded me of Ma in the bright years between Da's departure and the cancer's arrival.

'Aren't you going to introduce me?' she asked, whispering as an afterthought, 'I haven't met her before, have I?'

'This is my friend, Iona.'

Nan clasped Iona's hand in hers, the wrinkled palms and fingers folding around in welcome.

'Just a friend?'

'My girlfriend.'

Nan nodded and beamed her approval, gesturing Iona to sit down in the only other armchair. I plonked myself onto her pink duvet.

'About time too!'

'Sorry, Nan, it's been too long since I visited.'

'No, I meant it's about time you brought a girlfriend to see me.' She winked at Iona conspiratorially. 'Don't you know at my age I thrive on gossip? I need all the bars I can get in here. What was your name again, lass?'

'Iona,' I answered.

Nan scowled in jest at me. 'Men don't answer for women these days, Aidy! Fetch that green scrapbook from my dresser and a cuppa from up the corridor. This charming young lady and I shall converse. I've myriad photographs of your Aidy when he was just a tot. You will love these, petal.' She was theatrically ignoring me.

The scrapbook was worn and dog-eared, its pages patched with yellowed Sellotape that had lost much of its stickiness. I'd a vague memory of leafing through it, sitting on Ma's knee in Nan's living room when I was wee. The earliest photos were black and white or sepia – a baby Nan in a white lace christening gown; a formal family portrait of my great-grandparents, with Nan and seven siblings arranged stiffly in height order in front of them; my grandfather as a young man in a brown tweed suit. Nan's face lit up golden as she turned the pages. I watched her react with delight to Iona's interested questioning. Occasionally a pressed flower would appear in tissues between the pages and Nan would gasp with the beauty of its colours and shape preserved after all these years. There was her wedding photo on the chapel steps – she with a posy of wildflowers and Granda striking in a formal suit and tie with boots polished till they shone. Then Ma and wee Aunt Teresa appeared smiling with plaited red braids and hand-me-down dresses – peas in a pod except for the height difference. My grandparents only ever had the two girls – rare for those days when Catholic families were like Russian dolls.

It pulled my heartstrings to see Ma laughing carefree from the pages, full of childhood innocence. As a teenager, she modelled a long, knitted jumper, red like her hair which fell in loose curls past her shoulders. She was beautiful even in black leggings and baseball boots, the spit of Saoirse, who appeared as the bump under the white lace long-sleeved wedding dress over the page. So young. So full of hope. Iona's hand covered her mouth and she looked between me and another photo when the page turned. He had the same dark hair, same height, same jawline, even the same stance.

'You'd swear it was Aidy, wouldn't you?' Nan laughed at Iona's reaction to seeing Da on their wedding day. 'Except for the eyes, lass. He has his mother's eyes and eyes are the gateway to the soul. Saoirse now, Saoirse is the double of my Aibhlinn, God rest her.' She blessed herself.

Now there was Ma in a purple tie-dye T-shirt, Saoirse wriggling in her arms. Matching curls, high cheekbones and dark brown eyes. Da was there too, snapped in his black T-shirt and jeans, teaching a pre-school Seán how to solo a Gaelic football at Lisfannon Beach.

'Is that you?' Iona peered at the next photo. I was the toddler, clad in only a pair of cotton green shorts, barefoot, digging holes to Australia in the wet sand with a yellow plastic spade. Many of the photos were early childhood holidays in Buncrana or Bundoran. Good memories. The days before it all slipped into Da's alcoholic sludge on a one-way ticket. There were the three of us with candyfloss on a pebble-dash wall by the coast. Another of me grinning, aged four, with a poke of whipped ice cream – my chin milky white and the ice cream and red syrup dripping down the cone onto my fingers.

Saoirse's first communion was the next full family photo,

taken beside the statues outside Long Tower chapel, where St Columba stands at the foot of the cross pointing to Our Lord. We were scrubbed up to the nines; Da's tie matching Ma's burgundy dress, me and Seán in black school trousers and spanking-new white polo shirts fresh out the pack from Dunnes. I was hoisted on Da's shoulders. Iona was intrigued with Saoirse looking like a meringue. Nan's eyes flickered an unspoken question at me as she explained the mini white wedding-like dresses, symbols of purity and a reminder of baptism.

I groaned at the next pages: *Derry Journal* cut-outs. Set dancing in the *Féis Dhoíre Cholmcílle*. I'd have passed for the Gingerbread Man's twin, proud as punch buttoned into my wee traditional waistcoat. There was Saoirse too, red hair clasped loosely behind her head, playing her fiddle with a concentrated look. 'Kerry Polka'. Everyone played that; like all of Ireland only ever learned one tune. The *Gaelscoil Éadain Mhóir* trad group showed up with about ten older primary-school pupils. I was too young to be in it at that point, but Seán was there on the whistle as well as Saoirse with the fiddle. They'd won their category that year and were hugging silverware like it was the Sam Maguire Cup.

'Did you play?' Iona asked.

'*Bodhrán.*' I mimicked the Irish drum.

Nan laughed aloud before we could see the next images. 'Would you look at you there, Aidy! Ah but you were cute when you were wee. That face! Focused like you'd be up for an Oscar!'

Our school nativity show. 'Were you ever in one?' I asked Iona.

'Yeah, an angel one year, then Mary another time.'

'Really? Yous believe in Mary?'

'Course. How'd you think we'd have Christmas without Mary? What were you?'

'Lead Alien.' I laughed.

'Come again?'

'A profoundly serious part if I remember it well,' Nan said. 'A spaceship had landed in the playground and the school had to explain the meaning of Christmas to the aliens so that they could celebrate it. The lead alien had an extensive number of lines to learn that nearly drove his mother demented.'

We reminisced more about various school shows Nan remembered. Funny how she was crystal sharp remembering years ago and yet could forget if she'd eaten breakfast.

The scrapbook's ultimate pages were filled with more holiday photos at Portsalon strand by Lough Swilly. We'd gone camping there when I was seven. It brought bittersweet memories; the last happy family holiday of my childhood with five of us squished snug into a four-man tent. Ma had made Da take a Pioneer pledge and miraculously both him and the weather held out that summer. There had been sandcastles on the beach – digging mounds of sand big enough for the three of us and campsite friends to stand on top of as the tide swamped our intricate defences of moats and walls. I'd revelled in rock pools at that age – prodding the red sea anemones; crab hunting with fishing nets on bamboo poles; prising limpets off the rocks. By the following summer Da's drinking had kicked in with a vengeance and I guess Ma was too broke or too disheartened to plan more than a few day trips.

'What's in your sandwiches?' Iona asked.

'Cheesy Wotsits,' Nan and I answered in unison without a glance at the photo of me sat on a camping mat outside the tent.

'Cheesy Wotsits?'

'Absolutely. Best sandwich filler ever when you're seven, or eight . . . or eighteen for that matter.'

'Nope. Banana and sugar all the way,' said Iona.

'Did you ever do bananas stuffed with Mars bars cooked in tinfoil in campfire ashes? Or marshmallows or sausages on sticks? They're lethal!'

I licked my lips, almost tasting the childhood memories. We lost an hour engrossed in conversation before Iona remembered to check on Maddy. I passed her the keys. Nan waited until the heavy door slammed at the far end of the corridor.

'Ah, Aidy,' she sighed. 'She's a keeper!'

'You like her?'

'She's a wee dote, lad. A beautiful person inside and out. It would have done your grandfather's heart the world of good to see you with her.'

'Granda Michael?' I was perplexed at the sudden connection.

Nan closed her eyes, leaning back on the headrest. 'I suppose you never knew, did you, Aidy? Your granda was Church of Ireland. What we went through in them days trying to convince our families, never mind the priest.'

'Nan,' I interrupted. 'Granda was devout Catholic. I was at mass with him heaps of times. He took communion and everything. He's buried in the chapel graveyard.'

'Aye, indeed he is. But he wasn't always Catholic. He converted to marry me. Was almost shunned for it too, until his people got used to it. I forgot that Aibhlinn didn't tell any of you that. She was always afeared of your father finding out. Truth is, I think he knew anyway. It was always awkward there, even before . . . anything.' She fell into a silence that I couldn't break for a moment, still slightly stunned by the unexpected revelation.

'So, I'm a quarter Prod? That's why I hate mass so much!'

She looked me full in the face, lifting both her hands to cup my head. I used to be embarrassed when she'd kiss me on the forehead. I let her kiss me then without a flinch. Her eyes shone.

'I'm proud of you. Take this,' she said, prising a photo off the page with her nail. We were all beaming – Nan, Granda, Ma, Da and the three of us. 'You make your old nan so happy. God knows you've been through it, and I wish I could do more for you, lad, but look how well you're turning out!' She ruffled my hair, just like Ma used to. 'How'd your exams go? No school today?'

'It's August, Nan. School's out.'

'Where does the time go? So, how'd you do? Are you working now?'

'Results aren't out for a few weeks yet,' I said, as Iona rejoined us. Maddy was fit to be tied in the confines of the car. 'I'm painting here and there. Suits me grand for now.'

'What about you, lass?' Nan beamed at Iona.

'Hopefully university in September.'

'Now there's a great thing. Would you not take Aidy with you? You were always a bright spark, Aidy. Just like my Aibhlinn. Painting is a good trade, lad, but find a profession that uses your brain and the bills are easier paid. You mind that now – won't you? And bring this fine lass of yours back again sometime. I've plenty more yarns to spin. Now away with you young sweethearts and let me rest.' She dismissed us with hugs, a wistful smile and a handful of barley sugars from a tin on her dresser.

'She's sweet, your nan.' Iona relaxed back into the passenger seat and gazed out of the window as the Lough Swilly inlets passed us by on the rise of the road back to the border. It was a choice of either the flat lands of Inch Wildfowl Reserve or *An Grianán* fort on the hilltop at Burt. Iona picked the fort so Maddy could roam free. We parked at the chapel by the main road and followed the winding lane, striking a fast pace and sucking country air into our lungs. With the slightest whistle the Alsatian would be at our heel, tongue hanging out sideways and awaiting praise or instruction. The half-hour climb caught our breath, as did the views near the top on such a perfect day.

At the summit, a constant drift of families or couples climbed over the stile onto the plank path to the Gaelic ringfort. We'd come here as kids, letting on to be Columba battling druids or enacting Gaelic kings and warriors. The way *An Grianán* dominated the windswept hilltop with its thick, grey stone walls, solid structure and ancient presence always swelled my chest with a fierce sense of pride in our history. Like a mini Irish Colosseum; it commanded respect. On a windy day, ducking under the muddy archway through to the stillness of the centre was like being in the eye of the storm. Even on a still day, scaling its ledges and flights of flat-stone steps up the three thin circular terraces, we'd be prepared to be blown away by both the wind and the 360-degree panoramic view. In a storm, the gale blew your head clean off. You could see for hundreds of miles. To the north, Inch Island, Lough Swilly, Buncrana and Malin. To the west, the Donegal hills and Glenveagh National Park. Da had told tales of gun smuggling along all them back roads. To the east and south, Lough Foyle, glistening in the sun like a mirror, Derry City, and the Sperrin Mountains beyond.

Someday they'd build an all-singing all-dancing heritage centre to hook the tourists on the Wild Atlantic Way. Looking round me, I loved its roughness. Planting my feet on the rock, the power of it screamed into my being. *Know yourself. Breathe. Be. Stand.* I looked at Iona. She was quiet and reflective; natural and beautiful. I touched her hair, sensing her heart beat faster, like mine in taking in the outdoors.

I was craving to better understand what made her tick,

hanging on her words, watching her body language. Maybe it was kickback from Shannon; maybe it was because this felt different; maybe because she was Protestant. All I knew was I'd die to keep kissing her. Sure, I'd joked about it, but truth was, I'd never hung out with Protestants before. The fault lines were subtle, but it would've killed me to see them explode. Growing up we'd hung out at different ends of the city; I knew Donegal like the back of my hand, but Iona knew the north coast – even our holidays had been orange or green. When we talked about 'the' leisure centre, 'the' shopping centre or even 'the' dole office, we'd found we were talking about different places, Cityside and Waterside, ours and theirs, mine and hers. I'd found my eyes opening even wider to the voluntary segregation in our city. As I played with Iona's hair, I wondered how Granda and Nan had managed it all them years ago. If I told Iona about Granda, maybe that would balance telling her about Da having been in the IRA? Maybe. The real risk was Seán. What if he was making connections with the New IRA? No. Dylan and Luke had given Iona enough angst to deal with. That conversation was off-limits for now – just like the questions I wasn't asking about her dad being in the RUC during the Troubles. And as for my brother, that could seriously raise the stakes.

We leaned silently against the wall and each other on *Grianán*'s top terrace, high over the Wildfowl Reserve and patchwork fields below, shielding each other from the breeze. When she turned to me, eyes full of light and life, I kissed her. Her body moulded into mine. An intensity fired in me as our tongues played and the passion built. I could've lost myself in being with her and not cared if I never came back to reality. Her head in my hands, her breath on my neck. *This is heaven. This is new.* I opened my eyes to look at her as we kissed, and she was looking straight at me. Her eyes startled the words from my mouth before my brain censored them. 'Do you shag with your eyes open too?'

I kicked myself the moment I said it. Her eyes dimmed, not in anger, just something obscure, deep. Her arms slackened round my waist, slipping out of our embrace. Another girl might've jibed back or even chanced a come-on, but Iona wasn't just another girl. She said nothing. Her silence cut worse than a slating. She wasn't just my girlfriend, she was a *real* friend. In the same instant that I knew I'd screwed something up, it dawned just how much she was beginning to mean to me.

'Sorry,' I said. It wasn't that she'd run, she was still beside me. It wasn't even that bad, what I'd said, except I knew from her reaction I'd damaged something. I tucked her brown hair behind her ear. 'I'm sorry,' I reiterated, looking right at her so she knew I meant it. 'G'on, just forget I said that.'

We still talked, still held hands and brushed shoulders as we made our way back to the car. There wasn't hostility, just a slight distance. We even had a great lunch and a laugh in a Bridgend cafe, sitting at old upcycled school desks and wonky chairs with rough-hewn sandwiches and Cokes. It irked me that I couldn't quite fathom her reaction as we drove back. Pissed me even more when I spied the impromptu police-check ahead, just after the border.

'Pass me my driving licence – jacket pocket, back seat.'

'You won't need it, they're waving cars through. Probably just checking car tax electronically.'

'Watch this space,' I predicted, as they indicated for me to pull over. Again. Third time in as many weeks. Harassment at this point.

'ID?' I handed over my licence. The young officer was curt.

'Aidan Hennessey? Home address in Creggan, Londonderry?'

'*Derry*,' I emphasized. Two could play at that game. Iona shifted in the passenger seat and I saw him glance at her with a flash of recognition. She paled.

'Mind if I look in the boot?' That was new. I got out of the car and went to the rear. My gut turned over, as it crossed my mind that maybe I'd been looking for guns in the wrong place. I'd never searched the car. Maddy barked. Fifty different scenarios flooded my brain. *Was my brother involved in the New IRA? Did handcuffs hurt your wrists? Were the cops messing with my head? Was this routine? Would this torpedo me seeing Iona? Were we already sunk from my throwaway comment?* My head pounded and spun, my chest tightened, breathing quickening. *How dare they involve me in this. How dare my brother . . .*

Iona was beside me now. 'What's up, Leo?'

'I could ask you the same question, Iona,' he said.

She bloody knew the cop. Did that make it better or worse?

'They do say expect the unexpected in policing. John acquainted with your friend here yet?' Leo nodded my direction.

Iona froze.

'Thought so,' he said, as I loitered on the hard shoulder. 'Make absolutely sure, and tell John I was asking after him. You'll definitely get talking to him before I do. *Won't you?*'

Iona stood open-mouthed.

I coughed. Leo turned his attention back to me. Holding my breath, I squeaked the boot open. Empty. I exhaled. Not even a spare tyre in the dent where the puncture-repair kit was. I said a silent prayer of thanks to a God I hardly believed in, but it didn't calm the anger or dull the stress building in my blood. If Brexit was for installing cameras on the border, it'd bring a whole new meaning to photobombing.

'Happy?' I challenged, less than politely.

'Thank you, sir. You're free to go.'

I own my freedom. You don't control me.

'Tell John or he will? Was that an ultimatum?' I asked through gritted teeth as we rejoined the traffic.

'Yes.' Her voice had shrunk.

'Shite.' I banged the steering wheel. She put on the radio. I could see she was thinking. Hard. I wanted to spill my guts to her, but how? This stuff was dynamite. We drove without talking over the Foyle Bridge. For the first time, she didn't ask if I wanted to come in. I was relieved. I couldn't face meeting more cops. My two worlds were clashing and I was caught in the crossfire. It had been such a bloody brilliant morning and then with one throw-away line and one stop-and-search checkpoint it had all unravelled.

I slammed the door behind me as I arrived home. The house was a mess, the air thick with cigarette smoke and the unmistakeable sweet smell of dope. Striding through the kitchen, I jammed Nan's photo on the fridge with a Sacred Heart magnet. As I wedged the back door open with a chair, I fished in my pocket.

'Have your feckin' key back, Seán.' I lobbed the silver car key at him, not caring what his two friends slouched on our living-room couch thought. 'I'm not even going to ask who really owns that car or why we have it. *Three times.* Three times I've been stopped at the border by bloody RUC-PSNI cops. And once for a so-called random drink-driving check. Funny that, on the way back from a dissident funeral, eh? Pure coincidence. Really think I'm that naive or that stupid? Maybe you just *don't* think anymore. I don't care to know. I won't even bloody mention it again, but for

Christ's sake leave me out of it, all right? She even knew the policeman. My girlfriend knew the cop that pulled me over. Have you any idea how embarrassing it was thinking I was going to get frisked down in front of her? Worse, what if they had found something in the car that I knew nothing about? Think they'd have believed a word out of my mouth?'

I was seething by the time I finished. I didn't even bother waiting for a response from him before storming upstairs. When he shouted after me, I froze mid-stride on the landing.

'How come Iona knew the cop?'

Chapter 27. Collaboration.

IONA
Saturday 6 August.

Faced with Leo's ultimatum, there'd been no choice left but to tell John. Standing uniformed in our kitchen, my brother held the bag of Aidan's clothes like a bomb. His face matched.

'Dylan and Luke did what?' he asked again.

'She stood up to them, so they went for her at the pool. Don't make her repeat it,' Andy said. 'Can't you see she's shaking?'

I looked at John. 'Won't you help?'

'Solution's obvious,' he said. 'Split with your wee Republican.'

'I'm not asking for dating advice. I'm handing you a lead. Don't you want to impress on your first case?'

He hesitated. 'There is no case. Aidan never made a complaint. Read between the lines, Iona. Leo didn't pull his car in for nothing. What does that say about Aidan? Use your head.' John lifted his hat.

'What does it say about you?' Andy challenged. 'Use your uniform! Iona's scared.'

'You're just jealous you'll still be in a school uniform come September.' John squared up to Andy, shoving the bag of clothes into his chest. 'Police have rules. The budget won't pay to run forensics unless there's a complaint filed and more evidence.'

I dropped my gaze and kicked a random cornflake across the floor.

'What if *I* had more evidence?' Andy said.

My head sprang up. Andy was digging his phone from a back pocket. 'Sorry, Iona. I screenshot Aidan's phone in case Dylan came for me.' He scrolled through images as John and I crowded round him. Three pictures. They showed it all. Dylan and Luke, fists and boots. Aidan curled on the tarmac. Andy had been strategic. None of the rest of us in the frames. 'I know where they live,' Andy said.

'I know where they live,' John mimicked, sneering. 'Listen to Mr Hollywood.'

'Listen to Iona. You want this to happen to her?'

The silence was broken by the scrape of gravel as Dad's car pulled into the driveway. John looked at me more urgently. 'To run forensics, I'd still need Aidan to formalize the complaint.'

I shook my head. The car door slammed.

'Thing is,' said Andy, grinning, 'Dylan and Luke don't know that. Dylan's the ringleader. Luke's barely sixteen. Couldn't you knock his door in uniform and show the photos in front of his mum?'

Dad's key turned in the door. John grabbed the bag of clothes and shoved it in his nearby holdall. 'It's a long shot,' he whispered, 'but I'd have a case if I had a confession.'

Chapter 28. Deadline.

AIDAN.
Sunday 7 August.

Judas. My head and arms were scratched red, stinging from the thorns in the hedge, but this didn't feel like salvation. The weight of the black gun, cold in my hands, was distinctly like thirty pieces of silver. I hadn't expected the waves of emotion now engulfing me. Da's gun. As I knelt on the soil, I curled my fingers round the trigger and rubbed the nozzle in tiny circles against my palm. Had it, had he, ever killed anyone?

There was a sad, confused pride in me. Part of Da never survived the Troubles but, at one time, he'd been a man. They were days when it was easier to know what made you one. Days when injustice here was written in black and white, green and orange, and righted in red.

It looked Russian; a black star moulded in a circle on the grip, the kind of weapon the KGB bad guy shot in Cold War spy movies. Arms stretched, I raised the barrel level with my eyeline. Click. Son of a gun. Perhaps it was no bad thing there weren't any bullets. The thought of putting a loaded gun into Shannon's hands, and God knows whose hands after, was terrifying. Even with an empty chamber, this was killing my conscience. But there was no other way. I didn't want her threatened and I didn't need her threats.

Birds sang out the dawn chorus across the fields. Christ. Blue skies, yet my heart weighed heavier than the history in my hands.

Had I lived in the Troubles I'd have proudly lifted this, that I knew. Like him I guessed, I wanted justice, equality, a fair chance. It was just that the enemy was fuzzier now; it was *stuff* that stopped you, not people. Stuff you couldn't fight with a gun. At least Da had known what he'd stood for, what he'd fight for. Did I?

I looked in all directions as I waited on Shannon's doorstep. Perhaps for once she'd gone to early mass with her ma? I tugged the back of my T-shirt down again. Like some misguided cowboy, the gun was shoved into the back of my jeans, ice against my spine. *Eejit.* If I'd only thought to bring a rucksack. Even a jacket. People were up and about now and there was no way I was walking back through Creggan with this bulge. A bulge at the front of your boxers gave you six inches, bulge at the back, six years. I shifted from foot to foot, like I needed to pee bad. *Answer the bloody door, would you?*

'Aidan?'

'No. I'm a feckin' leprechaun. Let me in.'

She hid behind the door as I shoved past, closing it behind me.

'Your ma out?'

'Aye.'

She looked dazed, distant, her make-up smeared as she slumped barefoot onto the bottom stair, flicking her hair round her ears. Looked like she'd slept in last night's dress too.

'Got something for you.' I swung the gun in front of her to catch her attention back from swiping through her phone. 'Shannon! Feck's sake! I've brought you a gun. Are you on this planet?'

She looked at me with a glimmer of recognition.

'Gimme it,' she slurred, holding out her hand. 'Want your shag now then?'

'Hell no. I want you out of my life. I want my bloody reputation, what's left of it anyway.'

'Do you really not want me back?' she asked. 'I *am* sorry you know.'

'Me too,' I said, 'but I can't do this anymore.'

She glazed over again. 'Into your new girl more than me? See if I care.' She shrugged. 'Your loss.'

'Look, I've done my bit. You're safe now.'

She seemed oblivious to the tears sliding down her cheeks as I slipped the phone out of her fingers and sat beside her, gun between us.

'Swear you won't stir this up again? I need you to promise. It's important.'

'I promise,' she mumbled and leaned on my shoulder staring in a trance at the ceiling.

'You're wasted.'

'Aye.' She sniffed. 'On you. Sure, I'd rather screw your brother anyways.'

'Yer ma!'

'Least I have one.'

It caught me hard, a stab in the heart. A million words of spite flooded to the tip my tongue as I jumped to my feet but, as I looked back from the door, she fell over and something in me broke. I whispered, 'You were always cracker at cartwheels too.'

Chapter 29. Lisfannon.

IONA.
Tuesday 9 August.

Four days. It was the longest we'd gone without seeing each other. He'd been painting, I'd felt like I was watching it dry. There was nothing particularly wrong and yet there was. Four days, three hours. We'd texted and phoned. Still fine in theory for someone you'd only been going out with for five weeks, were it not for another phone call which had made me sick to my stomach. John. His opinions more forceful than the first time we'd spoken about Aidan. It was a conscious choice to disregard his brotherly advice, if I could call it that. It wasn't me in the police and I'd enough of taking orders waitressing. No, my head was clear – I wanted to see Aidan. I was just nervous. For once not about Dylan and Luke.

Aidan was upbeat, interacting with banter off the radio as I drove us over the border. I giggled at his quick wit. The skies were pencil-lead overhead, but the wind was warm. The tide was after turning as we piled onto Lisfannon shore. The sheen off the flat, wet beach, just cleared by the breakers, was patterned with feathery tributaries of ripples, the smell of seaweed in the air. We messed around, wrong-footing each other, skimming stones over choppy waves. After a while we grew quieter, walking side by side along the shoreline towards Inch Island, the crunch of shingle and shells underfoot. Gulls and black-capped seabirds swooped low over the salt water. Aidan was edgy. I was trying to find a way to broach the conversation, struggling to find the right words.

'Do we need to talk?' he asked.

'What about?'

'Whatever is bothering you.' He stopped and squished lugworm swirls of sand with the tips of his shoe before making fleeting eye contact.

'Who says I'm bothered about anything?'

'Just. You're distant. My clairvoyance skills are rusty. I can't mind-read.'

'My brother told me not to see you,' I said.

'Which brother?' he asked, sucking in air through his teeth and tensing his shoulders.

'John.'

Aidan turned, moonwalking backwards. 'Did he say why?'

'No.' I swallowed. 'Not specifically. He'd been talking with Leo. Something like you were bad news and that you were probably using me.'

'Using you?' He came to a standstill. 'Feck. What exactly did he mean by that?'

I shrugged. 'I think he meant using like . . . *politically*. To get information. Are you?'

'Sweet Jesus! No!' He noticed me flinch at his raised voice and went quiet, studying the ground.

I twisted my hair into a curl round my finger.

'So how come you're here if I'm such a monster?'

'What – you think I've no mind of my own? You think girls just do as they're told? My brother doesn't know you like I do.'

'Bloody hope not.' He laughed, looking at me again. 'Sorry. It's about the checkpoint, right?'

'How did you know they were for pulling you in?'

'It was the third time in as many weeks. It's the car, not me.'

His chocolate eyes held mine, jawline resolute. I didn't think Aidan had ever lied to me.

'So, who owns the car? Why'd they pull you in?'

'Who's asking – you or your brother?' He spoke curtly, eyebrows narrowing.

'Me. Just me.'

He hesitated, then relaxed. 'I don't know. God's honest truth. I'm not for asking neither. Seán knows. For what it's worth, I gave back the key. Look, I'm not *using* you. That's crazy. I *like* you. I thought that was obvious. If anything, maybe there's people trying to use *me*. I don't fully know. I don't even *want* to know. It's mental. I mean, do you still want to be with me? Do you *trust* me?' His shoulders dropped, feet shuffling.

I did trust him. My head was racing but my heart was steady. That made it even harder to tackle the other problem. Sometimes being an adult sucked.

'There's something else. I can't give you what you want, Aidan.'

His head jerked up. 'What are we talking about now?'

I breathed deep. It was my turn to study the sand. 'I . . . I can't tell you if I make love with my eyes open, because I haven't slept with anyone yet. And I can't sleep with you. I don't think it's right.'

He reacted, but not in any of the ways I'd thought he might. My heart had been prepared for challenge, frustration, even anger. He just went quiet, open-mouthed, and looked at me like he was searching for something in my soul or maybe his. I sensed his initial bewilderment, maybe hurt, and then suddenly, despite the strength of his stature, there was a raw vulnerability I'd never seen in his eyes before – not even that first day we'd talked in the cafe. It was like I'd broken something in him, but I didn't know what.

'Are you dumping me?' He asked in a voice so low I could

hardly hear it over the waves. 'I'm not good enough for you, right? Never mind my fecking politics, this is also because of what I said at *An Grianán*? Because I've slept with girls before now?'

'No. That's not what I mean!'

'What then? Like did I ever make you feel under pressure? I've only known you a few weeks, for Christ's sake . . . It was just one mad comment I didn't even think through and I'm sorry; I already said I was sorry. I'd no idea you'd react that way. I figured it must have been the pool thing. Was it so bloody wrong? Sweet Jesus, we're eighteen . . .' His voice wavered and he put his fist to his mouth, his eyes a picture of confusion and pain at a level that seemed out of place somehow. 'Did I screw up that bad?'

'Aidan, you didn't do anything wrong. Listen, I don't want to break up . . . I'm scared, that's all. I'm scared of getting hurt again because morally, with my faith and all . . . I can't give you what you want.'

'How the hell do you know what I want? *I* don't even know what I want. I don't get it. Faith? You're dumping me because I'm Catholic? You knew that from the start!'

'I don't want us to split! That's not what I'm saying!'

'So, spit it out. What are you saying?'

'I'm saying I don't believe in sex before marriage. It's not that I don't want to, I do, I just believe it should be one person for life. I'm terrified, Aidan, because . . . because I really like you and I know you don't believe the same, and if I fall even deeper it'll hurt like crazy when you ditch me over this . . .'

He rubbed his brow, then clasped his hands behind his neck, squinting at me. 'I think we're supposed to believe the same, but nobody our age does . . . You honestly . . . ? Like, come on, we weren't born yesterday . . .'

Finally, I could see the realization sink in. He looked to the clouds, then across the bay to the mountains, elbows bent pointing to the sky and combing his fingers through his hair. He turned and studied my face.

'That why Kyle broke up with you?' he asked as the wind blew sand round our trainers.

I nodded.

'World's biggest jerk. You were too good for him.' His smile was sad as he looked back out to sea where a couple of yachts played in the waves. 'You're too good for me too . . . You don't need my crap in your life.' He sighed without turning around. 'Your brother was right. I'm bad news. Just not for the reasons he thinks . . .'

He went mute then for some time, kicking razor shells and mops of seaweed by his feet. I felt a tear well up and slip down my cheek in the suspended silence between us. So this was it. We'd break up. The pain was already kicking in. I swallowed, waiting for the words. Leastways he played it better than Kyle, but it didn't change the score. Another tear fell, then another, and I fought them back but they refused to stop, so I lowered my head and focused on my shoes as my mascara drew dark lines down my cheeks. History repeating itself. Suddenly his shoes appeared in front of mine and I felt his warm hands cup my face and tilt it upwards until our eyes were only centimetres apart. The wetness glinted in the whites of his eyes. He touched his forehead to mine, his body trembling.

'Iona . . .' He ran his fingers through my hair, wiping tears from my cheeks. 'Remember in Belfast, the time you said honesty and sincerity was what you'd want?'

I couldn't speak but nodded again.

'It's like this . . .' He paused, breathing deeply but not breaking eye contact. 'I need to tell you something . . . something I don't want to talk about; stuff I never told anyone except Saoirse. I . . . Look, I really like you. Please know that. And I never used you. You mean mountains to me, but you need to know I meant it when I said I'm not good enough for you. You deserve better . . . How much honesty can you handle?'

He shoved his hands into his pockets and stepped backwards. I thought he was just looking for the right words to say it was over. Not so. Pain was etched on his face as he searched somewhere in the depths of his being to summon the courage to speak. When he did, it was almost on autopilot, like an essay he had to read in monotone for fear of breaking down.

'When I was fifteen and Ma died, I handled it real bad. I didn't handle it at all . . . I drank, did drugs, anything I could afford to blot out the pain of dealing with it . . .' He paused to gauge my reaction. 'So, there were girls too. One-night stands. It didn't mean anything. I barely knew their names . . .'

I watched him struggling to find the words to carry on; hands clenched in a knot behind his head, T-shirt riding high above his waist.

'I get it,' I blurted. 'You want a good time. You don't want me if you can't have me.'

He looked at me with an expression of anguish. Unable to speak, he just shook his head. 'No.' His voice wavered when he found it again. 'No. That's not it . . . This was . . . reckless. Scary out of control. I was so lost,' he said. 'People know about me. At least, they think they do, in my community. Bad reputations stick.'

He wouldn't look at me. Picking a pebble up from the shoreline he chucked it as far out to sea as he could, his jacket flailing around him in the exertion. 'I'm not proud of myself. Ma would've been so ashamed of me . . .' He threw another pebble far out into deep water. 'I was so broke, I lost hope of ever being fixed. You talk about faith and God . . . I'm no saint, Iona. Not by a long shot. Add that to politics and there's no point me pretending – I'm not what you need. I'm not what you want. Our families are explosive. Walk away. Do what your brother says – turn around and don't look back. You need to end this because . . .' His words petered out. 'Because I can't.'

He stole a sideways glance, then strode off up the beach as I stood, too stunned to do anything but watch him walk away. He kicked stones, kicked the sand and eventually sat on a grey rock at the far end of the beach, head in his hands, knees pulled up to his face.

I wasn't sure how long I stood. My heart and my mind warring to process his words; arms folded tight to contain the shaking. This was my cue to return to dutiful daughter, obedient sister.

As he perched on the rock, I could see in my mind's eye the photograph of the kid on the beach with a spade. The boy with the ice cream melting through his fingers. The boy somehow abandoned by his father. The teenager standing by a coffin in a graveyard. The guy beaten to a pulp who ditched the evidence. The stud I'd seen engrossed in the university bookshop. The glance in Belfast City Hall. Our first kiss at Mussenden. Our philosophical conversations over coffee. Our laughter with his white-haired grandmother. I saw *Aidan*. His world had been shit. Not him. I heard his words telling me to leave and instead I walked towards him.

He was motionless, a statue fixed to the boulder. The purple-green seaweed skirting the base of the rock floated in a small pool of salt water. I wrapped my arms around him from behind, waiting to sense what to say. His shoulders rose and fell.

'I can't imagine how much it must have hurt when your mum died.'

He turned his head to glance at me, eyes moist. 'See, only someone as good as you could take what I just told you and come out with that . . .'

I put my hand on top of his on the rock. He closed his eyes and lowered his head.

'Does it sound crazy to say there are times I wished I'd died instead of Ma?' He managed to look at me again, pausing before he spoke. 'For what it's worth, Iona, and I know it's a long shot, a very long shot . . . But I meant what I said earlier. I really like you. More than I've liked anybody . . . I'm not using you. That hurts. I have feelings for you and I'm not lying. I can't change who I am or where I'm from, but I'm not who I was two years ago either. I've only ever been myself when I'm with you. God's honest truth. I don't do drugs now and . . .' He hesitated, uncertain. I could see the inner conflict reflect deep in his eyes. '. . . I don't sleep around . . .' He swallowed. 'If there's any chance you still want to go out with me, I promise I'll be as chivalrous, as traditional, as holy as I know how . . . I won't ask for it . . . I can't promise not to want it, not to think about it, but I promise I'll never put you under pressure . . . I guess that's probably nowhere near good enough but it's the best I've got.'

I could've cried at how he set his heart on his sleeve, expecting me to trash it. I'd never expected to hear words like that from him. My mouth went dry. It was more than enough. Way more. I sat on the rock, leaning against him in silence, staring across the Lough to Rathmullan. 'I do want to be with you,' I said.

'Really? Why?'

'Because I've fallen for you.'

'What about Dylan and Luke? Or John? There's nothing I can do about them.'

'Forget John. Why don't we concentrate on the brother who wants to meet you, properly?'

'Andy? He wants to meet?'

'He feels guilty about what happened.'

'He shouldn't. He intervened. He stopped it. Why does he feel bad?'

'Guilty by association. He's like you – he's strong, proud of his roots, but he doesn't hate.'

'OK.' He shrugged.

'You'll meet him?'

'Sure.'

I hugged him tight, my arms wrapped under his jacket and feeling his body heat through his T-shirt. Warmth flooded me as I felt him relax and pull me close. Then he stopped and held my shoulders, looking straight at me. The deadness that had been in his eyes had vanished. 'Does this mean we're still on?' he asked incredulously, inhaling through his nose.

'Yes,' I assured him.

'Are you sure?' he persisted.

'Is the Pope Catholic?'

He looked at me for an instant and then laughed, under his breath at first, his shoulders shaking, and then an infectious laugh of relief burst out. He wrapped his arms around me and buried his head in my hair. 'You're an angel. You know that?' he mumbled, breathing onto my skin.

Chapter 30. McGrory's.

AIDAN.
Saturday 13 August.

McGrory's Backroom bar in Culdaff was jammed even for the support act, who were rocking the joint. Conal always had a knack for sussing out the best gigs. A knack and the right contacts. Half the crowd was from Derry, music heads and temporary refugees avoiding the parades; it was the second Saturday in August, when the Protestant Apprentice Boys paraded round the Derry Walls. We were never done with history here. There wouldn't be riots, no one could be arsed anymore, but it wasn't a day to be Catholic in the Waterside, where the bands and suited old men in collarettes strutted down Dungiven Road, over Craigavon Bridge and back, to commemorate the end of the 1689 Siege. Who cared what religion the King of England was four hundred years ago? It was like they were still stuck in the bloody siege. I'd spent so much time with Iona over the last six weeks it was good to get a lads' night out. Seán once took me, knee-high to a grasshopper, to a parades protest. I'd felt like a man, lapping up the profanities, rattling the spit guards. Foot-tapping to the music, I pondered my unexpected 'live and let live' attitude. Was Iona changing me?

We weren't drinking. Conal, because he was driving; me, because the appeal of being a pisshead was wearing off as quickly as my brother's enthusiasm for it was surging. I was running again and a clear head in the morning was precious. Plus, it didn't take a degree in fortune telling to know Seán would be hammered again by the time I got home. Money for booze, none for electric – and he hoovered the food from the cupboards at an unaffordable rate when he was half-cut. We'd nearly come to blows over it already, and the powder keg could explode if the two of us were drunk together. Like history repeating itself, I was watching him turn into Da. Frightening thought was, there were times I hadn't been far off the same road myself.

The bar-stool sages were talking world politics. After a few rounds they'd every world crisis solved and invented a few more besides. I was half intrigued, half riled by it. Closer to home, the local news was that Bishop Daly, the famous Bloody Sunday priest, was now pushing up daisies. Da had been just a tot when Father Daly waved the white handkerchief of truce, carrying out the dying Jackie Duddy from the Bloody Sunday massacre. 'Unjustified and unjustifiable,' the British Prime Minister had admitted forty years too late, as I'd stood, aged twelve, in the Guildhall Square crowds listening to the inquest verdict. It was the last time my family went to anything together.

Conal was now busy netting music contacts. Our band would be screwed once Jess got his shining exam results. He was for studying medicine. Conal had decided on a music technology course. I was still lost on the way to the start line – don't pass go, straight to jail. *Jesus. Touch wood.* I bit my thumbnail thinking of the looming exam results D-Day. I remembered the humiliating wake-up call of my GCSE results two years previous. I'd chain-smoked a pack of twenty, the crumpled printout in my pocket, before Saoirse had wised me up in no uncertain terms. 'Swallow your pride. You've a feckin' brain – use it for once. About turn and grovel onto whatever A levels they'll take you on! There's no bloody jobs in Derry for sixteen-year-old school leavers with lousy grades! Give up the fags too. You reek worse than your runners.'

Saoirse could still shock me. She'd been in touch during the week with unexpected news. She was coming home. As I tore bits off my beer mat and soaked in the trad-rock rhythms, I thought again about her message. Back before the end of August. No particular reason given. I didn't get it. If you escaped, why come back? I'd tried to chat to Seán to see if he was any the wiser, but he'd been as useless as a chocolate fireguard. Maybe she was broke. Sure as hell wasn't the weather. Hell would break loose though, if she saw the kip our house was in. We'd only two bedrooms. She'd want her room – my room – back. The possibility of bunking in with my brother didn't appeal. I'd wake up high by osmosis, reeking like a prison ashtray. The sofa was looking likely.

I sipped my Coke and switched my thinking. Iona. My blood warmed. Since the beach, we were living in each other's pockets and linking up more with friends. For the most part, any initial shock and curiosity was changing to an acceptance of us being together. Opening up to her hadn't triggered the expected kick in the teeth. My heart beat faster thinking about how close we felt now; to say it was going well was an understatement. She was rewriting my textbook on women. I liked that she made me think; that I couldn't always predict her reactions. I mean, I'd recited poetry on our first date – when had I ever felt remotely like doing that with a girl before? If my mates caught a whisper of that they'd crucify me for sport. She was bringing out a different side of me and I kind of liked it. I'd always fallen for the curved blondes, the come-ons with brash personalities, fake eyelashes and perfectly painted eyebrows. Iona was natural, real. She was genius, beautiful, yet she didn't even twig she was a winning ticket. And Christ but she turned me on. Honest to God, I was in love. I wiped my palms on my jeans. Like seriously. Romeo and bloody Juliet. My breathing quickened. I couldn't quite tell her that yet. I'd said those words to girls before, but now they really meant something.

It wasn't easy, what she'd said at the beach. I didn't have a one-track mind, but the track existed, even if it wasn't a monorail. She was one hell of a girl. I'd fully expected to be thumbing a lift back over the border. Did she know I'd nearly cried when she hugged me? Even without playing rabbit, I wanted to be with her. I sipped my drink. Unequivocal. I just hoped she wouldn't reconsider or that her faith wouldn't require me to broadcast my elected temporary celibacy to the world. Not even Conal was for hearing that. He was winding his way back to me now through the crowds.

'So, what's your story for after summer?' He straddled the three-legged bar stool and fired over a pack of peanuts. 'Made any decisions yet?'

I shrugged.

'So, talk. I'm your guru, mind?'

'Painting's grand.'

'Jesus, aim high why don't you, Michelangelo?'

I glugged my Coke. 'I'm being realistic. It functions.'

'What about university?'

'What about debt to the eyeballs?'

'Look, you know you want to go university. You slogged your guts out for grades. If it's the money, talk to people in school. Take a gap year and get loaded. At least do something that'll count on a CV.'

'Do you know anything about voluntary work abroad? Would Trócaire or Red Cross do that stuff? Maybe I'll move to Belfast. There's jobs there.'

'Aye right, like that's your only reason for picking Belfast!' he raised an eyebrow. 'You two seem to be getting on pretty well, all things considered . . .'

I returned his grin, setting down my glass. 'We are.'

'What, that's it? That's all I get?'

'Yip.' I laughed at his frustration.

'Why'd you want to work for free for a charity anyway?'

'Why not? I'd chase value over riches any day. Do something for yourself it dies with you; do something for others and it's immortal.'

'Exactly how much vodka is in that Coke?'

'None – not tonight anyway.' I laughed with him. Maybe I did need Dutch courage; somehow, I was going to have to tell Iona about Da. I'd dodged that bullet too long already. Could she handle hearing Da did time for the IRA? Could her family? Old sayings could be wrong; there was nothing fair about love and war.

Chapter 31. Match.

IONA.
Tuesday 16 August.

For someone who swore blind their closest encounter with tennis was swingball, he was sickeningly natural. Not that that was remotely the point. The point was that Andy was on the other side of the net. We'd all met at the Arena leisure centre in St Columb's Park. I'd stayed clear of the pool and steam room since being threatened, but no way were Dylan and Luke wiping my entire social life. Not being a practised mediator, I was hoping mixed doubles would distract from the pressure and initial awkwardness.

They'd exchanged a few words as we'd followed the shady path between the trees to the courts. I dropped back to chat with Rachel, straining to overhear.

'You're looking a bit better than the first time I saw you,' Andy chanced.

'Wouldn't be difficult. Was a rough night.'

'Sorry about that.'

They strode on, Aidan acknowledging the apology with a sideways look and a nod. He was fidgety, dragging his racket. I was strangely proud of him. If he felt outnumbered, off his own turf, he wasn't saying it.

'So, you and Iona are an item?'

'That a problem?' Aidan countered, edgy rather than aggressive.

'No. Just unexpected.'

'For you and me both.'

On court the tensions were fired into tennis shots. Aidan's height and co-ordination gave him a definite advantage, making him a fast learner. Though spin still perplexed him, it had taken him all of fifteen minutes to grasp the basics of overhead serve and volley. He was quick on his toes. The lack of experience only showed with his accuracy being hit and miss, and his speed of reaction to shots erratic. We'd lost the first few games, but now that he'd found his feet, were holding our own. The match was on. My real gameplay was the banter developing across the net; flashes of smiles and constructive rivalry. Despite the exercise, I breathed easier as we played on. It was working. So what if John remained a distant dictator with radio silence on the case? Andy would see the real Aidan.

People flowed through the park, inspired by the Rio Olympics and the drier weather. Echoes of teams and die-hard supporters carried over the trees from the grass pitches. As we rested between sets, Aidan left the courts to trawl for a ball he'd hit over the wire. Andy marched after him, catching him up on the grass slope towards the line of chestnut trees. They chatted whilst combing the undergrowth, spotting the ball under a clump of nettles.

Strolling back to the court together, Aidan flashed me a grin through the fence. Conversation snippets reached me – the Olympic diving pool turning green, the Irish rowers in the headlines for their dry double-act and medals. I smiled. The ice was thawing. This meant more than Aidan knew. Andy hadn't slept right in weeks. The first time I'd heard him up, I told him about Aidan deleting the video. He'd been speechless, then he'd cried quietly into his hand.

We played for the hour, then Rachel left us sitting under beech trees, drinking water from a shared bottle. Behind us was the cast statue of St Columba, bent backwards releasing a dove heavenward between his outstretched arms.

'It couldn't have been far from here, was it?' Aidan asked out of the blue.

Andy paled, looking at me and Aidan in turn.

'Would you take me to where it happened? I was wasted that night. I need to see it in daylight with my brain switched on.'

'Why?' Andy found his voice.

'Just. To get my head round it.'

More than just you, I thought. 'You're right. It's only five minutes away.' I sprang to my feet.

Following the tarmac path speckled with gum, we backtracked past the courts and down to the swing gate into the adventure playground. The timber climbing frames strung with ropes and swinging tyres cast shadows on the path. We'd hung out here that night in June, messing after the Northern Ireland match, the wooden pyramid with its staggered platforms the silent witness to our binge of cheap cider. Dylan and Luke had skulked off at intervals, returning with their eyes rolling. Park wardens had chased us at dusk.

Aidan, Andy and I reached the broad pathway skirting the riverbank, parallel with the train tracks. We scanned far across the river to the Cityside – Fort George, the former army barracks craving investment; Sainsbury's with its glass frontage; old shirt factories converted into student flats. Rising in the background, the spike of some chapel looked almost Russian Orthodox. The oak trees around us rustled in the sunlight from birds scavenging through their leaves. Pigeons cooed as a squirrel sprinted up a tree trunk. Kids raced, helmeted and serious on bikes, their parents strolling behind. Dogs. Owners. Cyclists. Bliss, yet my chest was tightening with each step. Until June, I'd loved this park. None of us had been back since. The Guildhall clock pealed the time, but it was the date that was significant – two months since it had all kicked off. Some days it felt like years, other times, like yesterday.

As we drew closer our steps slowed; air so still we could hear the insects among the spikes of gorse. A wire fence ran beside the path; broom, brambles, yellows of dandelions and greens of nettle clumps and dock leaves – where there was a sting, there was always healing. Andy stopped. 'Here,' was all he said, sitting on the back of a bench. Aidan looked around, quiet, then walked across the path till he stood opposite my brother.

'Here?' he whispered.

Andy nodded without looking up.

We shuffled and stalled as power-walkers nattering in Polish strode past. I stood on the mound between the trees by the path. It was where his mobile had skidded across the tarmac to my feet. Aidan leaned back against a tree and closed his eyes.

'Sorry,' Andy said.

'You've nothing to be sorry about,' Aidan countered, eyes flashing open.

'Get real.'

'I am. Mind, I saw it on camera. My head would have been a pancake but for you.'

'And I ran away while your blood pumped onto the ground at your feet there.'

Aidan looked down like he expected to be standing in congealed blood. He bit his lip, lost in thought. When he looked up, his shoulders straightened. 'It wasn't your fault, Andy. Hear me? Drop the guilt before it drowns you. Believe me – I know. Shit happens.'

I held my breath. They held each other's gaze, then my brother crossed over. 'I don't care what they say about you, Aidan Hennessey – you're sound.' He smirked. They high-fived like lifelong friends.

'See you back at the car in ten!' My brother rubbed his eyes, walking off in the direction of the leisure centre, leaving me alone with Aidan. I put my arms round his waist and drew into his chest. His heart beat loudly in his ribcage. His arms circled me, chin resting on my head.

'You're shaking,' he said. 'Ever think stuff happens for a reason? Ma used to say that.'

I nodded against his T-shirt, the friction warming my cheek. 'My dad says that too,' I mumbled.

'Speaking of fathers, there's stuff I need to tell you,' he said. 'I'm pretty sure it's why your John doesn't want you to know me.' He shoved his hands into his back pockets.

'Forget John. Andy's your ally for life now. Believe me – I need that.'

'He's a good guy.'

'So are you.'

'Glad you think so!' He smiled, cheekily. 'C'mere and juke at this . . .' He ran my fingers, laced with his, over the knots and crevices in a tree trunk. Droves of lovers had carved their initials in hearts into the rough bark. 'Let's join them,' he said. 'Make a new memory here. Would you do *that* with me?'

I returned his grin, recognizing the subtle innuendo in his question. '*That*,' I flirted, 'I can definitely do.'

We hunkered at the base of the tree in search of a sharp stone to make our mark. That's when we saw it; a shimmer of sunlight catching the edge of the silver. With a sharp intake of breath, he scrabbled in the caked mud and tangle of roots. Prising the small circle from the ground, he sat, ignoring the dirt, and rubbed the metal with his T-shirt.

He held out his palm. In it was a silver ring, broad and patterned with twirls in the band, hugging a jet-black oblong stone. 'It's Ma's.' He gulped, turning it over and over between his fingers; lost and found. Unknotting the cord of his leather necklace, he threaded the ring so that it hung safe by his Celtic cross. He double knotted it at the back of his neck. When he looked at me again, I realized he had been hiding the tears in his eyes.

'It's from Santiago. Her Camino. Thought I'd lost it forever . . .' His voice broke and he turned away, pressing the palms of his hands hard against his eyes. 'She wanted a ring to replace her wedding ring; to remember her pilgrimage.' For a moment he went completely quiet, clasping the ring at his throat, then he steadied himself. 'She gave me it when she was dying. My lucky charm. Like she's still with me.'

Our shoulders leaned together as we rested at the base of the gnarled trunk etched with lovers' memories. Carving our initials A.H. + I.S. in a ring instead of a heart, his mouth found mine and we kissed. Warm and deep. Places could change. So could people. It was going to work out. This was possible.

Chapter 32. Clash.

AIDAN.
Wednesday 17 August.

It was dark and I was happy-tired as I stood on the front doorstep, patting my pockets to locate my door key. The house I had been painting with Paddy was an empty rental and we'd worked late to reach the point that we knew it could be easy finished the next morning. Paddy had invited me for a quick pint as we locked up. At the same old man's pub where he'd first sized me up for the job, we'd sat on worn wooden bar stools drinking Guinness. I'd never drunk Guinness, but he hadn't asked, just presented me with the black pint, its creamy head still settling.

It struck me I'd never been to a pub with an older man – like in the father–son sense. People talked about having their first pint with their da or having a few at a family event. I'd never had that. Would've been Armageddon anyway.

Sometimes Paddy and I painted in silence with only the radio in the background. At elevenses, we'd chat about whatever came to mind as we dunked biscuits into coffee. We'd talked about the craziness of the 15th Night bonfire in the middle of Lecky Road in the Bogside. Headlines of hoods, backed by dissidents, who'd piled pallets and tyres two storeys high and clattered it with union jacks, Northern Ireland flags, an Israeli flag and even Sinn Féin election posters before igniting it with petrol bombs. That spoke volumes – the usual carry-on at our bonfires was burning Unionist posters. It was a cheap night out with a 'bring-your-own' policy for the two thousand-odd spectators. The road was wrecked. Predictably, my brother had landed home drunk, stinking of smoke, yelling a tuneless 'Fields of Athenry' at 3 a.m. My patience was frazzled.

I'd said goodbye to Paddy about half ten and, ravenous, headed home to get some supper. It had been sticky weather for a couple of days, but the clouds were building like messed duvets, ready for pissing cats and dogs through the night. Maybe there'd be lightning. I found my key. When I opened the front door it instantly felt wrong; an atmosphere you could cut with a blade. My head swirled with childhood memories – Da drunk in the kitchen, that sixth sense of pent-up violence. I clicked the front door shut and breathed deep, tension rippling through me, an imprint from ten years ago.

I called it before I saw it. Seán was sitting, hunched over the kitchen table, crushed beer cans spilling over the floor and a whiskey bottle down to the dregs in his hand. *Jesus. The gun.* Black star and circle clear on the grip. Unmistakeably Da's gun. How the hell did he have it? Was it loaded? It lay strewn by an overflowing ashtray, surrounded by silver popped-out strips of tablets. My head exploded with questions as he stared at me, pupils dilated as he slurred profanities welcoming me home. I'd seen him in a bad state before. Christ, I'd no call to judge but this was different. The gun made it different.

'Call yoursel' a fecking Republican, eh, wee bro?' He spat spitefully for the fifth time in increasing volume. 'Traitor more like! Lying tout! My own blood.' He slugged the last mouthfuls from the bottle and struggled to his feet. 'Worst thing is I didn't believe them. Hell no, says I! Then I find your wee phone all lonesome on the table . . .'

He almost fell over in the effort to pick up my mobile and

hurl it at me. I caught it on reflex. Then it dawned. In the rush out to work I'd forgotten my mobile. He'd gone through it. He knew about Iona being Protestant. Did he know about her dad and brother? I clenched my phone harder than my teeth.

'So she's Protestant. So what? This is 2016, not 1916!'

'British crown forces, that's what! Her family's crawling with police!' he shouted, staggering round the table, edging closer to where I stood by the fridge. 'What'd she do to you? Blackmail you with cash for your bloody university? Work you over till you couldn't resist? Make you a source for MI5? Some whore to win you over!' he yelled.

'Shut up. You're drunk. Off your head. Talking shite. She's no whore – she's my girlfriend!'

'Oooh! Defending her honour!' he goaded.

My blood was rising as I battled to keep my cool.

'So, you admit it then? Collusion? Bloody *tout*!' He spat in disgust as he screamed it.

'No way.' I refused to yell. My voice was raised but as steady as I could hold it in the circumstances. 'You *know* me, Seán. I'm your brother, for Christ's sake!'

'Only thing I had going for me was being a proper Republican. Da's name. Now they won't trust me. Reckon you're all pillow talk with your wee police girlfriend. Bloody snitch.'

'Lies! I've zero ambition to end up dead in some lonely ditch by the border. You're wrong. Whoever's telling you that I'm informing is wrong. They're just twisting everything because I wouldn't join. I haven't even met Iona's older brother or her da!'

'So why the shakes? Detox again? Fancy explaining it to my new mates?'

He was right. My hands and arms were shaking.

'Can I help it if you blew your opportunity?' he snarled.

'What? They couldn't recruit me, so now I'm a threat?'

'Listen *soldier*!' he spat. 'Unless you intend to represent your country in the Paralympics wheelchair racing, you'd better bloody break it off right now, because that's where your kneecaps are headed. Don't forget your heritage. *An dtuigeann tú?* Get it?'

'And if I don't? You're full of crap and you know it!' I countered, my irritation soaring.

'You sure about that?' he growled. 'On your head be it. Won't be a shocker if your girlfriend's brother finds a present under his car. What's she gonna think of you then? You live with that on your conscience?'

I stared, reeling at his words. 'It's not *my* conscience will be burning,' I said, teeth gritted. 'They might own you, but they sure as hell don't own me. You're all bloody insane. How's that crap going to get a United Ireland? Answer me that!' I was yelling now, full on.

'Just do as you're toul' and end it. You have no idea the shite your love life has caused me.'

'*My* choices caused *you* hassle? That's bloody rich,' I hissed back. '*You* end it! *You* quit! You're throwing your life away, Seán!'

'Big bloody loss,' he snarled.

Like Saoirse had warned, the truth was irrelevant. Useless trying to argue with a locked mind. As the conversation degenerated into more screamed allegations and filth, it was clear anything I could say was pointless. He'd made up his mind, or had it made up for him. That he'd spent his entire dole on the alcohol and prescription drugs was just the trigger. I tensed, smelling the reek of alcohol as he approached, the wildness clear in his eyes. For the first time I was conscious of being afraid. It was a feeling I hadn't felt in my own home since Da left. Even when Ma died it wasn't fear, it was grief, anger, pain. I squared my shoulders, muscles taut as I breathed heavily through my nose, the sickening knot tightening in my gut, waiting for the inevitable. I raised my chin, bracing myself, determined not to strike first.

My life didn't flash, but each millisecond was like high-definition slow motion. He raised his hand and I jolted as he smashed the base of the whiskey bottle down hard off the table edge, gripping the bottleneck tightly. Glass shards littered the dirty cream floor tiles. He ran the few short paces towards me. It wasn't Seán. It was a man possessed. Frozen in shock, I barely managed to raise my arm to block the broken bottle from gouging my face as he tried to glass me. There was terror in both of our eyes now. Brother versus brother. Chest pounding, I was wedged with my back flat against the fridge door and the razor sharpness of the jagged bottle lightly swiped the side of my neck. I didn't want to fight Seán. Even in the craziness with blood dripping from a gash in my forearm I was still yelling, trying futilely to reason with insanity. Then I felt the sting of the sharp glass brush my throat and my defences kicked in.

Fired up, I was stronger than Seán despite his stockiness. Taller by an inch, and sober. I rammed him backwards with the force of my weight and he slammed into the cupboards on the far wall, temporarily stunned. The whiskey bottle smashed into smithereens. Standing still on the glass and smears of blood on our kitchen floor, I'd one eye on him in case he came back at me and the other on my arm, assessing the damage. It wasn't deep. With a primeval roar he rallied, launching into me again, drunken arms flailing.

'Stop!' I screamed, trying to snap him out of his state of chemical-induced oblivion; but attack was the best form of defence and my punches were landing hard. He knew he was losing. I could sense the rage of it burning in his eyes – the affront of his younger brother outplaying him. That's when he lifted the gun. I ducked. Adrenalin surged in my bloodstream and as his fingers curled on the trigger, I threw all my weight behind a right uppercut. My arm shuddered as I felt the full force of it connect with his jaw. A blast. An explosion of sound. The blow picked him off his feet and he landed hard in a crumpled pile on the floor tiles, gun flung from his hand. A brass cartridge bounced past my feet. The air tasted burnt. My eardrums screamed with a metallic ringing. The hollow thud of the back of his head jolting off the ceramic floor sucked the breath from my lungs. I turned. Touched my fingers to the hairs standing on end above my ear. The bullet hole in the fridge door was a perfect 5p circle.

I waited, but his body remained motionless where he had fallen from the punch. Keeping my distance, I watched his chest rise and drop, but his eyes were closed. Edging closer I kicked the gun to the other end of the kitchen. Still I waited. Still he was motionless. I felt dizzy as my heart raced. The air stank of fireworks. My knuckles throbbed; terror closing in. Hell. I'd hit him harder than I'd ever hit another human being in my life. Cautiously, I hunkered beside him, concern he'd come to and retaliate hanging in the balance with concern I'd done serious damage.

'Seán?' I asked quietly. The air was pregnant with lack of response. The Wolfe Tones waxed lyrical with rebel songs, frying my head. I punched the stereo off. Even the music couldn't have drowned the gunshot. On autopilot, I grabbed a half-empty box of plasters from the cupboard above the kettle. Seán still hadn't moved. I was wary but he was my brother. My breathing was still heavy with the exertion; sweat soaked through my paint-splattered T-shirt. I approached him again and checked his breathing and pulse. It was there. My head swam, trying to process the last five minutes. Looking around the chaos of the kitchen, my decision was made. Fight and flight. I slid the Sacred Heart magnet and the photo over the bullet hole. No waiting to see whether it was neighbours, cops or balaclavas first through the front door. Grabbing the gun and cartridge, I put Seán into the recovery position and, leaving his mobile by his hand, fled out the back into the darkness.

My feet ran like they belonged to someone else. I must've sprinted the length of Creggan Heights and onto Westway. The reservoir was a hellish blur of panic, locked gates, five-foot fencing that tore my T-shirt; sliding over muck to the water's edge, gun jammed in my jeans. Then eerie stillness. I could barely stand, shaking like a vodka jelly. I ducked instinctively as a bat flew overhead. *God. Is this my fecking life? For real, like?*

Cartridge first. I'd have been a bloody brilliant rioter if I'd been born in the Troubles. Then the gun. Christ alone knew what past blood it had spilled. Mine was on it now, along with my prints. And my brother's. Maybe even my Da's. Please God it would sink like a cannonball to oblivion in the glar at the bottom of Creggan reservoir. It flew with a clean whistle and a near perfect arc as I peered after it into the darkness. The splash, like a trigger, set me to running again; past the bungalows, past St Joe's school and into Rosemount. At the old factory on the corner of Rosemount Avenue I doubled over against the wall, coughing, holding the stitch in my side and struggling to breathe. It was pitch black and the heavens had opened, pissing down in torrents; puddles filling the pavements; rivers flooding the gullies into the drains. The downpour which had been threatening all day had arrived in force with the onset of night. Soaked to the skin in minutes, I shivered in the archway of the converted factory. My knees were giving way. My stomach growled, then convulsed, with vomit splattering the concrete. I pulled my cotton jacket tight, but the night wind sucked the heat out from my body, and I slid down the wall, hunkered into a ball. *Was this my fault? I didn't ask for any of it.*

Impossible to think straight. My knuckles throbbed, fingers numb. Rubbing my hands, I breathed warmth onto them. Where the glass had sliced my arm and neck felt like razor-edged paper cuts, stinging as the fluff from my jacket stuck to the caking blood. Headlights from a couple of cars shone round the corner and I pulled back into the shadows as they sloshed past into Park Avenue. *Focus, dammit, focus!* My bones felt invaded by chill as the rain soaked through to my socks. I wanted to curl up in bed, duvet over my head, as if I could wake up and it wouldn't be real. *My brother. My own brother.* The cocktail of crazed emotions spun my head in different tangents – I burned, shivered and shook. I was clueless how long I'd stayed there, hunched up, barely sheltered from the driving rain bouncing off the sheen of the black pavements. Eventually the need for shelter pierced my consciousness over the avalanche of unanswerable questions. I couldn't go home. It didn't feel safe. *Was my brother safe? How hard had I hit him?* I imagined balaclavas hiding in the shadows round the streets. *How much of what he said was bravado? How much was true?* I hadn't a penny on me to take a taxi to Conal's. Going to Iona's was out of the question. I shuddered as rain trickled down the back of my neck. There was another option *if* I was prepared to bite my tongue and swallow my pride. They were family and only ten minutes' walk away in the Glen.

My aunt's house was in darkness as I dragged myself up the short driveway. Cupping my forehead in my hand, I peered through the front door. I glanced at my mobile. Just gone midnight, not ridiculously late. I tapped the glass lightly. If anyone was still awake, they'd hear me, but it wouldn't wake the household. I was frozen to the core, teeth chattering. No response. Stifling a cough, I pulled my sodden jacket tighter and contemplated the dull ache in my right hand. It was swollen. I winced moving it, praying it was just sprained. I tugged their car door on the off-chance it was open; the back seat would have been welcome even without company. No luck. Still the rain drummed, and I dodged puddles back to the shelter of their porch. It was all hitting me now. Sitting on the damp brick step, I leaned my back in against the door. Feck. I was out of it: out of options, out of hope. For the first time I gave in to despair, letting it flow through me like a tide and settle into every crevice of my body and soul. *It's useless, Hennessey; you're useless.* It was strangely comforting to give up. Maybe I'd pass out. I thought about sitting in the warmth of the bar with Paddy earlier. The thought bandied around in my head for a few moments before it registered. *Call Paddy.* As I reached for my phone, the door behind me opened and I found myself fallen backwards in the hallway at my aunt's fluffy pink slippers.

'Are you drunk?' she said in a pitched stage-whisper.

'No.' I tried to gather my thoughts, conscious of dripping onto her pristine wooden floors smeared with my footprints the instant I stood.

'Kitchen. Quietly,' she ordered.

Like a dog, I followed, blinded by the brightness as she switched on the halogen spotlights to inspect me.

'Mother of God!' She pulled her purple dressing gown closer and crossed her arms, challenging me in silence for an explanation. I stood dumb, faint with hunger and cold, struggling to find the right words.

'I had a fight with Seán . . .' I attempted to string together a coherent sentence, looking around the spotless kitchen surfaces and rows of shining utensils. There was no point sugar-coating it, though I kept my jacket pulled high around my neck to hide the evidence of the cuts. 'I'm soaked. Can I kip in the spare room? Just one night? I swear, I won't be any bother. Please? Honestly, I'm not pissed.'

'Will you never learn, Aidan Hennessey?' The incrimination in her voice was evident. I was dizzy just trying to stand upright. My gaze dropped to the floor. She was letting her words hang for effect. Every last ounce of my self-worth was draining out of me. *White trash*. It hurt sometimes just looking at Aunt Teresa, spit of Ma. I wished she were here; wished I still had her unconditional love; her encouragement. I didn't know its value until it was stolen.

'The spare room is full of stuff,' my aunt stated matter-of-factly, yawning and shaking her head in thinly veiled disgust. 'Take your shoes off. Sleep on the sofa. We'll talk in the morning.'

Chapter 33. Ultimatum.

IONA
Thursday 18 August.

The buzz from my phone woke me.

'Get up. Get the dog. Get your phone. Get out.' John's voice was harsher than usual.

'Wise up. I'm in bed. What time—?'

'No questions. I'm just off night shift. On my way back to Limavady. Do what I say, or I'll call Dad. Ring you back in five.'

The ground was still damp from its overnight drenching. Just gone 6 a.m. Barely anyone about. Maddy tugged me through a puddle, yelping and sniffing with the excitement of the unexpected early walk. I still smelled of sleep, pyjamas thinly disguised under Mum's big raincoat, heart thumping. The mobile vibrated in my pocket.

'On your own?' John said.

'Yes.' My skin prickled.

'Good news first. Luke lost his swagger when he was sidekick to his mum instead of Dylan. Didn't exactly take sleep deprivation or waterboarding. Reckon they're both nailed with the confession and evidence now.'

The chill of the air hit my lungs as I gulped. The relief of it caught halfway in my chest, then stuck. My toes curled from the water seeping through my slipper soles.

'You might at least thank me! I'm risking my uniform here.

Wasn't exactly orthodox policing.'

'Aye, like we've a history of that in Northern Ireland.'

A suck of air on the other end of the phone. 'Aidan brainwashed you? Say that to Dad and kiss your university fees goodnight.'

'I think for myself!'

'You're not thinking at all these days,' John hissed. 'You didn't listen before, but I'm telling you now. End it.'

'So your life choices count more? Is that it?'

'Bluntly? Yes. Teenage fling versus safety, family and career? Listen, I'm saving your skin in more ways than you know.'

'Like what?'

Maddy yanked on the lead.

'Can't say. Police business. You've got twenty-four hours. Call Aidan or I'll call Dad.'

Chapter 34. Shock.

AIDAN.
Thursday 18 August.

Having resolved to let me stay, my aunt had mellowed, taking pity enough to fire me one of my uncle's T-shirts and a spare duvet. Once she'd vanished, I'd raided the biscuit tin and peeled off my wet clothes down to my boxers in the privacy of the living room. I'd spread my painter's jeans and splattered green T-shirt over the radiator and hung my jacket on the door handle. Everything reeked of gunshot. Aunt Teresa would turn her nose in the morning. I'd drenched the lot with lavender air spray from the mantelpiece. My socks had been mud-coated and wringing wet. I'd taken them, along with the soggy box of plasters, and tiptoed into the downstairs bathroom. God knows why I washed them. It didn't matter a shred if they were minging, but I was like a robot. Standing with my hands in warm water in the washbasin I considered, almost like a spectator, what to do with my cuts. There'd been three. None deep enough to need stitches, but I'd battled to open the plasters with my shaking hands and attempted to patch myself up – I couldn't bleed on my aunt's duvet. I didn't dare risk further wrath. Like a dead man, I'd fallen asleep on the sofa; lost to the world within minutes.

One of the attributes which has kept me sane over the years is my ability to sleep like a log, no matter what life throws at me. I don't know if it's innate or developed from childhood to block out the impact of what happened in our house when Da drank.

The commotion at the front door around seven in the morning hardly registered through the fog of sleep until my fourteen-year-old cousin burst into the living room.

'Police is here,' she announced self-righteously. 'Looking for yeh!'

I fell off the sofa with a loud groan in an undignified tangle of duvet. Trying to squish into damp skinny jeans was not the best position to be in when Teresa entered the room with two police officers, one of them female. Whilst my initial reaction through the haze of abrupt wakening was mortification, the second was the fear and despair that came flooding back. *Had they found the gun that quick?* I straightened up, conscious not only of the bed-head, bare feet and oversized T-shirt, but of their gaze on the plasters on my arm and the bruising on my knuckles.

'Sorry to disturb you. Are you Aidan James Hennessey?' the male officer asked.

'Indeed,' answered Aunt Teresa as if I couldn't speak for myself. My brain was fighting to wake up properly and grasp what the hell I was facing. I wasn't alone in that either. My aunt was standing like one of those sci-fi stone statues, waiting to pounce. My eyes flitted between her and the peelers.

'Yes, I'm Aidan,' I confirmed for myself.

'What's this about?' demanded my aunt, simultaneously managing to smile civilly at the officers whilst glaring at me.

'What age are you, Aidan?' asked the female officer, sensing the tension.

'Eighteen.' *Feck. This was like Monopoly, I really could go straight to jail. Not remotely the ticket out of here I'd hoped for.*

'And your relationship to Aidan?' she turned to Teresa.

'His aunt. Teresa Donnelly. This is my house.'

'Thank you for allowing us in, Mrs Donnelly. Aidan, we need

to speak for a moment. Would you prefer your aunt to be present or to speak in private?'

I hesitated. It was more the 'What in God's name have you done now?' look on my aunt's face, that assumption of automatic guilt, rather than any rational thought that pulled the answer out of me.

'On my own.' I met her glare as she slammed the door. Her ears would be superglued to it anyway. The male officer spoke like a textbook.

'Aidan. Your neighbours reported a ... domestic at your house last night. There was concern you were missing.'

Jesus. No one reported gunshots in Creggan for fear of one in your head. Did he simply mean the fight or did he know more? My mind was trying to get a step ahead, to grasp which way the conversation was swinging. 'Do I need a lawyer? Am I being arrested? Questioned?' *Talk yourself bloody guilty, Hennessey.*

The officers exchanged looks. The woman sniffed the lavender air. 'Aidan, my name is Constable Rosie Conaghan. We're not here to arrest you. We wanted to ascertain your whereabouts to determine your safety. There may have been a weapon discharged yesterday evening?'

'I'm here. I'm fine.'

Maybe the gun was still drowned. Still, there was a sick feeling stirring in my soul as I began to think through my brother's allegations from the previous night. Here I was, alone with two uniformed police officers, talking. My aunt was already livid at the affront of their police car parked outside. Neighbours would talk, rumours would spread.

'There was evidence in your house of a fight. An assault? Our officers noted blood and glass on the floor; evidence of alcohol and substance abuse, a cordite smell?' I stared them out. 'Aidan, you're clearly injured. Can I ask how you got hurt? Were you at the house last night?'

'I slept here all night.' Panic began to filter into my conscience. I'd abandoned my brother. *Should I have phoned an ambulance?* My brain kicked. 'What are you saying? Is my brother OK?'

The officers hesitated, glances passing with unspoken words between them. It was Captain America's turn. He was straight to the point. 'We've arrested your brother, Aidan. We're holding him in Strand Road barracks for questioning. Anything you'd like to say?'

'What's he charged with?' I spoke carefully.

'Nothing at present.'

'What was he arrested for?'

'Suspicion of involvement with Dissident Republicanism and assault.'

I tried not to flinch as his words hit like a brick wall. *Stay emotionless. Say nothing.* I summoned all the wisdom I could milk from years of late night crime-scene TV; closing down my reactions; relaxing my body language despite the stress fizzing in my veins.

'When will he be released?' Cold sweat prickled my back.

'That's not clear at this point in time,' responded the male officer. 'Anything you wish to talk about? Can we be of any support?'

They always pleaded the fifth on telly. Useless here. Our fifth was probably something about the Holy Catholic Church. 'No further comment,' I stated in polite monotone.

The static on their police radios burst into life. 'I think we're done here,' Rosie said to her colleague as they headed to the door. 'Glad you're safe and sound, Mr Hennessey. We'll leave it at that for now.'

I was still standing numb, absorbing the shock of the encounter and the news of Seán's arrest, when my aunt stormed back, all guns blazing.

'No trouble?' she said, all Pontius Pilate. 'This is your idea of no trouble? Honestly, I thought you were learning, Aidan, but clearly I was over-optimistic. What's it now? Is this to do with what was on your Facebook a month ago?' The audience was building with my two cousins, still in pyjamas, peering round the doorframe and my uncle's footsteps thumping down the stairs. I tried to speak but the words wouldn't come.

'What have you got to say for yourself? You missed the soap opera, Niall.' She sought my uncle's endorsement in my humiliation. 'Two police officers, and sonny here has the cheek to exclude me from his interrogation under our own roof. State of you! Your mother would be ashamed, God rest her. She'll be turning in her grave.'

Pain seared at the mention of bringing shame to Ma. My breathing caught. Still I struggled for words. My aunt, reading it as an admission of guilt, turned her rant up a gear. Every past mistake was wheeled out again; every failure of the time I'd been a dysfunctional misfit in their family; all their efforts to help me, which I'd thrown back in their faces. I heard less than half of it, though it hit home blow by blow. It was the other words that were playing over and over in my brain. *We've arrested your brother . . . Suspicion of involvement in Dissident Republicanism.* It was like running into a concrete wall at full tilt on repeat. My brother was my family. The only place I fitted. My brother who had attacked me in a substance-crazed frenzy. My brother who needed help. I should've been strong enough to stay. If I hadn't abandoned him, he wouldn't be in custody.

'Listen to your aunt.' My uncle added his penny's worth of

cliches to the punches. 'You're throwing your life away! Wake up and smell the roses! Act responsibly! Take your education seriously! Get a job!'

'You're throwing your life away, Seán!' Weren't those my very words to my brother the night before? His answer slashed into my mental chaos. 'Big bloody loss?' All the warning signs had been in flashing neon, if I'd only read them. And now this. He could do time. If the cops found the gun, he mightn't be on his own. *Ma. Saoirse. They'd have known what to do.* Instead I'd screwed it up. I could feel my anger building like an uncontrollable surge. Finally, I exploded.

'Christ! Sorry for being born! If the world ended tomorrow, I suppose it'd be my fault too? Did it ever cross your simple minds, just once, that I'm not to blame for everything? I *do* try and make right choices. Just because I bloody *look* like my da doesn't mean I *am* him! But don't worry yourselves. I get it. I'm shit. And I'm out of your lives because I don't need you either. By the way, Seán's under arrest in Strand Road barracks, but hey – have a nice day.'

I grabbed my shoes and jacket, pushed past them, and strode out the door barefoot with as much dignity as I could muster. They could keep my sodden socks. I'd post my uncle back his T-shirt to save them accusing me of stealing it. I paused at the street corner to slip on my damp trainers. No one had followed me through the smoke of my burning bridges.

Focus on your feet. Feel your footsteps connect with the pavement. Listen to your breathing. I walked rapidly, attempting to calm myself down. They were tried and trusted techniques, except this time they weren't working. My brother. Arrested. God knew what they were asking him. Christ knew what state he was in to be able to give any answers, let alone the ones he needed to escape serious trouble. *Sweet Jesus, let him be coherent enough not to comment and to ask for a lawyer.* Why had they come for me if not about the gun? Had Seán blamed me? Had he confessed to threatening me? Were they digging for evidence to hang him on? Was I really under dissident threat? Had the New IRA made a connection with Iona?

The last question stopped me in my tracks. Mother of God. How on earth could I explain this to her? She already had Loyalists breathing down her neck. I hadn't yet told her that Da had been in the IRA. That confession paled into insignificance now that my brother had been arrested. What had Seán's exact words been? *Her brother could find a present under his car?* Please God let that have been the drink talking. Blow John sky high unless I stopped seeing his sister? Seán had threatened me, too, if I didn't break it off . . . Arbitrary 'justice'. Vigilantes. Wankers. I felt sick to my core. Was this really about me seeing Iona or were they mad because they didn't own me? Either way, they'd be riled about the gun now too. The New IRA wasn't exactly known for giving alleged informers the chance to argue their innocence. They'd just come for me and shoot.

I was drenched with cold sweat, paranoia pivoting me at the slightest sound. *It's not safe.* Every passing car was the police, or worse. Every dog bark made me shudder. My headache intensified to a pounding migraine boring into my forehead. My tongue stuck to the roof of my mouth. A siren wailed. I spun, expecting uniforms and handcuffs. *Get away! Away from streets. Away from people.* I legged it to Brooke Park and sank onto a bench overlooking St Eugene's Cathedral and the city beyond. Ma had always encouraged us to hope, to dream. *Why?* It was futile. I plugged in my earphones and blasted the volume. The lyrics screamed fighting and teenage freedom dreams into my bloodstream.

This couldn't actually be real, could it? My own brother. Ordering me to leave Iona. Threatening her family. I hated him. This was wrong. So bloody wrong. But I *needed* him. They couldn't jail him. He wasn't bad – he was hurting. Could I have done different? Iona's brother had demanded she leave me too. She hadn't. Maybe John had been right. It ripped my heart to swallow that thought. Maybe my brother was right. Maybe peace just didn't fit anyone from the arsehole of Creggan. Maybe you needed a radioactive spider to change your DNA.

The early morning dog walkers were out, taking advantage of the crisp air now the rain had cleared. I felt their gaze, sideways glances as they passed. I pulled my knees tight to my chin. Rocking. There were cars parked nearby. In my mind's eye I could see Iona's brother in a police uniform, sat at the steering wheel and then, boom, a fireball, people screaming. It wasn't real, but yet, it was. Iona standing over a grave, just like I'd stood; lost, shell-shocked and empty. Her tears streaming; staring blankly at me in accusation, fear. It was my fault. This was on me. My decisions. My choices. My problem. I had to solve it. There was only one way this was going down.

I stopped the music and brought up her number on screen, my eyes refusing to focus, staring as if it would dial itself. I couldn't. I just couldn't. There were no words I could imagine being able to say. Concentration was impossible. I attempted to hit the green dial button, but my fingers resisted. My phone clattered to the ground from my shaking hands. My mind was numb, overwhelmed with a level of emotion beyond what I knew how to handle. *You have to do this, Aidan. You have to keep her safe. There's no point anyway – her family will hate you. Your brother is going down. Let her go. Let her live her life.*

I was powerless to change what was going to happen to me or

my brother. My best throw of the dice was to shield her. I battled to find words. I heard Ma singing me to sleep as a wean, with the old Irish air:

'The river's wide, I cannot cross
And neither have I wings to fly.
Give me a boat that will carry two
And both shall row, my love and I
And both shall row, my Lord and I.'

Devoid of hope, I typed my message – every letter killing me.

I'm sorry, Iona. We're done. I can't see you anymore. It's not your fault. It's me. All of it. Keep on being amazing. x

I couldn't type the three words I wanted to tell her. As I touched the send button, I buried my head into my knees and tangled my hands tight into my hair. It was like being shot. Pain constricting in my chest. I pressed play and hiked up the music volume. *Drown. Don't think. Don't feel.* Was this what civil war felt like? Brother against brother? Lover against lover?

I was a zombie. People passed me. Maybe they stared, maybe they didn't. Maybe I cared, maybe I didn't. What difference would it make anyway? The Guildhall clock chimed and chimed again. Every quarter of an hour, religiously. The city was awake for a normal August Thursday. Clockwork. It was just my world which had fallen apart. Only me in silent Armageddon. I wasn't even sure I existed anymore, or whether it mattered. Then my phone rang.

'You OK, kiddo? Not like you to be late.'

'Grand.' I straightened myself back into reality, trying to get my brain in gear. 'Sorry. Give me ten. I'll be there in ten.'

Paddy looked me over as I arrived out of breath at the house. 'Hangover?'

'Something like that.' I avoided eye contact and sought out my brush and tray. It was just the final white gloss coat on the doors and radiators left. I prised the metal tin of paint open, stirring it with the old chisel. If I could, I'd have buried the chisel in my head to stab the throbbing in my brain.

'Hedge survive you being dragged through it? Must've been a good night?'

I suppose I did look rough. I hadn't shaved. I near fainted sniffing my armpits. My feet were stuffed sockless into my muddy trainers and my uncle's T-shirt hung on me, oversized and odd-looking. I ran my fingers through my hair in a vain attempt to spruce up. The only impact that had was Paddy noticing the remaining plasters on my arm that hadn't lost their grip. He stayed mute, the unasked question hanging in the air. My knuckles hurt as I concentrated on holding the paintbrush steady, the shake in my hands evident as my heart raced. Paddy's eyes burrowed my skull as I swore aloud, smearing dripped paint on the new tiles. I was too far gone to bring myself to talk to him.

My phone buzzed again in my back pocket as it had been doing every five minutes since I'd arrived. Every message I ignored was like a screw tightening the tension in my ribcage. My stomach growled for attention one minute and then threw up bile into my mouth, burning my throat the next. I swallowed and closed my eyes, lowering my head to curb the dizziness. I was beat. Burned out, and I knew it. I needed to finish this job. It was a constant in the chaos. I needed the pay. I needed normality and it was slipping through my fingers. My thoughts zigzagged from issue to issue, searching for a safe space to rest, some sign of hope to hang on to. My phone rang this time. I jolted, brush clattering, spattering bright wet gloss over the floor. Something inside me exploded. I shouted, swearing at the top of my voice, punching walls in meltdown. I grabbed my phone from my pocket and in the instant before I flung it across the kitchen, saw fourteen logged messages from Iona and Conal. Conal's call was still ringing as the mobile fell with a contented plop and a quiet fizz of electrics into the bubbles of washing-up liquid in the sink.

Paddy moved fast, his hands raised. I expected anger from him. His strong hands tried to grab my shoulders, but I shoved him in the chest. He was a rock. I'd lost the plot, overcome with situations beyond my control. Terrified. Floundering. I hated the world, I railed against what it was doing to me. My torrent of language was beyond chronic as I kicked rings around me. Undeterred, Paddy reached for me again and again, dodging my blows. On the third attempt, despite my struggles, his grip held my upper arms pinned to my sides. Years of labouring had honed his physical strength.

'Calm down,' he was repeating over and over. 'It's OK. Whatever it is, it's gonna be OK.'

'It's not fucking OK!' I yelled back in his face. 'How can you say that? They've arrested Seán. He's guilty as hell, Paddy. They've arrested him and he'll do time. I can't do this on my own. I just can't. First Da, then Ma. Then Saoirse left. I mean, she's coming back, but she'll never stay. Now they've taken my brother. He's all I've got left, Paddy. They can't take him. My aunt hates the sight of me. No matter what I do I'm never good enough. Why all this shit? Why do I never get a break? It's results day. That's why Conal's calling. It's supposed to be the day I get a chance and instead I had to dump my girlfriend, the first girl I ever really cared for, and they're gonna shoot me over it. So much for bloody peace! Can't I track my own path? Didn't Bobby Sands say my generation gets to laugh? What's my crime, Paddy? Falling in love? Since when was that bad? What the hell did I do so wrong to deserve this?'

Paddy released his grip tentatively as my rage cooled after the outburst. To my surprise his blue eyes reflected deep concern, not anger, under his greying eyebrows. 'Sit down a minute.' He pulled up a chair to the kitchen table for me. Meekly I obeyed. My fight had gone. As I buried my head in my folded arms on the wooden surface, I heard him fish my phone out of the sink. He boiled the kettle and the aroma of coffee filtered over as he stirred in spoonfuls of sugar with a clink. Tinfoil rattled, his footsteps crossed the floor, and there was the hollow knock of two mugs set down by my head.

'Here.' He prodded my hand. 'Drink up. When did you last eat? Take a ham sandwich.' He offered me his lunch. I cupped the warm mug in one hand, my head in the other. He sipped his own coffee. The silence was like therapy as the hot, sweet liquid warmed me from the inside. My eyes wandered. Amazing how much damage you could cause in a two-minute meltdown when there was paint around.

'Sorry, Paddy,' I whispered as the fuzz in my brain cleared enough to speak. 'I'll fix it. Give me a minute.'

'Look at me, kiddo. Cleaning paint can wait. I've never been much of a counsellor, but you need to know you're not on your own. Hear me? That's serious shit you're dealing with. If you need me, I'm here for you. If there's anything I can do, I'll try my best. If you want to talk, I'll listen. If you don't, I'll feed you coffee till you do or I'll take you to someone who's better at this than me if it helps.'

'You're doing just fine.' I managed a weak smile. It took until I'd finished my first coffee, and a second, and slowly digested a triangle of sandwich before I considered if I could talk more. I remembered Saoirse helping me deal with my grief two years ago when I had finally started to open up about Ma's death. Saoirse was my saviour then, Paddy now.

Knowing I had to talk didn't make it easier. I drank another coffee and hoovered all of his sandwiches before I felt human enough to speak. Once I started, it gathered momentum like a flood; frustration, confusion and fear spilling out over the table. Paddy was a rough-edged angel without wings, listening for over an hour, occasionally asking a question or confirming his understanding.

I told him about Shannon, about the attack in the park, my terror that I was a clone of Da. That should've been enough for one summer, but then there had been the attempt to recruit me. Seán had been a saga since then – I was at the edge of my sanity, walking on eggshells to handle his mood swings, the drugs, the drink, his complete disengagement with everything practical. And John; to be hated by someone I'd never even met felt degrading. Understandable, but it hurt all the same. I rubbed my temples hard, struggling to convey the events of the previous night. The blackmail. The gun. I still couldn't figure it out. The fight with my brother. The threats, real or perceived, dissidents and cops, hanging over me. No matter how I tried to spin it, the fact was the bullet my brother had fired had narrowly missed my head. My heart was in the gutter, my throat burning. I knew if he'd been in his right mind it would have been a different story. I wished I'd been more attentive weeks ago. The betrayal of trust cut deeper than the scabbed slice wounds on my arm and neck. I explained how I'd sought sanctuary with my aunt and uncle. How their negativity stung no matter how hard I'd tried to straighten myself out. I slouched in the chair, knackered, tension leaking from my muscles. I still felt sick to the core but at least someone had cared enough to listen. The pressure valve was finally opening.

'What about your girl, lad? Iona, was it?'

I looked at him a moment, his chin resting on his folded hands, elbows on the table. It was the one part of all of this mess I had avoided talking about, consciously or subconsciously. I shook my head. It was too raw. Too recent. *Don't make me go there, Paddy, please, I can't.* My eyes pleaded with him. He nodded in silent acknowledgement, letting me hang on to the shreds of my dignity, and stirred his coffee before speaking.

'Hell of a lot on your shoulders, kiddo. That's for sure. You've also a shedload more maturity than I did at your age. Things I might be able to help with, if you want. No promises, mind. Other parts, I have to admit, are beyond me. You know what strikes me the most? You're way too hard on yourself. If half the young lads I see around had half your decency, half your courage, it would be a much better place. Your mother would've been proud. If I dare say it, despite his many faults, so would your da. There's people I know. I can ask around. To be honest, the threats smack of alcohol-induced crap, but I'd rather be sure. Do you want my help, kiddo? I don't want to interfere if you'd rather handle it differently, but you're a good lad. I hate to see you hurting.'

I nodded. I wanted, needed, to know. Even the possibility of being dragged up a back alley to be shot by appointment at point-blank range was terrifying.

'I'm also taking you to the college to collect your results. You're a good worker, Aidan ... generally ...' He chuckled into himself, looking around at the paint-splattered walls and skirting boards. 'But if someone had told me when I was your age that I'd the chance to make something of myself, I'd have grasped it with both hands. Do yourself a favour. Don't give up just yet.'

That was how I ended up in my old school assembly hall, sitting in front of my form teacher, a sheet of paper in my hands.

Politics: A. History: A. Irish: A. English Literature: A. Given the day that was in it, it was like a sick fairy tale. There wasn't a single ounce of me felt able to celebrate.

With the catapult of clarity I'd craved all summer, came the full blow of disillusionment. Despite my self-doubt, something deeper inside of me had known I could achieve, yet when I finally knew what I wanted, it was impossible. Four simple grades on the page said, *You can*. Sitting there in painter's jeans, my brother in custody, my life shredded, my heart broken, everything else screamed louder. *You can't. Why would you even try? Why would you ever dream you could fly?*

I wondered how Iona had done. Our day in Belfast flooded back: standing in the bookshop, conversations on the bus. I hoped her results would take her where she felt destined to go. The acute ache in my soul told me in no uncertain terms what I'd tried to fathom all summer – I wanted to be with her at Queen's.

My form teacher's voice was an incomprehensible drone. I fled the first chance I got. My chair squeaked as it scraped backwards on the varnished wooden floor. The same room I'd sat my last exam in two months ago, a different lifetime.

Ghosting unseen through the crowded conversations of lads in the school foyer, I wove back across the car park to where Paddy sat reading the *Journal* in his blue Toyota.

'Aidan! *Comhghairdeas!*' Mr Ó Súilleabháin's unmistakeable voice rang out congratulations behind me. I hesitated, hearing the pace of his steps quicken across the tarmac behind me.

'Hold up a minute!' He drew level, pumping my arm in a handshake. 'Knew you could do it, lad. Knew you had it in you.' The enthusiasm was as genuine as his smile. 'Stay for the photo! Straight As is always a formal photo for the papers.'

I imagined my photo in the *Journal* next to a shot of my

brother, jacket over his head, being led into a courtroom. 'I'll look like a scarecrow.'

'I'll borrow you a jacket. Stand in the back row.' He looked me over in mild amusement. 'So, what's next? You must be thrilled the hard work paid off!'

I didn't know how much of my despair was visible. I battled to maintain my composure but the best I could muster was a fragile mask of indifference. My shrug as I walked away stopped him in his tracks, falling well short of the Oscar I'd have needed to convince my favourite teacher that all wasn't far from well.

As I piled into the passenger seat and yanked the door shut with a thud, Paddy peered from behind his paper. 'Bad day at the office?'

'Think it's safe for me to go home?' I asked. 'I just want to go home.'

He flung the *Journal* on the back seat and was turning the key in the ignition when Mr Ó Súilleabháin tapped the driver's window.

'Your teacher wants to talk, kiddo.'

I looked away, across the sports pitches. 'I can't do this. Not today. I just want to go home. I don't even care if it's not safe. I don't want to be here.'

Like I was invisible, I heard bits of the conversation as Paddy stepped out of the car and spoke with my teacher. Mr Ó Súilleabháin singing my praises over the grades. Paddy taking it all in, glancing through the glass at me. Lowered voices of concern as Paddy mentioned my brother. I wondered if Seán could be released yet. But wasn't it forty-eight hours they could question you for? Then formal charges or special powers or something? You heard it on the news. Always with dissidents. 'Prevention of Terrorism Act', was that it? I felt for my phone, thinking I'd google the law, then realized the handset was lifeless on a rag at my feet, victim of its unintentional swimming lesson. I thought of Seán with the mother of all hangovers trying to evade truths he couldn't admit to. I could see a grey plastic chair in a bare room with a wooden table. Like the movies, there was a two-way mirror, the interrogator playing to both audiences. It probably wasn't like that, but I'd never been in a police station. No matter what, he was screwed.

'You're a dark horse,' Paddy said as he returned to the car. 'And yes, I will take you home, but it's on three conditions. One – you open the door to no one. Two, you do nothing stupid – keep calm and don't even think of taking this into your own hands.' Driving along Buncrana Road he made a point of looking at me until I acknowledged I understood. 'Three, we're not done talking about these grades, but that's for another day.'

I nodded, gazing out the window at the traffic.

I was coming round slowly. The front door had had the hallmarks of a patched-up forced entry when we'd arrived. The kitchen was worse than before – trashed like a riot. Upstairs was unscathed. After Paddy had left, I'd nose-dived onto my bed and had lain there in a mental and emotional coma until dozing off. Awake again, I hadn't yet opened my eyes. My ears were taking in the comfort of routine sounds – the hum of passing cars, the banter of kids on the neighbour's doorstep. The radio informed me it was just gone two in the afternoon, not that I cared; I currently had the emotional capacity of a stranded jellyfish. My fingers clenched the duvet. I was still mad at my brother; pissed with life in general. Jesus, if I'd the life experience of Gandhi I still wouldn't have handled this. 'I wish she was here,' I spoke aloud to myself, and then realized that for the first time in my life the 'she' was neither Ma nor Saoirse. My eyes shot open to avoid seeing the mental image of her.

'On your feet, soldier,' Ma would've said if she caught us moping. She never meant it how Seán had taken to it. She was right though, I needed a distraction to prevent me from curling into a useless ball. After a long, hot shower, I fired on my old slacks and took to cleaning the house. Saoirse could land home any day and God knew what she was coming home to. She'd not be expecting a red carpet, but being able to see the carpet might be a plus. The glass and blood shifted easy enough off the kitchen tiles compared to scrubbing the ingrained dirt. Jesus's Sacred Heart took a lashing of Fairy Liquid, as did the fridge door. Seeing the bullet hole put the fear of God in me. I slid the photo back in place, covering it. Righting the furniture, I vacuumed, bleached, polished, mopped. I even threw the kitchen curtains into the wash and near died when they came out white, not cream. After a few intensive hours' work it struck me with a heavy dose of irony that this was what my father did before a binge. An odd sanctification, like kneeling through Saturday night mass before getting plastered. I leaned on the fridge, reflecting. Maybe there was more of him in me than I cared to admit. The sudden crash of front door jolted me.

As I turned, a gun muzzle whacked the side of my skull. 'Where's the Tokarev?'

I blinked, taking in their two-tone army khaki, face-scarves and sunglasses as they twisted me to face them. A second blow to the temple and I crashed to the floor. The bleach from the tiles stung my eyes, but I recognized the shoes, even with the new laces. Gerry kicked me hard in the shin. 'Answer the question.'

'Where's the bloody pistol?' The second man had grey hair under his black beret and a Belfast twang to his voice that seemed vaguely familiar.

My head throbbed as I tried to stand. He slammed me backwards, dragging me up against the kitchen wall, hand choking my windpipe. My arms flailed. Useless. Nothing but a strangled gurgle escaped. Gerry grabbed my wrists and swung me hard into the doorframe.

'Jesus . . .' I gasped, heart racing.

The cold of the gun muzzle was thrust under my chin.

'Talk or get lead in your head.'

'There is no gun,' I shouted. Inside I was burning. *Holy Jesus. Ma.* 'Fuck off, Gerry!' I screamed and screwed my eyes tight. The punch floored me, arms and legs like jelly on the tiles.

'Let me cripple the bastard,' said Gerry. I could taste his rage.

'One more chance, lad. Where's the gun?' The older spoke calmly, like interrogation was old-school, his boot flat on my spine.

My brain spun and twisted like my limbs wriggling for an escape, blinded with panic. 'Don't shoot! Don't shoot! I did nothing. Nothing!'

'That gun was ours. OURS!' screamed Gerry. 'Still want to stand up to me? No chance.' I heard the click as he pulled back the top slide.

'That's lies. I—'

A kick in the jaw silenced me.

'Bite your arm, son,' said the older. 'Keep still.'

My fingernails dug at the grout under the fridge as the gun pressed hard behind my knee. Ready to shoot. A punishment attack. No trial. No appeal. I held my breath. Gritted my teeth. *God. Please God.* I twisted my head, the Sacred Heart magnet and the family photo blurring into my vision. *Ma.*

'Ages since I saw your old man.' The Belfast twang had followed my gaze.

I recognized the voice now from the pub. Maybe Da could still have his uses? 'I'll tell him you were asking for him,' I whispered.

'What'd you say?' He kicked me in the gut. I doubled up in pain.

'Liverpool.' I groaned. 'Phones most weeks. Talking of coming home.'

'Your da's coming back on the scene?' He hesitated.

'Am I shooting or what?' said Gerry. The gun rammed onto my joggers again as my knee twisted on the floor. A car horn beeped twice in the street. The explosion rang in my ears. I screamed and kept screaming, but I couldn't hear myself, gagging with the bitter smoke and voices everywhere. Racing. Shouting. Doors slamming – front and back. Radios with garbled voices. Muffled thuds. I felt nothing. Felt everything. Felt my feet. Both of them. I turned. Blood. Trickles of it, like shaving cuts. Shrapnel and dust had showered my joggers. I stared at my knees, then at the bullet hole in the tile beside them. The cartridge was still spinning on the kitchen floor as more cops invaded the house. The gun by my ankles where Gerry had dropped it.

Constable Rosie crouched in her uniform before me. I could see her talking. The same words over and over. Gradually my ears tuned in again to make sense of sound. The back door flapped. Commotion in the yard. Male voices . . . *right to remain silent . . .* radio static . . . *backup, backup . . . weapon on scene . . . one in custody . . . one AWOL . . . shot fired . . . ATO . . .*

'Are you OK?'

I turned to Rosie and nodded. 'How come you were here?' I asked.

'Fluke,' she said. 'We wanted to talk to you again about the gun.'

I groaned, pulling my knees tight to my heart and smothering my face in them.

'It's OK,' she said. 'We've the pistol and plenty of forensics right here. You've been through enough.'

The randomness of it was freaky. Chunks of time went missing. The handing over my clothes for DNA and gunshot residue. The crossing the street to sit in a neighbour's while the Bomb Squad and Land Rovers took over our terrace. Other images burned into my brain in fine detail. The acrid whiff of the damp patch on Gerry's jeans as they shoved him through the kitchen in cuffs. The back-to-front collar on the padded olive suit of the Army technical officer. The neighbours reminiscing like old hands about raids and police procedures, as I tranced out to cartoons on their sofa. Hours passed while the police did forensics. They offered me casualty. Victim support. Asked to take a statement. No. No. And No. My brain was mangled. The cops, the community, everyone wanted this done before dark. Otherwise they were risking riots. I wanted . . . I didn't know what I wanted anymore.

Later, when the police had gone, the neighbour walked me back across the street. Every step was Christmas. Through my own door. The miracle of two intact knees. Into my own kitchen. The magnet was still there, fixed over the bullet hole, gripping Nan's photo. Sacred Heart of Jesus, my da and the police – the unholy trinity of my salvation.

'You could eat your dinner off the floor,' the neighbour announced. 'Cops left a right mess, but you can't beat the Creggan women for the oul' cleaning.' They'd even filled the kettle. Maybe a strong coffee was what I wanted.

I was stirring it for the millionth time, my gaze flitting between the bullet hole in the floor and Da's face in the photo on the fridge, when I froze, hearing a key in the front door.

'Bloody hell! We expecting royalty?'

I couldn't have predicted how I'd have greeted my brother. Ten thousand scenarios and as many emotions had whirred through my mind, tangling with the rest of the chaos. In the moment, it was simply instinctive. I leaned against the kitchen doorframe as he loitered in his leather jacket and jeans at the end of the hall. It didn't need words. It was all there in that look we shared, bridging the silence. He was exhausted; shoulders hung low, black rings under his eyes. Wrecked, like he'd crossed mountain ranges to be stood there in front of me. His eyes spoke of a story he'd never tell. I was too tired for anger. We were brothers. Family.

'Kettle's boiled,' I said.

Relief flooded his face. We hugged in the hallway, slapping each other on the back then breaking like true Derry men who daren't show too much emotion.

'I'm so bloody sorry, Aidan. So, so sorry.'

They'd released him without charge. No call to hold him. They had a gun, a shooter, police witnesses, forensics and their own walls had given Seán an armour-plated alibi. Paddy appeared in the doorway minutes later. He'd collected Seán from near the police station and frog-marched him straight home. If he hadn't, my brother would've been drinking a river in the nearest pub. As it was, he went upstairs to sleep. Paddy accepted coffee, but not for purposes of small talk.

'They got Gerry,' I said.

'On his own head be it.'

241

'The other shooter, I knew his voice. I know who he is.'

He nodded. We talked. Like father to son he drilled me in do's and don'ts, promises and procedures; not a lecture but a life jacket.

'Not a word to anyone, kiddo. I'll talk to them. Vouch for you. They know me. Some of them owe me from days gone by.' Before leaving, he hugged me tight.

'Keep your cool, kiddo. Your Seán's a different kettle, but you've a wise head on you. I'll sort it. You'll be OK.'

I slid down the wall in our hallway after he clicked the door behind him. I was still a wreck, but with Paddy's reassurances I'd enough healing to hang on to.

At dusk, I heard my brother stir and brought him cup-a-soup and toast. 'Mind if I ask you something?' I said. My voice sounded smaller than usual.

'Fire away. I won't guarantee an answer though.'

'You still want to be involved? Like, you've obviously made a conscious choice. Any regrets?'

'Think I'd have been drowning myself in drink and drugs if this was a walk in the park?'

'I don't know what to think anymore. So why not leave?'

'Can't. I'm sworn in. Think I didn't try when they started talking about you?'

'The Ra used to let people buy themselves out. Not everyone, but if you weren't in that long . . . if you didn't know too much . . .'

'June. I only joined in June. Three thousand quid to leave. You got that in your back pocket?' He flopped on the bed. 'Cash . . . or a gun.'

I stared. And stared. 'It was you all along?'

He nodded. 'Saoirse's idea. She said offer them a gun instead of the money. They were up for it too. She remembered the walk

242

with Da. Reckoned you'd find it.'

'Christ . . . Couldn't you just have asked?'

'Saoirse said to, but I didn't reckon you'd get it for me. Not after Strabane. So I figured I'd try it different. I told Shannon the New IRA would be interested in hearing she'd drugged you at a party. That it was her fault you got beat up. That there was plenty I could say about her . . . But that I'd say nothing if she did me a favour.'

'You blackmailed her?'

'Didn't take much – implying a threat, bribing her with a few tabs. Easy carrot-and-stick stuff.'

'Jesus. Manipulation and abuse more like. Two-faced as well. Makes sense why she's so wired now.'

'Look, I needed the gun. Besides, she was so up for the acting anyway, I reckon she missed her Hollywood calling.'

'Why?' I asked. 'Like, I said sorry for the party – even though *she* drugged *me*.'

'You lied to her. Two-timed her.'

'Not true.'

'You were in Belfast with Iona. Told Shannon you were on your own.'

'Christ Almighty . . .' I tipped my head against the wall. No matter which way I looked at it, my life was screwed. 'Why'd you join in the first place?' I whispered.

'Look at me. I've nothing. I'm out of school years and the best I've ever got is some part-time dead-end job that finishes after a couple of months. It's shit, the dole sending you on placement after placement for a tenner a week more than your benefits. There's nothing here. I just wanted to feel alive; part of something; make a difference . . . I don't know. I was bored mindless. They understood. They wanted me.'

I stared at the wallpaper as if it held the solution. He crunched his toast.

'What if we just leave? Go someplace else? Like Saoirse did.'

'You should,' he mumbled through a mouthful of crust. 'In fact, if you don't, I'll hound you personally until you do. Go to Australia or New Zealand. The States. Canada. Everyone's leaving these days. It's not for me though.' He blew over his soup.

'Would they take instalments?'

'Are you off your head?'

'No. I could pull together a hundred from painting. Three thousand's not impossible if we both worked at it a year. I'm not leaving you in this. I'll cut grass, clean windows, wash cars – whatever. You'd be a good spark – mechanics, electrical stuff – you used to rave about it . . .'

'Yeah and look where that got me when other people found out . . . Look, if there was a simple solution, I'd have found it. Trust me. Anything to get out of the torture of this last month.' He reached into his bedside drawer and pulled out cigarette papers, loose tobacco and dope. It wasn't unusual. I'd watched him roll dope hundreds of times. 'Let me ask *you* something. Most stuff I said last night was probably exaggerated shite, but what about Iona? You still together? If you are, that's bloody complex.'

My head hung limp. 'You honestly think I could still see her now, after all this?'

For once he didn't offer me a drag of the spliff. He didn't need to. It had been a hell of a day. No, it was me who gestured for it. Me who inhaled deeply and lay back waiting for it to kick in.

Chapter 35. Melancholy.

IONA.
Thursday 18 August.

I didn't care that it was 5 p.m. and that I was still in my PJs skulking around the house. My brain was bubblegum; I couldn't think. It was warped that I'd decided to defy John's ultimatum only for Aidan to meet it. Part of me longed to spill my guts to Mum. She'd switch on her therapist mode and bring pepperoni pizza. But it felt like everything was way too complicated.

Results day was meant to be brilliant. Instead, I couldn't see my bedroom carpet for crumpled tissues. I wanted to kill him. I kept switching my phone off to banish him from my life, then minutes later switching it back on in case I missed his call. Within the first hours of his message my fingers were sore from speed dialling and texting, my head aching. Something had happened, for sure. The last time we'd been together we'd carved our initials on the tree. I'd scrolled through all his messages since then – no sign of any change of heart. He had even finished the 'It's over' message with a kiss.

Surely he was messing? Had someone hacked his phone for a joke? When he didn't reply I'd paced around, hugging myself, tears welling. Was it his results? Maybe he'd looked them up online early and was crushed. Over and over I kept phoning but it always rang out, then went to voicemail. Despite the state of my heart, there'd been no choice but to go into school for results. By late morning Aidan's phone wasn't even ringing. I'd switched to messenger so I could see if he read my messages. Nothing.

Rachel had found me in the school toilets. I'd tried to put a brave face on collecting my results; my ticket to Queen's. I'd smiled, masking how I felt. I'd chatted with friends; done the group hugs, posted the selfies online, and then the not knowing about Aidan had become overwhelming. The instant I locked the cubicle the tears flooded. Hand over my mouth, I'd tried to stifle the sobs, wondering how long it would take to muster enough dignity to flee.

'It'll be fine,' Rachel had tried to reassure me. She'd give him a piece of her mind. Typical bloody bloke. I deserved better.

I argued. He wasn't 'just like Kyle'. I didn't want it to be 'his loss'. I wanted to talk to Aidan; hear *him* say it, *his* voice. He'd have had the decency at least not to dump me by text. *Why? Had he really only been after one thing?* He had been gorgeous. The way we talked, the way he held me, the way we kissed. He had a warm soul. I could still sense him with me; the smooth of his lips; the dark tones of his hair and eyes, the scent of his aftershave, his hands and body pressing against mine. We couldn't be broke up. If we were, I'd trust the Agony Aunt horoscopes quicker than men the next time. I hated love.

Only the walls of the house had witnessed me drag myself in with my results page. I had swallowed deep, practised speaking, then phoned my parents. We'd celebrated over the airwaves, excited for me to go to university. Sure, I was heading up the town with friends – see you later.

It was Andy, first home, who'd discovered me floundering in the ocean of Kleenex and hate-the-world rock tracks, firing carpet fluff at my feet.

'What's the story? Thought you aced it? Two As, a B and a C? Wasn't that what you needed?'

I slammed the door in his face. Footsteps down and back up the stairs; a tentative knock and he appeared with Maltesers and sidled onto the edge of the bed. I accepted his offering, wishing he'd brought WKD with it. I didn't want to talk. I did want his opinion. Initially he had narrowed his eyebrows and swore at the phone when I showed him Aidan's message. He bear-hugged me. Then he'd studied the text again.

'Cold comfort I guess, and you two freaked me at the start . . .' he said with a brotherly dig in the ribs, ' . . . but I liked him. He seemed decent. I thought he really liked you. Nothing else happened?'

Something else did happen just then. Dad's car engine cut in the driveway. The driver's door banged and the front door followed in quick succession. Dad surged up the stairs two at a time and barged into my room.

'John's been on the phone. Andy, out. I need to talk to Iona. Now.'

Chapter 36. Pain.

AIDAN.
Saturday 20 August.

I'd woken up on Friday morning with a pounding headache and serious cotton mouth. *Never again.* I wasn't sure if the best move was to drink the Foyle or jump in it. My own fault. As I'd tried to wash away the brain fog under a cold shower, I knew I was at a crossroads. I was capable of seriously bad choices. I turned up the temperature, leaned back against the cold white tiles and let out a deep sigh into the building steam. My head split the spray of water in different directions and I'd watched the drips trickle down the glass doors to the foam of shower gel at my feet, wrestling my thoughts. *Not this time*, I'd decided. *Not this time.*

I'd grabbed a towel; it would have been so easy to let them win. That's the course my brother seemed to have chosen, waiting on the sidelines, a marked man in a belch of cigarette smoke on the sofa. If they'd been in contact, I wasn't aware of it, not that I really wanted to know. Appealing as wiping myself out with drink was, I made a conscious choice as the water bounced off my skin – *feel the pain, Hennessey.* I didn't mean physical pain. It wasn't even the horror of what happened with Seán, or the dissidents. It was that I missed her. *Chronic.* I missed her so badly I ached every time I thought of her, which was every, bloody, minute. Tears were a non-starter: they had to be, or they might never stop. Instead I was going to follow the pattern that Saoirse had instilled in me. Exercise. Eat. Sleep. Repeat. That's why I'd got my feet out pounding the pavements again, even if it had felt like a Lambeg was drumming in my skull.

This morning the air was fresh, and being Saturday, half of Creggan was still asleep as my earphones pulsed playlist beats. Perspiration rivered through my hair, sweat soaking my T-shirt. *Find your feet, Hennessey. Find your fight.* Losing myself in the physicality of it would keep me from meltdown if I could just break through into that zone where I ran beyond feeling. I needed that void where I moved free, hearing my heart, feeling the cool intake of air from my nose, hitting my lungs like liquid gold, the exhale of warm air through my mouth. I ran wherever my feet took me, the loop of Iniscairn Road, Circular Road, Creggan Heights, through the neat rows of terrace houses with drawn curtains. Doubling back by Central Drive, I swore I heard my name shouted. Slowing, removing one of the earphones, I heard it again, and copped him smoking by the cube frontage of the Old Library Trust. I stopped in my tracks and blinked. Christ. It was him, beckoning me over.

'You lost? Last place I expected you,' I said, catching my breath and wiping the sweat off my forehead. This was my backyard, not his.

'Free country last time I checked,' Andy jibed back.

'Ireland or Britain?' I exhaled, hands on my hips.

He grinned. 'I'm on a training course. For doing door work. It's free. Condition of cross-community funding that they got a few of us Prods onto it as well as your lot.'

'You want to be a bouncer?'

'Qualifies me for other things too – like marshalling parades.' He winked as he stubbed out the cigarette. 'And if you're ever asked, I don't smoke and I wasn't here. Mum would have a fit at one. Dad the other.'

I wiped my palms on my shorts. We stared at each other, neither of us sure whether to risk the unspoken conversation. It was bloody raw. *Could I even speak about it? Could he?* I'd bounced back from other girls. This was different. Each day was worse. The reality of it kicking in more brutally than I'd imagined possible.

'What's up?' he ventured.

'Nothing much.'

'No. Like really. What happened? It's like you broke my sister. She won't talk. She's holed up in her room, avoiding everyone. Why'd you give up?'

I looked at him bleakly. God. The moment he said it my throat tightened and my voice failed. I stepped back, trying to steady my breathing. 'You know my da was in the IRA? He did time. You must know. Your brother knew, right?'

Andy nodded, eyes shifting.

'I never told Iona,' I said. 'Does she know?'

He shook his head. We dipped closer.

'My brother got arrested. Did you hear that too? He wasn't charged. Just questioned . . . dissident stuff.' I stopped before my voice shook too much. It was impossible to hold Andy's gaze now. I'd no idea what he was thinking as I kicked the rubber front of my trainer off the pavement.

'What about you?' he whispered.

My eyes connected straight with his. There was no hatred there. I shook my head and sucked in air. 'They almost shot me. I'm not involved, Andy. I swear. Never have been, never will be. Get real, though – you think that makes one ounce of difference to what your family think of me?'

'It makes a difference to my sister.'

My voice stuck. I looked to the clouds and swallowed.

'Could you tell her . . .' I stalled again, choking on emotion.

'Could you tell her I'm sorry. I didn't mean for this . . . Look, just tell her I said she's beautiful. She'll know. Tell her hold her head high. Be herself. She's better without me. Just tell her I'm sorry; that I'd no choice, will you? Please?'

I turned away from him, knotting my hands to the back of my head, throat burning.

'I was right. You are sound, Aidan Hennessey. She misses you like crazy.'

Those were the words I held on to, almost despite myself, as I walked into our kitchen thinking I would at least try to kid myself into enjoying breakfast. When, for the second time that week, my brother was lying on the floor. This time he was unconscious; the last of the three empty paracetamol packets cradled in his hand and a handwritten scrap on the table.

I thought of a way to fix it.

Chapter 37. Bubbles.

IONA.
Sunday 21 August.

If it wasn't for the influence of preachers and therapists on my parents, there'd have been champagne not Shloer in the glasses. I could hardly bring myself to be there, the smile Sellotaped to my face.

'A proud moment, son,' said Dad.

'Wonderful your first case being a success,' added Mum.

John and I joined the chinking of crystal, bubbles and smiles, hiding daggers in our glares. I'd a feeling that John and Dad knew something more about Aidan's family than I did. The grief Dad had given me over Aidan didn't fully make sense otherwise. Maybe I was missing part of the picture. Then again, so was Dad – he still didn't know about the attack in the park. Andy, John and I'd all be in for it if he knew about that.

Dead if you dare sink me about covering for you and Andy.

Tout. Lording it over my love life. Don't think this is done.

'And here's to Queen's, Iona.' Mum raised her glass again.

'You've earned it, pet,' said Dad.

'Loads of nice men in the university Christian Union, I hear,' nudged Mum.

Andy wrinkled his nose. 'No toast for me?' He winked.

'Your day will come,' said Dad.

Tiocfaidh ár lá, my head replied. Our day will come. The only sentence I knew in Irish. Aidan had smirked at my efforts to say it. I'd splurted my Coke at the spelling. We'd laughed. The memory of it ached. Adults remembered our past. Would they ever remember our future? Smothering the frustration of it building in my gut was harder by the hour. Would our day ever come?

Chapter 38. Family.

AIDAN.
Monday 22 August.

The days blurred. The only saving grace was that I'd found him soon enough. After an eternity of frantic searching, I'd found his mobile stuffed down the sofa and dialled 999. In A&E, the paramedics had swarmed like bluebottles. Dazed, I'd watched as they pumped his stomach and pumped me for questions until I had no more answers to give. He had been admitted onto a ward, hooked up to a drip and roused enough to stare like the living-dead before zonking out.

I'd drained his credit almost dry leaving international voicemails. I needed someone, anyone. Where was Saoirse when I couldn't see the fan for the shite? Paddy's number eluded me without my phone. I'd debated calling my aunt but there was a limit to the 'anyone' category. Instead I'd spent the night in my running gear, a twisted knot in a ripped green armchair, with a thin blanket wrapped over me. I don't know why they didn't kick me off his bedside vigil.

I'd been sipping milky lukewarm tea that tasted like piss when Seán came round the next morning. It had been like a role-reversed déjà vu from June. They'd questioned him, handed me the leaflets and I'd got us the taxi home. As we'd stood on the doorstep, me fumbling for the key in the zipped pocket of my running shorts, the front door opened. Miracles. My knees buckled and I fell into Saoirse's bear hug, uttering a 'Thanks be to

God' before collapsing zombified onto the sofa. I could hardly believe she was back.

Seán was still sleeping upstairs, despite having spent all day yesterday in bed, and Saoirse and I were lounging around the living room in slacks watching Monday morning TV, talking for the first time. Her body clock was out of kilter with the jet lag and I was rough as sandpaper. Sleeping on the sofa had made me stink of smoke, but I wanted Saoirse to have my room. It felt like I was having hallucinations, waking up to her sitting cross-legged in the armchair, red wavy hair tied up behind her head like Ma.

'Mind when we were kids and we used to fight over the stupidest things?' I yawned. 'Like nabbing the last cola ice pole? I wish we could rewind; that we didn't have to be grown up. The way Ma would click her fingers and have it sorted.'

'It's going to be fine, Aidan. Trust me.'

She'd used those words before. She wasn't a saint, but she was my sister; always exuding calm, seeing the possible. Like Ma. Like Iona. My migraine had gone but not all the questions.

'What about Seán?'

'Give him time. He'll get there. More to the point, what about you? Seán couldn't even tell me your exam results, but he did say you're cut over your girlfriend.'

'When were you talking?'

'Middle of the night. Couldn't sleep. Heard him awake. He's mad guilty over it. Says you really liked her . . .' Her dark brown eyes looked me over.

'Can't believe you got him to talk.'

After all this time she could still read me. War and peace. There was no point trying to disguise the hurt.

'CV the length of my arm in getting brothers to talk. Leastways, it worked with one of you . . . So, if you won't talk about your girl, what about the exams?' She winked, acknowledging my evasion.

'Straight As.'

'I knew you were adopted. Seriously? You're a bloody brainbox. So what's next?'

I shrugged. 'Clear as muck. Gap year maybe. Paddy's been good. I'll probably stick with that.'

'Da's mate Paddy? From when we were kids?'

'Guess so. Wouldn't have known him in a line-up but he knew me. Think I was just a wean.'

'Must grab a chat with him.' She frowned, thinking.

'Why?' I raised my eyebrows.

'Many reasons. Seán for a start. I also need to convince him to release my wee brother from minimum-wage cash-in-hand work so that he'll think properly about his future. I need my bump to have at least one functioning uncle as a role model when it arrives . . .'

It took a long moment for what she said to really filter into my consciousness, then I sat bolt upright, staring.

'You're pregnant?'

'Four and a half months. I'm due around Christmas. Virgin birth, obviously.' She smiled. 'Fix your face before the wind changes.'

'Like, what do I say? Congratulations? Who's the da? How are you about it all?'

'I'm fine, Aidan. I'm twenty-two. It wasn't exactly planned but it's not the end of the world either. Ma had me when she was nineteen, mind? Least you handled it better than Seán. He was all joking about being up the duff and buns in the oven. Rafael's the da. Argentinian. Double of Che Guevara. Guess I bought more than the T-shirt.'

'Is he here? Are you still together?' I asked, trying to compute.

'No and not exactly, though I wouldn't completely rule it out. Seems he's taking their "Don't Cry for Me" anthem to heart. Only told him six weeks ago. He might test the waters if he can sort the plane fare and visa. If he doesn't, I'll live with it. Be chuffed for me, Aidan, please. I'm freaked but wild excited too. I'll need a human shield when I tell Teresa – she'll be hell-bent on bringing back the Magdalene Laundries.'

I grinned wide, rubbing away the remnants of sleep and stretching off the sofa. 'Some chance me persuading Aunt Teresa you're a saint. Coffee before I clear my room? No hope fighting you over it now.'

My sister's optimism was infectious, but it had limits. Waiting for the kettle, my head chewed over our fortunes; her news, the mess with Seán and the cut of my heart. Did Iona still think about me?

Chapter 39. Choices.

IONA.
Tuesday 23 August.

'What's the point in peace if you still *think* like we're at war? At least let me think for myself.' I'd said it under my breath, but they'd all heard it. They were meant to. There was a clink as my father set down his fork. Andy kicked me under the table. We knew how this worked and it never ended well, not unless you apologized and admitted he was absolutely right, as always. I gritted my teeth but refused to look up.

'What did you say?' He'd never quite lost that clipped military tone.

Mum did one of her fake happy sighs. 'She's just tired, honey. Aren't you, darling? Away upstairs. I'll clear up.'

Lifting my head, my eyes locked with Dad's. 'I said, I'm eighteen. You've got to let me make my own choices.'

His hand twitched.

'And you can, darling, you can.' Mum tried to mediate. 'You're choosing university, you're choosing English, you're . . .'

'I mean Aidan.'

My brother stuffed another forkful of mash into his mouth like chewing it made him invisible. Dad sipped water, eyeballing me. It was building; we were already past the point of no return.

'Sweetie, he's not even a proper Christian.' Mum's eyes pleaded with me.

'Aye, just like that's not sectarian.'

The glass slammed onto the table, sending the coaster flying.

'Iona. Apologize to your mother this instant. And you listen here . . .'

'No. I won't. You listen. All my life it's been, *Don't upset your daddy, tiptoe on glass, say nowt.* We're stuck in the same old tune forever . . .'

'In the Troubles . . .'

'Don't you get it, Dad? The Troubles are over. And Mum, just so you know, Aidan's more of a Christian than half the sweet boys singing on Sundays. He's just –' I struggled for the right words – 'he's just honest about it.'

'Honest?' Dad roared, standing and thumping the table with his fist, making the cutlery rattle. 'Honest in how he forgot to mention his dad and brother were terrorists?'

'What?' I said, staring at Dad.

'You heard me,' he sneered. 'He'll tell you he loves you but won't tell you where his real loyalties lie?'

'And what?' I said, head spinning. 'Maybe I did wonder about his dad, but Aidan's not like that. Just because you and John have guns, doesn't mean I do.'

'Enough. That. Is. Out. Of. Order.'

'He told me,' Andy said.

We stared at him. He gulped, then continued.

'And he told me you're beautiful and swore he's not in the New IRA. I believe him. Iona's right – you can't stop her. You let John choose the police and me choose a band, even though you hate it.' He stood, shaking, but equalling Dad's height. 'Bet you didn't know two of my mates nearly killed him in June just because he's Catholic, or that he ditched the evidence and never pressed charges to protect us! Ask John.'

'I am not hearing this!' Dad shouted, throwing his glass across the kitchen.

Mum froze.

For once, I was having the last word. 'You'll never hear if you're scared to listen.'

Chapter 40. Disillusionment.

AIDAN.
Wednesday 24 August.

'Hi, Nan!' I began hopefully.

Her once red locks of hair curled silver around her wrinkled face, but today she was a young woman again, in her mind at least. I had found her sagged in an armchair staring out the bay window up the corridor.

'Aren't you a fine lad,' she responded. 'Are you waiting for the bus too?'

'Remember me, Nan? It's Aidy. Aibhlinn's son?'

'Sure my Aibhlinn's just a lass. She'll make a fine mammy someday, but not yet, lad.'

You saved my life with a photo and you've forgotten my face. She was always happy, lost in the past. Like her heart rooted out the good memories and buried the bad. Priceless. I tended to play along in her sepia-tinted time warp. I nattered on, figuring maybe she'd find her way back as we talked.

'All's grand at home, Nan.'

Christ, you could do a PhD in what folk really meant when they said that. *I'm sleeping on my own sofa; Derry feels like a life-sentence; throw me a line – I'm drowning.*

'Smooth bus ride today.'

We've lost the car. Saoirse made Seán give it back. 'Seán says hi.' *He overdosed, nearly said bye.*

I chatted as I led her by the hand, back to her room where her

261

dinner was waiting by the bed. She went quiet. At least the banter was back in our house. As the three of us had sat up to stupid hours goggle-boxing some two-star flick on Monday night, I'd fired in the curveball.

'Did ye's know Granda Michael was Protestant?'

'Wind yer neck in. He was Catholic,' said Seán.

'He wasn't. He converted. Nan told me.' I'd kicked my shoes off the sofa.

'Nan must've been in Wonderland when she told you that.'

'I knew,' said Saoirse. 'Ma told me.'

Seán had tried to argue black was white but my sister held her ground.

As I sat with the threadbare recliner pulled up close to Nan's bed, it didn't matter a button what religion Granda had been. I wondered was Nan for joining him anytime soon or for staying suspended between worlds for years yet. Did they have peace walls in heaven? She leaned forward for the next spoonful of champ. I fed her again, smiling reassurance.

'I know your face, young man. Do I know your mother?' She paused mid-chew.

'I'm your grandson, Nan. Your Aibhlinn's son . . . but don't worry about it. Here – fish finger?'

Her brow wrinkled as she trawled through elusive memory banks. 'I have you! You were here before – with a young lassie! Does she work here too?'

'No, she doesn't work here but yeah, you're right. She was here.'

'Your wife?'

I shook my head. It was a wearing conversation on so many different levels. 'I'm too young to be married. Do you mind your wedding day with Granda?'

'Lordy, how could anyone forget their wedding day? The band played Glenn Miller and we danced! You're not too young to be married. What are you? Twenty-five? You should ask her.'

'Eighteen, Nan . . . That bird's flown.' I fed her an extra-large spoonful of beans. Nan's dinners put me in mind of the free school meals you got when your family was broke. If I kept talking, she might just listen and keep eating.

'Seán's asking for you – sends his love. Saoirse's home too. Mind my sister? She's back from globe-trotting. Imagine she'll visit you soon. You'll know her when you see her. The spit of your Aibhlinn. And she has news! There's going to be a new arrival – another wee Hennessey. You'll be a great-grandparent by Christmas, Nan, and I'm—'

'She's what?' Aunt Teresa interrupted from the open doorway. I dropped the spoon with a clatter.

'She's pregnant!' Nan celebrated with a joyous clap.

Aunt Teresa and I exchanged a glance. I wasn't sure how long she'd been standing there, or whether my nan was back in the room with us or still in cloud cuckoo land. The shock on my aunt's face couldn't have been worse if I'd been up the duff myself. Maybe it was a double blow that I was the last person in the world she'd expected to find feeding her mother.

'Lost track of time. Bus soon. I'll be off.' I jumped off the chair and leaned to kiss Nan's cheek. 'Bye.'

'There's a bus stop just there,' Nan said, gesturing vaguely in the direction of the bay window up the corridor where I'd found her earlier.

'Aidan. Sit. Wait. I'll give you a lift back to Derry.' For once, my aunt managed a string of sentences without a condemnatory note. She even smiled, but only in so far as to indicate it was an order, not an option. It would be a grilling. A twenty-minute journey-cum-interrogation. I messed with my phone. It was a miracle it had sparked into life when I'd reassembled it. I should've logged it towards my sainthood. As the minutes ticked, I folded my arms tighter, fidgeting, withdrawing into a ball of numbness. A lecture was the last thing in the world I wanted. There'd be a barrage of questions I either couldn't, shouldn't or didn't have the heart to answer. A cold knot coiled in my gut.

'So, let me get this straight.' My aunt began the cross-examination now we were alone in her car, Nan left snugged, hugged and fed. 'Seán was questioned over dissident activity. That's what your fight was about? You were nearly shot and Seán attempted suicide? Saoirse's home but no one told me because she's pregnant? Anything else I should know? You never talked about what happened in June . . .' She tapered off and went quiet.

What struck me wasn't what she said, but her tone. She wasn't angry. It was a mixture of exasperation and hurt. But for that, I wouldn't have answered at all. 'Ask them, not me.' I scratched at the upholstery on the car door and drew smudges on the window. I was tired of life dealing shit hands; if this was as good as it got, maybe it was time to stop playing. My feet kicked the car mat. She glanced between me and the road.

'I didn't know you still visited my mother,' she said, lost in a different train of thought.

'Mad that, when you know me so well,' I jibed back.

'Aidan, for God's sake cut me some slack. I'm trying to understand what on earth's going on in my family!'

'Your family?' I sniped.

'What, you think I don't care?'

'Do you?'

'You're my sister's kids, for crying out loud. Of course I care! I just didn't realize . . . Oh, I don't know. I can't juggle everything.'

'Didn't know we were a circus act,' I sulked.

'Enough!' she shouted in frustration at the windscreen. I shut up. Fine by me to travel in icy silence. To put my earphones in might have been pushing it, but I could stare out the window till the cows came home. The blackberry brambles whizzing past at the roadside were laden with their first fruit of the season. We used to pick blackberries every year with Ma and make jam, bubbling thick, gloopy and syrupy in the pot. We'd argue over licking the spoon; the saucepan was the jackpot. Sometimes when we'd got home from school in September, she'd have made a blackberry and apple pie with custard. At Halloween it had always been a special apple pie with lucky charms hidden in it for superstition. 'A penny for poverty, pound for a chance, thimble for work, a ring for romance.'

Saoirse was always mad for the ring. Sean and I had vied tooth and nail to find the pound coin.

'Didn't you get A-level results the other day?' my aunt asked, breaking the silence. I nodded, gazing at the passing hills and blue-green seascapes of Inishowen. 'How'd you get on?' she pressed, trying to get a conversation going.

'Straight As.' I rubbed my nose. It made no difference what I'd got. I was who I was. That was that.

'Straight As?' I could feel her eyes swinging between me and the road. She slowed. Gravel crunched. She pulled in at a viewpoint on the Wild Atlantic Way and switched off the engine.

'Aidan Hennessey. You're serious, aren't you? Straight As? You'd nothing on Facebook. You didn't phone! How'd you celebrate?'

I shrugged. Celebrating had felt as relevant as the Ten Commandments in a brothel.

'Aidan!' she thumped the steering wheel. 'Look at me! What's going on?'

I turned. There was something unexpected about her look that reminded me of Ma. She was concerned. She didn't have the same shock of long wavy red hair framing her face, but her eyes . . .

'I'm sorry, all right?' I gulped before turning away, seeking some obscure point across the windswept landscape.

'Aidan?'

'I'm sorry I always screw up. Sorry I brought the police to your door. Sorry for all that stuff I said that morning; for kicking off at you; for my language in front of your girls. Sorry for all the times I threw up on your carpets or caused havoc. Sorry I'm a constant disappointment. Sorry I wasn't strong enough to hold it all together . . . And I'm sorry I remind you of Da, just by walking into the room. I can't help it. You remind me of Ma.'

'Look at me.' She spoke softly.

I could see the wetness in her eyes, the drawn look on her face.

Her lower lip trembled. 'You were only fifteen, Aidan. *Fifteen.* You weren't the one who was supposed to be able to hold it together. I was the adult. I'm sorry. I let you down. I let your mother down. I miss her too.'

I pulled a knee up to my chin. For once she didn't bark at me over shoes on the car seat. 'It's OK,' was all I could say after a minute.

'It's not though, is it? Even setting aside the bigger picture, you got straight As in your exams and not a single family member asked or celebrated it with you? It's not fine that I've under-estimated you; grown so out of touch that I haven't noticed you've changed! Did you expect to do so well? Have you plans?'

I was getting sick of people asking me that question, as if I had any real choices.

'Painting and decorating. I'm good at it.' I gazed out the windows again. I wasn't used to my aunt, or any adults for that matter, being so interested. I bit my thumb. If I left the car I'd just walk and keep walking to somewhere, anywhere.

'Aidan.'

'What?' I groaned.

'Did you apply to university? Have you offers?'

'Yeah. They're online. Don't know when they expire, but it's irrelevant. I can't take them. Can't afford it.'

'Where did you want to go?'

'Queen's.'

'To study what?'

'Politics and Conflict Studies.'

'Who's your principal? Who should I talk to in your school?'

I shrugged. 'Any of them. Mr Ó Súilleabháin maybe.'

My will to communicate had exhausted itself. If Aunt Teresa wanted to try to sort out my life, she was welcome. I'd given up. 'Can we just go?' I asked her before she could delve any deeper into my disillusionment.

She started the engine again and rejoined the dual carriageway, but she hadn't finished with me yet. 'So, who's the girl Nan mentioned?'

'Doesn't matter. It's over. We split.' *Just bloody shut up and leave me alone.*

'Sorry to hear that.'

'Me too.' *End of.*

'Did she break up with you then?'

'No.'

'Doesn't sound like you wanted to break up with her?'

'No.'

'That doesn't make sense. Why'd you break up then?'

267

'Just.' She wasn't getting the message at all. My throat burned. My whole chest was tight. Having family be interested wasn't all it was cut out to be. 'Just,' I repeated.

'What's her name?'

Jesus. Kick me in the balls. She was clueless.

'Iona,' I whispered, almost inaudibly. Any other time I'd broken up with a girl I'd have been fine by now. This was a different league. Each morning I woke up, crap as before, and pulled the duvet back over my head. I wasn't coping because I didn't *want* to cope. I didn't want it to be over. I wanted her back. I gritted my teeth and pulled my other knee up on the car seat, burying my head into my jeans and hoping my aunt would quit questioning. She got the message. *I should send another one – an SOS in a bloody bottle.* My circumstances hadn't changed. Seán was a mess. I was a wreck. Saoirse was reassuring but no magician. Feck 'feeling the pain'. It was murder. It was practically *all* I was feeling, every day.

Did Iona miss me? Did she hate my guts? I'd dumped her by text. *Chronic.* If I'd looked at my phone once, I'd looked at it fifty times, trying to summon the courage to call her to apologize and then talking myself out of it because I was scared it could open a whole can of worms. More scared still that she'd diss me completely. Freaked that I'd put her family in danger. *It can't get worse.* The thought clicked a switch. I just decided. *Feck it.* Since I couldn't ask Iona back, I'd do the next best thing. She at least deserved an explanation. She deserved to understand that it really wasn't her. Just me. I scrunched my face, wiping my palms on the seat belt as I thought it through over and over before asking Aunt Teresa. 'Could you do me a favour?'

'I'll try.'

'Drop me to the Waterside? Kilfennan? Save me a taxi fare?'

Chapter 41. Doorbells.

IONA.
Wednesday 24 August.

I whacked the guitar strings as I contemplated dying my hair purple, or blue. They'd notice me then. Was it even possible to be grounded at eighteen? I'd handle it today for Mum's sake. Not like I'd anywhere else to be. If we'd still been together, it would've been two months this week. A whole summer. My best summer. Ever. He'd been different. Was there 'the one'? I twisted the peg on the bottom E string; strumming so hard had knocked it out of tune. 'All things work together for good,' Mum had said. There was nothing bloody good about this. Crap. I was even starting to think the way he talked. Me, trying to be all positive, singing worship songs; miracles, trust, faith. It wasn't exactly mirroring how I felt. My eyes were Halloween-bloodshot; my hair limp and unloved.

The A string snapped and sprang out with a twang that scratched my finger. Dropping the guitar, I curled back on my bed and sucked the blood. Nothing was working, not even music. Downstairs, below my window, the doorbell rang, but I didn't budge. Dad's footsteps marched along the hall floorboards to the front door. At first there was a lull, like no one was there. Then I heard a voice, *his* voice, an uncertain edge ringing to it in the stilted conversation. I jerked upright.

'Erm . . . Hi. I'm Aidan. Is Iona in? Could I talk with her a minute?'

Dad's sarge-in-charge voice rang out a response that, judging from the hesitation that followed, shook Aidan as much as me.

'You look scarily like him you know.'

'Like who?'

'Like your father!'

I heard Aidan's two steps backwards on our gravel path even before I reached the window to peer out the blinds. He was stood, hands stuffed deep in his pockets.

'You knew my da?' he asked, colour draining from his face.

'Wouldn't say *knew*; I met him. Once. Arrested him, to be specific.'

Aidan shuffled further away, gaze lowered to where his feet toyed with the loose stones. 'Jesus . . .' he exclaimed, his voice faltering into nothing. My heart went out to him. I reminded myself to breathe. The uncertainty, the fear, flitted across his deep brown eyes and furrowed expression. Silence. I couldn't see my father in the porch, but since the terse conversation he'd had with me, he was generating all the positivity of a black hole.

Aidan's hands grasped the sides of his head; eyes wide. He folded his arms, trying not to shake. I desperately wanted to touch him. It was torture watching from the sidelines. 'No contact,' Dad had ordered me. 'No phoning, no texting, no nothing.' I was still fuming, but Aidan had broken it off with me, maybe there was no point.

'Leave. Now. I'm sure you understand why,' instructed Dad.

Aidan nodded, biting his lower lip; desolation mixed with pent-up anger on his face. I watched as he turned and strode away. The front door closed. Out the window he was pacing in his ripped jeans and black V-neck. He marched to the end of the street, then plonked himself on a low wall, head buried in his hands, heels kicking off the brickwork. Footsteps downstairs as my father returned to the kitchen. My mother's muffled voice in concerned conversation. I collapsed onto my bed and had my head shoved under the pillow when the doorbell rang a second time. My father shouted and his footsteps thumped. I leaped. My face hugged the blinds and I prayed to God that he'd remember David and Goliath. If miracles were real, it was high time they showed up.

'Mr Scott.' Aidan spoke immediately when the door opened and carried straight on before Dad had a chance to halt him. 'Look, I get it. I am going. I'm not thick. I know I can't be here. I know it's over with Iona. Please, for what it's worth, which I know is like nothing to you, but I'm Aidan Hennessey. I'm not my da, Liam Hennessey. I'm not my brother, Seán Hennessey. I'm just me. Last time I checked I don't have a criminal record. I've never been arrested. I'm not involved. On my ma's grave, I swear. I never have been and I never intend to be. I finished school. I got decent grades. I didn't mean to cause any harm. I didn't mean to hurt her, or your family. Maybe, could you just tell her I called to say sorry. I know I should've told her earlier. I was just . . . scared. Mr Scott, you have an amazing daughter. You should be so proud of her. She's a credit to you. All I wanted to say was that I'm sorry. I wanted her to hear it from me. That's all.'

He'd raced the whole spiel without a break, looking directly to where I assumed Dad was. The instant he'd finished, he legged it, not waiting for a response. He'd been out of sight for some minutes before Dad gently closed the door.

Chapter 42. Prayer.

AIDAN.
Saturday 27 August.

I'd gone where I always go. My thinking place, where I attempted to process the chaos in my mind into something manageable. This time my head wasn't wired though, and her ring was secure alongside the cross on the leather cord round my neck. I'd come here as a man with a mission.

It was still early, for a Saturday anyway. Behind me, half of Creggan, and the city sprawled below, was still tucked under its duvet, though the sun was awake, filtering through the hazy cloud. The end-of-summer breeze was moaning through the graveyard, playing with grasses, blowing petals from dried-out wreaths.

I laid my posy of wildflowers at her headstone. I could've bought flowers, but the wild ones reminded me more of Ma, and remembering her was the essence of the day, her birthday. I remembered how she'd taught us to make daisy chains – selecting the wee yellow-centred white-petalled flowers with the strongest stems. She'd smiled, showing us the way to use your nail to slice a small hole right near the end of the stem to thread through the next daisy. We'd make chains to magic her and Saoirse into princesses; garlands strung like crowns round their heads. Royal fanfares on grass trumpets – I'd loved it when she'd shown me that. I'd been about six. Finding a wide piece of grass, piercing a slit into it. It had taken practice to stretch it taut between my thumbs, cupping my hands to amplify the sound of the vibrating grass as I blew. Squeaks, low owl hoots, kazoo sounds – I'd squandered summers mastering it.

Above all else, guard your heart, for it is the wellspring of life (Proverbs 4,23).

The silver-painted script still declared her motto boldly against the contrast of her gravestone. She'd have been forty-two. Many's a time she'd whispered those words to me in life, in death. Still I struggled with them. Guard my heart from love, even if it breathed life into my veins? It was a double-edged sword – deal with hurt or die from loneliness. Guard my heart from hate? Shield myself from attitudes and actions of others? Did that kind of guard face the wrong direction? Guard against hating? Was it about forgiveness? Inner-peace guru crap? At any rate, there was nothing left of my heart to guard. It beat strong but it was tattered as January flags; broken beyond what I could fix. *Time's a healer*, they always said. Time never healed the Troubles – just recycled them different and passed them on. I'd plenty of time on my hands anyway, just nothing to do with it. The pain of Ma's death had seemed impossible to overcome; the ache of Iona would fade. Eventually. I still missed her. Every day. Her perfume. Her hair. Her smile. Her. Just her. I hadn't known I was capable of feeling that much; that deep.

I scanned the skyline. Find Altnagelvin Hospital, then move a little closer and to the right. Kilfennan. Was she there? I ruffled my hair, determined not to focus on her. I wanted to remember Ma. That's why I'd come early, before Seán or Saoirse had surfaced. Far as they were concerned, I'd just be out jogging. Most people remembered anniversaries of deaths. I marked Ma's birthday. It made it about her life, rather than the cancer that stole it. The memories were getting more elusive. I plucked weeds and shifted pebbles from the grass. My eyes drifted over the grave; over the

Republican plot with its row of imposing seven-foot Celtic crosses and across to the Waterside again. The Foyle sparkled like a mirror in the morning sunshine, the blue cross on the top of the Long Tower chapel glinting as the bell pealed 10 a.m. That decided me. I'd go to mass and mind her that way. She'd have liked that. It was a 'her' thing rather than a 'me' thing. She'd know it, wherever she was, and I'd even make a point of praying for her soul, not that she needed it. I shook the loose grass off my joggers. I'd be late for the mass; no change there. Still, it would be symbolic.

The wooden pews were empty apart from a scattering of elderly women gathered round the centre aisle. They'd reached the gospel reading. I crossed my head, lips and heart on autopilot, sliding into a side pew, avoiding eye contact with the priest at the altar. As chapels went, I liked Long Tower best; the way the light beamed through the stained-glass windows, illuminating the yellow-green ceiling. Religion oozed from its candles and statues. How many whispered prayers had it collected from centuries of hopeful souls? Maybe it was making our first communions and confirmations here that made it homely.

Ma wasn't always religious. She was brought up all bells and incense, but she ditched it, at least till it got mental with Da. After he left, she drifted back to mass. Cancer made religion her lifeline. I suppose that's why she did Santiago after her diagnosis; her last two-finger testament to the world before the treatment bled the energy out of her. Someday I'd do that hike. Her holiness wasn't in her prayers, it was in her smile, her free spirit, the snippets of songs she hummed randomly round the house.

I'd mumbled through the prayers and responses, lost in the memories. Now it was communion. The wafer held high by the priest; the bell to mark the holiest moment. For her and her alone, I joined the ritual – in the name of the Father, the Son and the

Holy Spirit – queuing up amongst the blue rinses to receive the Body of Christ before hiding back in the oak pew, varnished by the finger grease of penitent parishioners.

Somehow, I missed the end of the mass, lost in my thoughts. I was remembering the last days when they'd put the morphine driver in and we'd comforted her in turns, holding her hand, wiping her brow with a cold facecloth. I jumped, suddenly conscious of a Franciscan brother in his brown tunic, hovering by my bench. One of the few clerics that didn't look like he'd survived the Reformation in person.

'Think you single-handedly reduced the average age in our mass there by half.' He smiled. 'Did you find it meaningful?'

'Honestly?' I scrunched my face. 'No. I only came to remember Ma. It's her birthday. Thought she'd have liked that I made the effort.'

'She died?'

'Few years back.'

'Sorry for your loss.' He paused. 'Would it help to talk?'

'Not really. I just thought that, wherever she is, it'd make her day to see me in mass. It's not exactly the most common occurrence.' I grinned.

'Like me to hear your confession while you're here?' He inclined his head.

'You got five years?' I joked. 'I don't really believe in confession anymore. It's been a while . . .'

He sat at the opposite end of the bench, thinking – that spiritual look when they're reflecting on something but not quite telling you what. I half expected a sermon, but he didn't preach.

'What's your name?' he asked.

'Aidan.'

'Aidan – ardent and fiery, like the monk.' He reflected on the

Irish roots of my name. 'I'm Brother Daithí. This might sound strange, but I felt drawn to you after mass. I'm not sure why. Do you believe in God?'

His question triggered the memory of Iona on our first date, standing absorbing the view over Downhill beach. 'Mental. You're the second person to ask me that this summer!' I rolled my eyes.

'What was your first answer?'

I hesitated, picking candle wax off the seat. It seemed different saying it to a monk. 'That I believe in God, but I'm not sure he believes in me anymore.'

The brother scrutinized me with a kind face. 'Interesting answer. Why would you think God wouldn't believe in you?'

I stretched my hands across the smooth oak, considering whether I wanted to have this conversation. 'Because I'm too screwed up. I went off the rails a few years back. I'm not sure I fit them anymore,' I admitted eventually. 'I can't be holy. I never manage it. No difference whether I believe or not. If he is real, he never listens, and I don't think he cares. I mean, maybe he listens to people like you, but not me.'

His blue eyes concentrated on me carefully, fingers interlocked like a prayer. 'I think that's why I was meant to ask you about confession. What you just described – that feeling that you can't ever be right with God because of something you did – that's what confession is about. It's a reset button for your soul . . . We all make choices, some good, some bad. You chose to come here today – that was good.'

'What made you choose to be a monk?' I slid down the bench, fidgeting with my shoelace. 'You're not really old. Don't you ever miss girls?' I wondered if he'd ever had an all-nighter, and not of the exam-cramming kind.

'Sure I do.' He laughed. 'I'm human. Especially at the start, if

I'm honest, but I'm used to it now. I knew this path was right for me though. Choosing holy orders was an urge I felt deep within me; a calling if you like.'

'And if you couldn't have your choice? What then? What if it was impossible to follow what your heart chose?'

He studied me. 'I'd have prayed,' he replied. 'That's probably not the answer you were looking for, but it's an honest one. I'd have prayed until it either became possible or until another way forward opened up.'

Both of us sat in silence, the only two people left under the high roof arching above us. He knew I hadn't really been asking about him.

'Do you know the Hail Mary, Aidan?'

'Yes. Why?'

'It's an appropriate prayer for your mother's birthday. If you'll forgive me a moment before I go, I'd like to offer you something. You were meant to be here today, Aidan. I feel it in my spirit to offer you a general absolution. That's like a forgiveness for sin without you having to verbally tell me your confession. It's conditional, though. If you're up for it, I'd like you to do two things.'

'Shoot,' I said. It couldn't hurt to hear him out.

'First, choose somewhere this morning, somewhere that has some spiritual meaning for you, and say one Hail Mary as your penance.'

'Just one Hail Mary? For forgiveness of all my sins?' I raised my eyebrows. He'd clearly mixed me up with Mother Teresa.

'Yes. But think about it as you say it. Whatever comes to mind, try to work it through in your spirit.'

'Fair enough.' I shrugged.

'Secondly, whenever you feel like it in the next couple of weeks, find a way to make a fuller confession that feels real and meaningful for you. Here's what I suggest, but it's only a suggestion, understand? Find a stone or a pebble. Whatever you think has messed up how God sees you, whatever you need to confess, say it straight to God in your heart. The stone's symbolic of whatever guilt you feel. When you're ready, chuck it as far as you can into the sea or a river so you can never ever find it again. Let go. Let yourself start over with God. You don't have to do this, Aidan. Make your own choice. Just promise me you'll think about it. Yes?'

I half nodded, half shrugged. No harm in trying. It'd be a holy way to mark Ma's birthday. He shook my hand and told me his Franciscan order had a Facebook page in case I wanted to contact him. Mad that: monks on social media.

Other locals had filtered into the chapel to pray. A tourist wandered in, raincoat, shorts and backpack – dressed for four seasons in one day. I sidled out of the pew, looking round the chapel, reflecting on Daithí's words. I didn't feel like trying to pray in front of others, all obvious and Pharisee. The heavy door creaked as I emerged into warmth and daylight. At the railings round the statue in the corner, I hesitated. Good a place as any – so long as no one else came by a minute. St Columba in his white tunic and gold cloak pointed up towards the crucifixion scene. Jesus, arms splayed and head dropped; Mary in her traditional blue and white at his feet. They never looked Middle Eastern in our statues. Always white.

I glanced about and rubbed the back of my neck. There were no footsteps or voices interrupting the birdsong around the chapel, so I focused on the cross. If I was doing this, whether for Ma or me, I may as well do it sincerely. I blessed myself. *In ainm an Athar, agus an Mhic, agus an Spioraid Naoimh, Amen.* My prayers still flowed better the way they'd been learned me, in Irish. I took a deep breath, even though I wasn't praying out loud. I'd never read the manual about how to tune in to my soul. Confession as a reset button – that made sense. I could use a fresh start.

Hail, Mary . . . Word by word, I focused myself on the familiar phrases. Searching for meaning in them. I prayed for my own ma, for her eternal rest. For her to be at peace in heaven. Mary must've been bloody amazing to stay full of grace.

God being with you. Like, how did you really know that? Old folk talked about having a 'peace'. I'd never felt that in mass; it never felt right that God was boxed in a building. If I believed, would he ever show up? You weren't meant to ask questions. Ma did. Outside – that's where I felt peace. Anywhere with a view and the wind buffeting your senses. Did that make me pagan? I thought of parables they'd taught us. Jesus spent a lot of time outside. Pilgrims, like Ma on her Camino, outside. Maybe I wasn't the only one.

As for being blessed among women, nothing holy came to mind. Iona did, like a wrench in my gut. I sighed and moved on, trying and failing spectacularly to keep my thoughts pure.

Mary pregnant with Jesus. I prayed for Saoirse. Her pregnancy. I smothered the other thought, my own past behaviour, balancing instead the prayers for my siblings, praying for Seán and the tangled mess with the dissidents . . . Still a prodding, a shadow over my soul. Nan. I fired a wee petition her direction . . . The gnawing from my past still shamed me . . . 'Whatever comes to mind, try to work it through in your spirit,' that's what he'd said. I glared at Jesus on the cross. Only a bloody statue. Why was my head swirling? My mouth was dry, heart racing as my hands gripped the black rail. Nothing logical, just a knowing. I swore, and in the same breath apologized to God for my words.

Us sinners. No avoiding it anymore. That included me. In a painful whisper, sucked away by the wind, I prayed for forgiveness for myself. Forgiveness for the anger and chaos I'd fired round me at fifteen. The drink. The drugs. The girls. Forgiveness for shaming Ma with my actions. I prayed for mercy. For peace. For a second chance.

In everything that had happened – the fight, the shooting, the break-up, the hospital – my flood defences had worked. I'd learned well off Da. *Bottle them tears.* With a sharp intake of breath, I let them flow, trickling down my cheeks, tasting their saltiness before scrubbing them away with my sleeve.

As I came to the end of the Hail Mary, I blessed myself in a whisper of Father, Son and Holy Spirit. A lifting, fizzing, shaking surged through me. It caught my breath something unreal. Was it stress release? Outside I was still; inside, my whole body was electric. Closing my eyes, it was there. Peace. Real. Powerful. Present. 'Amen.' I exhaled as the breeze blew round my face and a dog barked in the street.

I felt different the whole way home as I cut through Stanley's Walk and up to Eastway. I had no words, like no experience I knew. A weight off my shoulders. Out of this world, yet real as my runners on the pavement, the sweat on my skin, the sun bouncing off the concrete. Pure spiritual. Not scary. Not weird. Genuine. Like God knew I'd been serious. It was making me think, sending crazy thought patterns through my consciousness, blazing in every direction like my whole world was impacted. Like the first time I'd taken tabs, knowing I needed the trip, yet clueless where it would take me. *Christ.* I swallowed. Was I morphing into a Jesus freak like Brother Daithí? I feckin' hated sandals. Likely the whole thing was just psychological. *Wise up, Hennessey*, I reflected on the doorstep, *you're still you.*

I swore as I entered our kitchen. The United Nations of Derry was assembled around our scratched table, drinking tea out of every presentable mug we owned. It was obviously about me – there was no other logical common denominator. Saoirse was plumped like the arch co-ordinator in the middle; Seán, fidgeting on a stool, closest to the fig roll biscuits; Aunt Teresa, fingers clasped; Mr Ó Súilleabháin scratching his beard; Paddy, for once not clattered in paint; and at the far end, sat back from the table, *Mother of God*, it was him. Iona's dad. My chin dropped as I stood there clad in running gear. What the hell was I supposed to have done wrong now?

'Where've you been?' Saoirse piped up. 'You jog a marathon?'

'What's this? The Inquisition? I went to ten o'clock mass in the Long Tower.'

My aunt's face adopted a faintly surprised look of 'Hallelujah', whilst my sister's eyebrows expressed unequivocally that further explanation was warranted.

'It's Ma's birthday. I felt like marking it. Plus,' I added, 'life's been such a breeze recently I figured a drop of holy water would do no harm. Guess more of you realized than I was aware of. What's the story? Why's he here?' I frowned at my sister. At least in part this was her doing; only she knew me well enough to co-ordinate this round table convention – with the exception of Iona's dad. My skin crawled as I squinted at him.

'Don't panic. You didn't do anything,' Saoirse said. 'Leastways, nothing wrong. It was my idea along with Aunt Teresa. I wanted to help but I didn't have all the answers.'

'So, what's the craic?' I surveyed the faces focused on me.

'Your call.' She beamed. 'Tell us what you want – we'll try to help.'

'What I want?'

'Yes. Now you've finished school and all.'

I hesitated, scratching my scalp. All eyes were on me as if I'd have something prophetic to utter. 'I just want to keep working for Paddy, I guess. Pay the bills, help put food on the table, maybe help towards Rafael's ticket if that's what you want and . . .' I glanced at Iona's dad, picking my words carefully. 'And get Seán free from his *responsibilities* so we can get back to normal. That's all.' I lowered my head, noting my runners still mucky from the graveyard.

'Aidan,' my aunt intervened, 'that's all great stuff, but none of it is really about you. What do you want for you?'

A lump stuck in my throat. I didn't want to talk about what I bloody wanted. Verbalizing it was torture. None of it was possible. I'd struggled through the last ten days convincing myself to bury my hopes. It was the only way I knew how to cope with the pain. *Guard your heart.* Don't dream. Can't fall if your feet are glued to the ground. *Man up, Hennessey. Don't cry.* Turning round, forearm shielding my eyes, I walked stubbornly into our living-room-cum-temporary-bedroom with as much composure as I could muster, closing the door behind me. My mind was swimming again, headache back with a vengeance.

Concerned mumbles from the kitchen penetrated the plasterboard as I paced in circles. The mantelpiece was strewn with my hairbrush, gel and deodorant; my duvet piled at one end of the sofa with my jeans. Dirty socks and yesterday's T-shirt stuck out from under a chair in the corner. I didn't even have a place in my own home anymore. Saoirse rapped the door and peered in.

'Hey,' she said. 'I never thought of it freaking you. Sorry. Didn't realize the date. I just want to help. I think they can help.'

'I don't need help. I'm not a charity case.'

'No. Far from it. But you don't have to be an island. You don't have to handle everything on your own. These people *care* for you, Aidan. *I* care. We just want to know what you're interested in doing; what you feel ...'

'What I feel? You expect me to talk about what I'm feckin' feeling in front of a room full of people? I'm barely managing to stay sane. What d'you want me to do? Break down in front of them? So, maybe I had a pipe dream of going to university. Get real! I checked it out. I thought about it. It's crazy money. I could work twenty-four/seven for years, paint until the cows came home, and still not sniff at the fees. As for how I feel ... Did Seán care about that when he got involved? Did Da ever think about how his choices closed down ours? What I really wanted got stolen by other people's decisions – not mine. Iona and me? What the hell did we do that was so wrong? Our brothers made choices, our fathers made choices – who thought for one second about our feelings? We just got caught in the crossfire ...'

'That's why people want to help. It's called community. Listen! Your teacher has checked out some local trust fund. They're head-hunting you. Even your principal's on for endorsing it. They'd cover your university fees. Every penny. They only pick a handful from Derry every year – brainy but broke. You were born with a schoolbag. Our circumstances, your grades, make you a cert.' She shook my shoulders and eyeballed me. 'Wouldn't do any harm either to get out of Creggan a while. Get back out there and engage, Aidan. Opportunities like these are godsends. What I'd give to be anyone's number one right now. Paddy's sorted Seán too – if you go to Belfast, he'll take Seán on as payback for some backdoor deal they've negotiated. Bingo. No more threat.'

'Paddy's paying them?' I asked.

'For all I know he's painting their houses for life. Ask no questions.'

'Who invited Iona's dad?' I challenged, stalling to digest the information. 'He's not here to help! Last I knew, he made it crystal clear I was as welcome as shit on your shoe! Any idea how hard that was to take and not explode? You know what I really wanted, Saoirse? I wanted to go to university with Iona. I was in love with her, Saoirse. I still bloody am – and I never even got to tell her! I can't get her out of my head and it's driving me mental. You think they've a solution for that round the table other than blow my head off?'

'Yes. I do.' The deep voice startled us from the doorway where Iona's father stood.

Feck but I needed a spider-sense.

'Nobody invited me, so don't blame your sister,' he began. 'I wanted to speak with you. Didn't know I'd crash a committee meeting. Can I borrow five minutes of your time before you rejoin the all-party talks?'

I traded glances with my sister. Her eyes indicated tacit support as she walked out, leaving the door ajar.

'Mind if I sit?'

I grabbed a book and my shirt off the armchair he was aiming for. I debated standing but angled myself on the sofa arm.

'Firstly, I want to apologize. I've already apologized to my daughter and I need to do the same for you. I gave you a rough ride when you called. It wasn't justified. Secondly, I wanted to introduce myself properly. I'm Ian: Iona's father, not actually the devil incarnate. I love my daughter. Doesn't mean I always get it right though. Are you up for a man-to-man?' He paused, his hazel eyes shining just like Iona's, seeking out my response.

'Guess so . . .' I replied, afraid to consider whether this was about sex, politics or both.

'Last couple of weeks I've heard about what we'll call

circumstances impacting my thinking.'

I nodded, shifting uneasily.

'When you left my doorstep I was accosted, so to speak, by not just my daughter, but Andy. It was enlightening. I know how you met, what you went through. I've always striven to be unprejudiced, but I had you in a box, Aidan. Andy, for all his flute bands and Loyalism, showed me up. Judging from the ferocity of my daughter's arguments, you're a courageous and decent young man and you mean a lot to her. This is not easy territory, Aidan, on either side – hear me on that. What I've come to understand though is that just because I or my eldest son chose a certain path, doesn't mean that our choices should restrict Iona. You can follow my drift and apply that to your own family if you wish. I came here today because I wanted to tell you face to face that I'm not standing in your way. I retract my words from Wednesday. Forgive me – this is new to me and, put bluntly, seriously challenging as a father. The proverbial ball, as they say, is back in your court.'

I blinked, processing his words. 'Are you saying I can get back with Iona? Does she still want me? Did she say that? Did she get her grades for Queen's?'

He smiled one of those parental all-knowing smiles. It wiped all his stern features in an instant. 'My daughter's pretty vocal on not having men speak for her right now. You two will have to work things out for yourselves. What I will say is, what I overheard you express to your sister, is what I believe Iona feels about you. You underestimate the impact you've had on her, Aidan. I don't think I need say more.'

He offered me his hand. Tentatively, I shook it. His grip was firm.

'Can I tell her to expect a call?' he asked.

My grin said it all.

Chapter 43. Kinnagoe.

IONA.
Monday 29 August.

The Monopoly housing with its rectangle front gardens by the border gradually gave way to the randomness of older cottages and freestyle houses with boulders, wildflowers and hedgerows. The roadside markers switched from white to yellow and the speed limits from miles to kilometres. They were saying Brexit would bring back customs checks, or create a United Ireland, but for now we just drove.

'G'on, pull in,' he said at the wee shop by Redcastle crossroads. He jumped from the passenger seat, leaving me daydreaming to my shuffle playlist, engine idling. I was high as a kite being back with him. He reappeared with a stuffed plastic bag and a cheeky grin.

'What'd you buy?'

'A childhood experience for when we get there. Doubles as lunch.'

'Exactly where are we going?' I quizzed him again.

'Told you – it's a surprise. I can't believe how little you know Donegal. It's my favourite beach. Your gourmet cuisine, cooked by the best male chef in this car, will be barbecue sausages in floury baps and smores for dessert. I also bought a tomato,' he added. 'Girls always let on to be healthy, besides, they'd no ketchup. Let's go! I'm starving!'

I stole a sideways glance as I drove. It wasn't just his stomach that was hungry; my heart flipped at his new-found attention, his eyes all over me. Following the twists and bends of the road, the Donegal hills fell away to the sea on our right; the Foyle estuary opening to the expanse of the Atlantic. Signage filtered bilingually into Irish and English.

'Da used to swear that even the air breathed easier as you crossed into the Free State,' Aidan mused aloud. 'I'll grant him, he didn't get everything wrong.'

A tractor slowed our progress to a second-gear crawl before cutting into a field dotted with sheep. The road curved through a tree tunnel, hedges high as we skirted the fields into Moville port, water lapping at the Gaelic football pitches. The estuary was flecked with buoys and boats, the fields a patchwork of dark green farmland interspersed with wild grass, reeds and bracken. He sat up straighter, concentrating through his sunglasses as we passed through the fishing village.

'We turn left somewhere here. It's either in the village or just past it.'

'Sure you know the way?'

'I'll find it. Years since I was here. Past a chapel, then keep left, I think. I'll know the turn for definite when I see it – it's a wee thatched cottage called Charlie Brown's, then an immediate left into a back hill road.'

The road veered left past Moville as we coasted along on the navigation memories of his early years.

'There!' He pointed and I slowed for the turn.

On the hilltop was a lay-by viewpoint for the Wild Atlantic Way, the fence posts and chicken-wire fencing strung lopsided, angled into the peat soil and braced ready for the autumn gales. Pulling in, we got out of the car and viewed the panorama that showed Greencastle village, nestled below, hugging the coastline.

The wild grasses rippled in the breeze as we scanned across to Magilligan Point where the ferry operated. The far mountain was where we'd had our first date nearly two months ago. The colours lost their immediacy as they phased into the distance, shrouded by the heat haze of bank holiday sunshine. Aidan was leaning on the warmth of the car bonnet, gazing to the horizon. 'Lot of water under the bridge since Mussenden.' He winked, stretching for my hand, pulling me close into him for a kiss. 'Ten minutes and we're there.' He beamed, touching my nose with his and smoothing my windblown hair behind my ears.

The single-lane tarmac road with its ditches and peat lands either side was strung with one solitary line of cabled poles, the ups and downs and loops of the high road curving by tumbled stone cottages and whitewashed holiday homes in the valley. Around us in fields skirted by flat stone walls, black-faced sheep with fleeces painted different colours paused to stare. Daisies and dandelions rimmed the Gleann Mhíc Dhuibhne viewpoint.

He pronounced the Gaelic words out for me. I repeated them. 'You're a natural,' he said.

I'd never realized how many place names stemmed from Irish. Like his name, Hennessey, Ó hAonghusa, the choice.

'Kinnagoe Bay,' he yelped. 'We're here!'

Crawling down the hairpin, we were met with the roar of the ocean surging on the black rocks. It echoed off the steep hillside, the tumble of shrubs and dune grasses to the orange-gold sand and the choppy bay where they found the *Trinidad Valencera* wreck.

'Whoa.' I exhaled, pulling into the tiny car park. 'It's stunning.'

'You like it?' He tilted his head as he sprang out of the passenger seat in his shorts and vest top, opening my door like a gent.

We weren't alone on the beach, but the hideaway bay wasn't busy for the heat of the end-of-summer day. Dotted here and there were families on picnic blankets; kids playing with bright-coloured buckets and spades. Aidan steered me to the firm sands by the outgoing tide and we kicked off our shoes to feel the damp smoothness of the beach underfoot. Blankets of seaweed, browns, purples and greens, floated in the shallows. The acoustics of the steep-sided bay were awesome – even the small breakers roared as they sucked the shingle rhythmically, methodically, like nature's jet engine. I breathed the smell of salty seaweed in its mops and clogs, deep into my lungs. Kinnagoe was a world apart, the cliffs a shield from cares and worries.

'You came here as a kid?' I looped his arm as we dandered.

'Couple of times we camped rough at the back of the beach. I always loved the freedom, the ruggedness of it. Biggest adventure of my life back then.' His hand smoothed my skin and his eyes caught mine.

The farthest part of the beach had the most pebbles and the least people. We clambered round bigger rocks to reach its privacy, relishing the sun on our backs as we sat facing the sea.

'That why you wanted to bring me here? Childhood memories?'

'Mostly . . .' he replied wistfully, staring out to the blue line of the horizon, his muscled arms wedged at angles into the sand behind him as he leaned back. 'Or maybe for making new memories. I also wanted the chance to talk. Like, *really* talk. To get away from it all and just be with you; maybe ask you stuff. Just me, or was this summer crazy?'

He left the question hanging as we soaked in the sunshine and vastness of the outdoors. The carefree wildness of him that I adored was back. Digging the barbecue from the bag, he hoked a pit out of the sand and surrounded it with pebbles, washed smooth from seasons at sea. Fishing out matches, he shielded the flame against the breeze with his body, cupping the match in his hand until the fire took. The charcoals were black. We'd have to wait until they burned ash grey to cook our lunch. We were chatting, burying our feet in the sand and turning over pebbles when he stopped mid-sentence, becoming reflective, mulling over a small black stone.

'Don't go anywhere,' he said, jumping up. 'I've to keep a promise. Back in a tick.'

He strode across the sands, picking a route through the seaweed and shingle at the tideline before edging his feet into the salt water. Smiling over his shoulder, he turned and waded in slowly, until he was knee deep. He seemed oblivious to the larger waves seeping into the hem of his shorts as he stood stock-still, lingering almost reverently with his head bowed. After about five minutes he lifted his head and looked out to sea. Surprised, I watched him make the sign of the cross, before leaning back with a swing of his body and launching a pebble far, far out into the deep water with a distant *plop*. He trailed his hands down into the white-topped breakers and threw sea-water round his head in a shiver before weaving his way back up the beach towards me.

'I'm intrigued. That was keeping a promise?'

'Aye,' he confirmed, flopping onto the sand by the barbecue. 'A spiritual one, actually. Think you'd be proud of me,' he said, stripping off his top over his head and running his fingers through his hair.

'You're doing that on purpose!' I protested, blushing.

'Doing what?'

'Seducing me with spirituality, then taunting me with your torso!'

He rolled his eyes at me and flexed his bicep, making the Celtic tattoo ripple.

'Call it revenge.'

'Revenge?'

'Yeah. For what you do to me every time I so much as look at you. Besides which, it's hot!'

'Are we talking about the weather?'

He fell back onto the sand laughing. It was a beautiful game.

'Did I ever tell you I'm in love with you, Iona Scott?' He sighed happily, covering his face with his hands to hide the flush of his cheeks as he said it.

'I love you too.' I leaned forward and whispered into his ear, trailing my fingers across his chest.

He rolled over onto his stomach beside me, touching his head to the ground before propping it up with his hands under his chin. I played with the dry sand, letting it drift between my fingers to catch the sea breeze.

'Promise you won't laugh?' He looked at me intently. I nodded, raising an eyebrow. 'I was praying last week . . .' He searched me for any reaction. 'I went to mass to pray for Ma and ended up praying about me; like seriously praying. Actually, you kind of sneaked in there too, but not in a particularly holy way,' he admitted with a flash of charm.

'What'd you pray about?'

He paused, a fleeting shadow crossing his face before he spoke. 'It was a confession: asking forgiveness about my past. I've already told you about what I mean. It felt like a release. I didn't tell anyone else in case they thought I was crazy, but I thought you might relate. That's what I was finishing there, with the pebble.' He smoothed his fingers in the sand. 'A monk suggested I make a fuller confession – any way that was meaningful. I just did. As part of it, if there's anything you want to know about me, anything at all, I don't want any more secrets. I've no more chronic skeletons in my cupboard anyway, in case you're worried.'

'Always knew you'd a spiritual side!'

'Maybe I've crossed over. The Force is with me, and all that . . .' He grinned.

'Since we're talking, what was it you wanted to ask me?' I prodded the barbecue coals with a stick.

'Remember asking me on that bus back from Belfast if I'd ever been in love? Thought I had, before this summer. I was wrong. With you, I'm like a virgin all over. No idea what I'm doing, I just know this feels different. It feels right. I want you to know I'm serious about you. Like, when we're at university we'll know that it's not just a passing thing? I swear I won't clock anyone else. I'd really like to give us a proper chance. What do you think?'

'I'm already serious about you! Don't you know that?' I wiped sand from his shoulder.

He looked taken aback. 'That was a big deal for me to say that!'

'Sorry! I know that. I'm not making light of it. I love that you asked!' I reassured him. 'Course I want us to be serious, especially now we're for Queen's together.' I lay back on the warm sand and closed my eyes as the wind tangled my hair round my face. He caressed my thigh, stroking the sand off it.

'There was one other thing,' he said, voice serious. 'I've been thinking about the Camino Ma did. You know, the pilgrimage?' He sat back onto his haunches, holding steady eye contact. I loved when he did that – like we were trying to see into each other's souls. Looking down, he messed with his fingers in the sand, then breathed in deeply. 'I'd like to walk it next summer. Would you come with me?'

'Absolutely.' I smiled.

His whole face creased with joy, his deep brown eyes afire with life. As he leaned down over me and his lips met mine in a slow kiss, I pulled him onto me, the heat and physicality of him melting through my summer clothes. It crossed my mind, more than once, how my body urged and pulsed to disappear with him into the privacy of a lover's entanglement, hidden in the long grasses backing the beach. I knew he felt it too, and yet whilst our hands explored each other he understood me and the significance of honouring his promise.

'I am so in love with you,' he breathed passionately into my neck, both of us lost in the moment.

'If this does work out,' I mumbled hopefully through a mouthful of sticky marshmallow a while later, 'it would make a great first novel.'

'Aye, right.' He laughed.

Chapter 44. Peace.

AIDAN.
Santiago. Summer 2017.

Peace is not merely the absence of war. It is the presence of something positive, so they say. Einstein reckoned it was government. Martin Luther King believed it was justice. Me? I'm still learning, but I think it's something different.

The Spanish sunshine made us blink as we spilled out of the Cathedral of Santiago into the square and found a quiet corner to sit. Pulling off our hiking boots, we slouched against our rucksacks. She held my hand as my eyes took in the red roofs and bustle of pilgrims in the cobbled streets. It was like she knew I was thinking of Ma. She waited till I spoke first.

'So, what'd you make of the mass?' I asked.

'The swinging incense was class.' She smiled. 'And you all holy – crossing yourself.'

'I still don't believe the half of it,' I said, messing her hair.

'And the other half?'

I shrugged. 'I didn't rate the relics. Weird, worshipping bones from the past. I'd bury them. Let them rest in peace.'

She wiggled her toes in the warm air. 'I wish everyone thought that,' she said, looking at me. I still loved the hazel of her eyes. Digging in my pocket, I handed her a ten-euro note. She squinted.

'Think I didn't notice you making your official first holy communion there? It's tradition. I've to give you money and take you to lunch.'

'And the white dress?' She winked.

I grinned and kissed her. 'Ma would've loved you,' I said. 'She'd have been proud of us.'

She squeezed my hand. 'So, how was your Camino? Did you find what you needed?'

I closed my eyes. Listened to the hum of voices in different languages, the footsteps around us, the thump of my own heart. 'It really is about the journey, isn't it?' I said, smiling. 'But yes, I've found exactly what I was looking for.'

Author Note.

Thank-you for reading this book. That means a lot. I grew up in Northern Ireland during 'The Troubles'. Blessed with amazing parents, I learned that bridges could be crossed and that all people mattered. At eighteen, I studied European Studies in England and France. Then came a critical decision. Would I go back to Northern Ireland? I decided to give it one last chance – with a secret condition attached. In my heart, I would only stay if I could help to build peace.

Some doors opened. In Belfast, I qualified to teach History and Politics. The following year, 1998, I moved to Derry to gain a Masters in Peace and Conflict Studies. I remember the feeling of pure joy when the 'Good Friday' peace deal was signed. The deal marked the end, to a large extent, of violent conflict here. Put another way, it changed how conflict happened – moving it from violent to non-violent, guns to democracy. What it didn't do overnight was to build peace.

There are many brilliant novels set during The Troubles, but teenagers today weren't born then. I wrote *Guard Your Heart* to show Northern Ireland one hundred years after violent events which formed it and a generation after peace. Society has changed – but we are still on a journey. Aidan and Iona, 18, were both born on the day of the Northern Irish peace deal, but they live in a society where identity is still tattooed under your skin, in your blood. They live in the legacy of the Troubles. The complexity of peace. What if peace is harder than war?

Often Northern Ireland is explained in simple terms - 'It's about Catholics and Protestants . . .' When it's put like that, it's easy to think 'Why don't they just get over it?' The truth is much more complicated. Religion is just the simplest label for complex political, historical, cultural, human rights and identity issues. Similar issues are found in communities and countries worldwide. Sectarianism in

Northern Ireland is a form of racism. Political tension is a colonial legacy. Prejudice, grief, radicalisation, faith, hope, battling against circumstances – these are universal challenges and themes. Big questions explored in the book resonate elsewhere. Can teenagers escape identity conflicts inherited from their parents? How do poverty and marginalisation impact a teenager's life choices? What empowers a new generation to move forward into a shared society?

The novel is a Romeo and Juliet, a love story across divides. It's fiction, but the context is real. *Guard Your Heart* was inspired by the desire to tug hearts and minds into empathising that wherever it takes place, and in whatever form, reconciliation can be a fragile process. A courageous risk.

2021 marks the 100th anniversary of the Partition of Ireland. The creation of Northern Ireland. Brexit and changing politics in Ireland, north and south of the border, are generating conversations around a 'New Ireland' and a potential border poll. The issues in *Guard Your Heart* remain very relevant.

As a young adult, I made choices to build peace. Personal choices and career choices. After teaching History for 7 years, I switched jobs. For over 16 years now, I've worked in community peace-building for local government. For me, peace is about a lot of things, but it's not about everyone being the same, brushing the past under the carpet and polite avoidance of tough conversations. It's about understanding and respecting diversity, listening and talking, changing unfair systems and engaging with the issues. Failure to do this, hands the space over to extremists and propaganda. Don't take peace for granted.

Why do I write? I like to make people think. I hope that *Guard Your Heart* will do that. Conflict dehumanises the 'other.' Stories connect us to the 'other'. I write because fiction is a powerful tool for creating empathy, and empathy is a powerful tool for creating peace. In life, just as in my writing, I believe that hope happens because of risk takers . . .

Acknowledgements.

Thank you to everyone in my life who helped make this book happen. It has been a journey.

Thank you to my friends, Noelle, Anne, Emer, Brenda, Emma, Claire and Ciara, who chewed their way through horrendous early drafts before I knew the meaning of the word edit. Thank you to Dave Duggan for initial insight over the muggatay. Thank you to the X-Borders crew, Irish Writers Centre and Maria McManus who first persuaded me to own the title 'writer'.

My deep thanks to Bernie McGill for mentoring and encouragement in windswept cafés in Derry and Portstewart and surprising sunshine in Armagh. To those who beaver away behind the scenes to run the annual Caledonia Novel Award and Irish Writers Centre's Novel Fair – you are stars. Without you, Aidan and Iona may never have had their chance to shine.

To my incredible agent, Laura Williams of Greene & Heaton, thank you for your wisdom, enthusiasm and for finding me in Dublin that February. I am eternally grateful for the email that said 'yes'. To Rachel Petty, my editor at Macmillan, thank you for your faith in this novel and for understanding what lay at its heart.

Writing may be an individual task, but without community, in two senses, this story would not have been told. To the writing community in this wee corner of the world – ye's are a class act. Keep 'er lit. I have lived and learned so much from listening, networking and performing at your platforms and events. I am grateful also to the Arts Council of Northern Ireland for the Support for the Individual Artist award. To the peace community, those unsung heroes (often heroines) and visionaries at the gable end of bringing hope to local communities, you are my inspiration.

Beyond writing, indebtedness, hugs and lattes to those who sustain me in 'real' life. To the 'girls' night out' crew for friendship and laughter. To Trinity, for creativity and the quiet whisper to switch off the television and turn walls into words. To Michelle and Tom who were a wellspring through the years when the guard on my own heart was wounded. To my parents for their unconditional love and, in particular, my mother for always being there with reassurances, dark chocolate bounty bars and a listening ear. Know that you are appreciated. To my sister, Anita, who must surely have been a literary agent in a former life, thank you for sunshine, sushi and astute critical feedback.

And finally, to Ethan, my amazing son. Thank you for sharing life with me through the ups and downs. For your patience and understanding all those evenings and Sunday afternoons when I typed at the kitchen table or in the living room armchair. I hope that my generation will pass on a better story, a better place, to you and your generation. At least you will know that I tried. Keep on being fiercely you. Make a difference. Your way.